MARRYING UP

By Nina Foxx

Marrying Up
Going Buck Wild
Get Some Love

MARRYING UP

Nina Foxx

AVON TRADE

An Imprint of Harper Collins*Publishers*

Interior text designed by Elizabeth M. Glover

ISBN 0-7394-5624-5

TORTURE

His tongue was warm. Paris gasped, then arched her back as Tyson moved gently down one thigh and then up the other. It felt so good it was like torture. Tyson knew how to please her and, right then, she wanted to enjoy him for that. She would worry about the rest later, the baggage that came with being intimate with someone this way.

A moan escaped her lips, and her legs tensed. Paris gripped his head with both hands, her fingers digging into his chin-length locks. She twisted them between her fingers, holding on as if they were a lifeline that could keep her head above water and save her from drowning.

Paris and Tyson were in the hotel where they always met, downtown, overlooking the lake. She had told herself that the last time was the last time, but Tyson and his charms had once again proven too much for her to resist. It was a historic place, the kind with no thirteenth floor and hidden passageways rumored to have been built by Lyndon Johnson. Antiquelike furnishings were crammed into an old-fashioned room retrofitted with modern fixtures where gas lamps used to be. Marble and mahogany meet glass and chrome.

A vanilla-scented candle was burning. His favorite. The gentle scent mixed with that of their lovemaking. Paris's clothes were carefully folded across the back of the desk chair, his strewn across the floor. Tyson didn't speak, but his actions conveyed his message loud and clear. He had no intention of letting her get out of that hotel room without a struggle. He was trying to do everything she liked, extra well, to try and convince her to stay. *Where did you say you had to go?* He exhaled and looked up at her, his almond-shaped brown eyes full of questions.

Paris answered his questioning eyes. "I have to meet my mother. I promised I would be there." His unspoken offer was tempting, but Paris knew how important it was to her mother that she show up.

They never went to his place. It was too small and very guylike. Sparse. And the bed was too hard for Paris. It made her parts fall asleep.

She never invited him to her place either. That would be too intimate, and Paris had no desire to get that close. It was her unspoken rule.

"Uh-huh." Tyson buried his head between her legs again, and Paris squirmed, pushing him away.

They tussled for a minute until Paris managed to turn over onto her stomach. Tyson lay on top of her, his head on her behind. He reached up and cupped her breasts from underneath.

"Paris?"

"Hmmm."

"You sure you can't stay? I could make it worthwhile."

Paris chuckled. She knew his deep brown eyes would

have that look in them again, the one that said it was time for her to go. Her watch was on the Victorian nightstand by the bed. She reached over and picked it up to check the hour for the fourth time.

"I'm sure you will, but if I stay here any longer, you know that Alexis will be calling me. I don't want to explain our business to her either. You know how she can be."

"That cousin of yours is far too nosey," Tyson said. He had listened to many of the things Paris had told him about Alexis over the past few months. He wasn't sure he would like her if he ever met her.

"She is also my best friend. And since you haven't met her, that means you do not have license to talk about her." Paris regretted her words the minute she said them but was unable to help her defensiveness. Alexis was almost perfect, at least in her family's eyes. She was almost married to the right kind of man from the right kind of place. That made her one step ahead of Paris.

Paris pushed a little, and Tyson rolled off her, sliding onto the bed. Paris let her eyes roam over him, taking him in as he sat up. He was beautiful.

He ran his hand through his hair, training his locks back into place. His hair fell down, framing his squarish jaw as perfectly as a professional job on a museum print.

His chest was covered with light hair and chiseled. She liked that, too. The little silver ankh he wore around his neck on a black string found its place and rested perfectly in the middle of his chest.

"You could stay if you wanted to, you know. Or I could go with you." He paused. "Better yet, you could come back. I rented this room until tomorrow." His sly smile hinted at his mischievous thoughts.

She shook her head. "You know how it is. No can do." They'd had the same understanding for a while. They had made the segue from casual friends to lovers a little more than four months ago. Paris liked him, but the relationship had gone as far as it was going to go.

She planted a big sloppy kiss square on his mouth and ran her hand over his chest. He was sexy and rugged. *Too bad he can't get it together otherwise,* she thought.

"Hair is looking good."

"You should lock, too. It liberates you."

Paris shook her head. "Can't. Too straight. Who says I need to be liberated anyway?" She flipped her head, and her straight hair moved obligingly.

He reached up and touched it. "There is no such thing as too straight. Everyone can lock. You got enough *African* in you."

He liked to refer to her African-ness, the part of her she had been taught to ignore all of her life. She rolled her eyes.

"You are good at changing the subject."

Tyson obviously knew her well enough to be onto her ways. He didn't take her bait. He wanted to make her uncomfortable and was not ready to give up that easily.

Paris ignored him. "Time for a shower. I can't go to one of my mother's functions smelling like I just had sex, now can I?"

"You are good." Most of the women he knew wanted a commitment. He was handing her one, or something like it on a silver platter, yet Paris was running away from him faster than he could have imagined.

Instead of answering, Paris gave him a noncommittal wink. She knew that he wanted her to talk about their relationship, but she wouldn't. She didn't want to move to whatever he imagined the next step between them would be. In her mind, things were fine just the way they were. There was no need to complicate matters. When she needed him, she called. They would get together, sometimes have lunch or dinner, sometimes not. The sex was always good. Then they would go back to their respective lives. Less complicated that way.

"And what is the occasion for this soiree?" Tyson was referring to the barbecue her mother was hosting that evening.

Paris measured her words. She got up and stepped over to the windows, opening the blinds with one push of her slender arm. The midday sun poured in, and they both squinted, shielding their eyes from the brightness. It was a clear day, and the almost still water of the lake below glistened in the sunlight. Paris sucked in her breath and paused. The view was always as breathtaking as the first time she had seen it.

"Who knows what my mother has in mind." She lied. Her mother never really needed an occasion to host one of her parties, but this time, she knew full well what the occasion was, but Tyson didn't need to know the truth. Paris turned so he wouldn't see her face, heading to the shower.

No use in hurting his feelings. The truth of the matter was that this particular party was actually a husband hunt. For her. This was her mother's modern-day way of trying to get her hooked up with a suitable bachelor. And *suitable* was the operative word. This wasn't an unusual thing in her life. In her mother's opinion, Paris was long overdue for a husband.

Tyson watched her walk away. His eyes warmed her

back. Paris glanced over her shoulder. Their eyes met. He followed her to the bathroom and stood in the doorway. *Damn, he is fine,* Paris thought.

She looked over her shoulder at her backside in the mirror. Firm as it ever was. She was not old by today's standards, but by her mother's, she should have already pushed out at least one kid. She and Alexis were the only two cousins their age who were yet unmarried. But at least Alexis had a ring. And after last weekend Alexis had a live-in fiancé, too.

Paris moved the plastic, industrial shower curtain back and turned on the shower. She didn't want to look at Tyson, knowing that a glimpse of his rock-hard midsection would weaken her resolve.

"Can I join you?"

She shook her head. She knew he only wanted to slow her down and try to get her back into bed. This was part of the "don't leave" dance that they played, his way of showing that although she wouldn't make any further commitment at the moment, he still had some power over her.

Let him think that. But he did have more than he realized or than she wanted to admit.

She stepped into the shower, inhaling as the warm water hit her.

Tyson followed her anyway, a light smile on his face, completely ignoring Paris's *no.*

She smiled. It was kind of charming how he never listened to her.

"What are you doing?"

"Making sure you get clean."

Paris smirked, leaning against the shower wall. Tyson reached around her, massaging her thighs. He ran his soapy hands first over her stomach, then her breasts, and finally probed between her legs with his fingers.

Shivers coursed through her body like electricity as she parted her legs slightly to accept his touch. Paris tilted her head back and let the water hit her face. She liked the way he touched her, as if he knew exactly what she needed. She closed her eyes. The man was skilled.

"Tell me again why we can't live together."

Not that again, she thought. "I don't want to discuss it. I told you. I don't do that. It's not proper." She didn't have to do everything Alexis did.

His hands stopped moving. "And this is?"

"You know what I mean." Tyson had been asking about them living together a lot lately. Pushing. *I have a master plan. Living with a man again is not in it.*

"Actually, I don't. Why don't you tell me again."

Paris exhaled heavily. She was at a loss as to how to make him understand without hurting his feelings. "I want to be *married,* not just live together. To someone who has the same values and ideals."

"And you are saying—"

"That we are in different places."

"Are we? That isn't what you were saying this morning. We seemed to be in exactly the same place."

She stepped out of the shower and grabbed a towel. He was right about that. They were in the same place, marching to the same drummer. *He had hit all the right notes, too.* "A relationship should be about so much more than sex."

Tyson turned off the water. They were both tense again. Silent.

Paris held her breath. She didn't want to spoil the wonderful time together by saying the wrong thing.

"Why can't we just enjoy the way things are? We discussed it, and you agreed with me that we would not be good together. I can never think straight when I'm around you. That's just not good. We would be too . . . irrational."

He grabbed a towel and rolled his eyes. "And you would build a future on what then? Money?" He watched Paris closely for her reaction.

She knew he would go there eventually. A lot of men thought with their dicks first, but Tyson was not stupid. She should have known from the beginning that he would want more from her. "It helps. Money is the number one thing most couples fight about. I told you. My daddy left my mother because he was poor. He couldn't provide for us, and the stress was too much. So he left. My mother married my stepfather because he was not poor. They were happy. End of story."

"I won't always be poor. It's not like I'm starving. I have good ideas. You even think so. And I am not your father. It's a different time, and things are different."

"No, you're not him. But ideas don't put food on the table. Or build a dream house. Can we please not spoil a perfect morning?" She tried to smile and softened her voice. "I just don't live with men."

The discussion was over. Paris did not understand why Tyson wanted their relationship to go somewhere they never planned for it to go all along.

They didn't talk as they continued to dry themselves with the rough hotel towels. The air in the bathroom was still. Paris looked down at the tile floor to avoid looking Tyson in the eye. If he kept this up, she was going to have to end it. That wasn't exactly a welcome idea. She would miss him.

Tyson stayed in the bathroom after she left. Paris knew he was upset, but he would come around. Hopefully, he needed her as much as she did him. She picked up her phone and scrolled through the messages. Three from Alexis.

She grabbed her purple Cosabella underwear and pulled it on. Her lips curled into a half smile as she noticed Tyson peeking out of the bathroom at her. Paris slowed down a little, acting as if she didn't see him. Purple was his favorite color. Her bra and panties matched perfectly. She had a thing about her underwear matching, especially if there were a chance that someone might see it. Paris also liked to feel nice fabric next to her skin and had been thinking of Tyson when she bought the set.

Finally, Tyson stepped out of the bathroom.

"See you later?" he asked.

Paris slid her jeans over her hips. She looked up and gave him a big smile.

He liked the show.

She nodded. "As long as I'm done early." She sidled up to him as if they hadn't just almost had an argument and placed her arms around his neck. She gave him a slow, lingering kiss, the kind he liked.

He patted her ass in that way he did, and she let him, smiling. *Tyson is good for me.*

His penis rose and pressed against her stomach. She smiled. *And I am obviously good for him, too.*

Tyson stood shirtless in the rented room and watched Paris leave. He inhaled, still smelling her scent on him through the heavy perfume of the hotel soap. *Paris is like that,* he thought. *She takes over everything and everyone that crosses her path, in a magnetic kind of way.* He sighed, cringing as the door slammed shut behind her, and glanced around the room. The bedspread and sheets were crumpled, halfway off the bed. The room smelled heavily of sex. He smiled, enjoying the way his scent intermingled with hers.

He dressed methodically, thinking about Paris. His daydreams drew him back to their chance meeting in Home Depot. Even in the well-worn jeans she sported that day and with paint splatters on the edges of her hair, she had been amazing. He followed her for two aisles before he even said hello, then had made the mistake of thinking that she needed help. She had run into the store to pick up an extra gallon of paint and knew exactly what she wanted. She smirked, then left him openmouthed as she asked the guy in the paint aisle to mix her paint with the expertise of a pro. Her intelligence about things that were supposedly in the male domain was very sexy, but then intelligence was a powerful aphrodisiac. It was then and it still was. On their first date, he found out that paint wasn't the only thing she knew a lot about. Paris blew him away with her knowledge of finance and politics, too. She knew things about the local political scene he could never begin even to grasp.

Tyson jumped as his phone rang. It was on silent, but it vibrated across the top of the small night table. Unlike Paris, he had forgotten about his cell phone. She thought he hadn't noticed how many times she checked that phone when they were together. She had been preoccupied a lot lately, almost as if she couldn't wait to move on to the next thing.

He reached for the phone. Paris was gone, and it was time for him to get down to business, too. He could think about her and her issues later. He had a business meeting to attend. He might actually have a chance at selling his tiny company. He grabbed his keys and his portfolio. Paris would surely take him seriously then.

SWEET POTATO QUEENS

I hate leaving. Paris put on her shades before she even got outside the hotel. She tapped her foot as she waited impatiently for the elevator. Her phone started to vibrate again. She answered just as the elevator doors opened. She knew without looking at the number that it was Alexis. Again.

"Yes?"

"Why are you talking so quietly?" Alexis's voice was as bubbly as ever.

"Maybe I don't want anyone to hear what I am saying." Paris's nostrils flared slightly. She couldn't help being annoyed with her cousin. Alexis never resisted the urge to get in her business. She was relentless.

Paris could not tell if Alexis dismissed the annoyance in her voice or had just missed it, as usual.

"I hope you are on your way. You never get anywhere on time. Your mother says you put too much into one day, just like your father used to. I agree—"

Paris rolled her eyes, thankful that the elevator was

empty, and only half hoped that her cell phone didn't cut off. "I'm coming right now. I was occupied." She chuckled to herself, despite being annoyed at the comparison to her father. Alexis knew she hated that.

"Oh," Alexis said. "I see. That means you were having sex with that mystery man of yours. I don't see why I can't meet him."

"I never said you couldn't meet him." She grinned from ear to ear.

"Uh-huh. That's why I haven't. So, I'm right. You were having sex? Right? And right now you are leaving wherever you two were at, feeling guilty, right?"

"How could you know that?" Alexis was right about the guilt. Paris felt as if she were sneaking out of somewhere she was not supposed to be, or at least out of a pay-by-the-hour motel. For some reason, she always felt that way after being with Tyson.

The elevator door opened, and she stepped into the lobby, looking around to make sure Alexis wasn't somehow sitting there watching her. Something like that would not be above her.

"I knew you before you knew yourself. I felt you kick your mama. Is he married or something? Ugly? What is the big deal?"

"No big deal. And no, he isn't married."

"Then is he unemployed? Is he white? What?"

She liked that Alexis was curious. "None of the above."

Alexis sucked her teeth loud enough that Paris could hear her through the phone. "Unemployed would kill your mother."

Paris flinched. Alexis was right about that, too. Gainfully employed or independently wealthy were some of her mother's major requirements in a man. Paris ran her hand over her face. *My thing with Tyson is mine alone*. It was the only part of her life that Alexis knew nothing about, the one thing neither she nor her mother could offer advice on.

"Just hurry up. There are a lot of people here," Alexis said. "And if he is employed, you better get your hooks in him while you can. You aren't getting any younger."

"Like you did?"

"We aren't talking about me."

Paris could almost feel Alexis's mind working hard through the phone, trying to figure out why she still hadn't had the pleasure of meeting Tyson.

"I will be there in twenty minutes."

"Wash first."

She laughed and handed the valet-parking attendant her ticket. "I showered." She resisted the temptation to tell her that she showered *with* him.

"Hmph. His stuff must be good. This is the second time this month."

Third, but she doesn't need to know that.

"So, is he your boy toy? Or are you his thing on the side? Every woman should have a boy toy. Someone to fulfill her needs. But being the thing on the side isn't good. The other woman never wins."

"Is that the Miz Alexis theory of life? What are you, one of those women in the *Sweet Potato Queens* book now or something? So, is that what Walter is for you?" She paused. "I'll talk with you in a minute." Paris pictured her stomping her feet in that spoiled-brat Alexis way, annoyed because she wouldn't share.

"Fine. Don't tell me. But it can't be too serious. You tell me everything. I just hope all this sneaking around is worth it. Does he go down on you? Because if he does, you need to just go ahead and introduce him to the family. Walter did that the first time we were together, and you see I'm going to marry him. Tongue magic is better than chocolate—"

"Alexis?" She was still trying to find a way to give her advice, even in the absence of details.

"Huh?"

"I'm hanging up now." She snapped her phone shut. The suspense was really killing Alexis. And Paris loved it. She smiled and tipped the parking attendant. Contrary to whatever her mother thought, Paris felt like she was beating Alexis at something. For once.

WE ARE FAMILY

Athena's party was held in a community center in northwest Austin, in a corridor now populated by people who had moved to town when the high-tech companies were really booming. Everything, including the park, was well kept and still looked new. Paris drove into the parking lot, swearing under her breath. Alexis was right—the party must be packed; there were almost no spaces left. Knowing her mother, she had probably rented the center and tried to find a way to keep the community residents out. They would be beneath her in some way.

Paris finally pulled into a space being vacated by a young, Hispanic family. She made eye contact with the man driving; he looked as if he were trying to get out of the park as quickly as possible. Paris couldn't blame him. Probably running from the influx of her mother's friends and acquaintances, rolling up in their overpriced cars acting as if they owned the place. She would run, too, if she had any sense.

Her mother was good at throwing parties. At fifty, she was still the life of the party and loved to get people together for a cause, any cause. Athena was the master of making life look fun. This event had been billed as a barbecue, but Paris knew that there would be no hot grills anywhere to be found. Her mother had surely had it catered, probably ordering barbecued turkeys and brisket by the pounds.

Paris flipped down her visor, reapplying her lipstick and smoothing her hair. She could hear the music coming from the small brick building before she even opened the door. Music from the sixties and seventies, stuff her mother and her friends liked. Her mother tended to stick to the old ways of things. *Music and marriages.* Paris chuckled to herself. She was calling this party of hers "Athena's Love Affair." It was supposed to be about getting together with friends to share the love, but it was no secret that her mother was trying to help her daughter find some love. A double entendre. Like she couldn't find it by herself.

The door to the building was wide-open. It was still technically the middle of the afternoon, but the old folks were dancing to Al Green like they were in a club back in the day, or at least at an old-fashioned house party in somebody's basement. A smile crossed Paris's lips. Her mother spotted her and made a grand dramatic approach like she was onstage. The way everyone was watching her, Paris could almost swear that she was.

"Here she is." Her arms were outstretched, reaching out to Paris as if she had not just seen her the day before.

Athena grabbed her elbow, prodding her farther inside the building. Paris looked around as she was swept into the party. Several of the people she recognized from other events her mother had given. They were already in various stages of inebriation from imbibing the spiked punch. If she knew her mother, Paris was well aware that they would probably be that way well into the night, or at least until they were kicked out of the center.

"'Bout time," she said. She lowered her voice so that only Paris could hear. Athena spoke through her teeth, keeping the smile plastered to her face the whole time.

"I was held up."

"Um-huh. I have some people I want you to meet." She cut her eyes at her daughter, showing her disapproval. She wouldn't dare ask her what the holdup had been, but she operated as if Paris was not allowed to have a social life of her own.

Paris cringed, then braced herself for the onslaught of introductions. She wanted to bask in the aftermath of being with Tyson, so instead of fighting, she went with the flow.

Alexis came through the crowd, saving her. She smiled at her mother, but Paris recognized the glare in her eyes.

"Aunt Athena, let me," she said. "I want Paris to meet this gentleman over here. One of Walter's friends."

"You sure? You should be having a good time."

Sister Sledge started to play, and her mother clapped her hands together excitedly. Paris knew the song was a hit when her mother was in her club days. She had heard the College-in-New-York-Disco-Days stories many times.

"Don't go far," she said. Athena started to look for her husband, so they could dance and relive their glory days. Relief flooded over Paris. She and Alexis waited for her mother to leave.

"She wasn't wasting any time. Still not telling?"

Paris shook her head. "Some things are better left unsaid. You want me to meet one of Walter's friends? He's so straightlaced I can't imagine him knowing anyone even remotely exciting." Walter was Alexis's fiancé. "And besides, the last time you tried anything like that I ended up on a date with that Pillsbury Doughboy look-alike who could only talk about himself, remember?"

"That mystery man must be something." She was still fishing for information. Alexis raised her eyebrows. "I just said that so I could steal you away from Auntie, hoping you would give a sister some information, but I can see I was wrong." She sighed and ran her hand through her copper-streaked hair. As always, it had been straightened to within an inch of its life and blended with a weave that was far too long for Alexis's tiny five-foot-two body. "I hope this doesn't mean that you are not open to meeting people. The man your mother wants you to meet this time is a keeper."

"There's only one? Usually she has them ready like a police lineup. You know she thinks I'm an embarrassment to her, being the only cousin nowhere near marriage and all. And if he is such a keeper, why did you rescue me then? You should have let her get on with it. I don't know why I keep agreeing to do this."

"You don't embarrass her. At least not *all* the time. And cousin David is unmarried. But then again, he is gay."

They laughed.

"You keep doing this because although you hate to admit it, you are just like the rest of us. Deep down, you want a man."

"How would you know what I want? I'm just fine without a man, thank you very much. They are much more trouble than they are worth."

"Really? So are you saying you are into women now? Because if you are, I can help you with that, too."

"Alexis, you are a divorce lawyer. You know lots of men who have been newly divorced. That comes with its own set of problems."

"And don't forget newly separated from their money, too." She laughed. "Don't get smart with me. You don't even know what you want, so what can humoring your mother hurt? Seriously, this guy is pretty cool. Good thing for you I am already taken." She winked at Paris. "He is from the East Coast somewhere. Athena says he went to camp with us one year as kids, but I don't remember him." She shrugged. "But I think you will find you have a lot in common." She put her hand on her hip. Her engagement ring caught the light. Paris blinked. Alexis was going to blind someone with that thing.

The faces of all the people Paris went to camp with over the years flashed through her head. She shuddered at the thought. "Camp Atwater? Between the two of us we must know everyone anywhere near our age who went through there."

Alexis nodded in agreement.

"Not a good sign. If I wanted to keep in touch with any of them, I would have."

"Well, this one must have gotten better with age. I have to remember to check the alumni files. You know that the camp still exists? Maybe we can find a picture that will help us remember. I got the whole scoop from your mother. And, he seems to have a reputation for being very enterprising." Alexis winked at her cousin.

"Why does that not surprise me?"

"Just looking out for my girl. You know how we do." She laughed and playfully hit Paris on the arm.

"Uh-huh. I know you as well as you claim to know me. The real deal is your ass is just nosey."

"I'm going to ignore your ungratefulness." She rolled her eyes and the dark lines of her eighties-esque eyeliner came closer together. Alexis cocked her head in that way she did when she was about to tell some juicy stuff. "Anyway, your mother says that he only went to camp one year, then his family fell on some hard times, and they couldn't send him back for a while."

"Drug money run dry? That is so unlike her. Why is she rushing me to meet him if he is broke?"

Alexis chuckled. "You need to stop. This is your future we are talking about. Hear me out. He isn't broke anymore. He is a big-time investment banker turned lobbyist or something. He went to the right schools, and it paid off."

"Oh, he's one of *those* New Yorkers." Memories of being teased at the very northeastern camp about her now-defunct Texas accent ran through her mind. She'd worked hard enough to lose it. Ever since then, Paris felt that people from the coast often looked down on those from the center of the country. Either they didn't really want to mingle or held some outdated stereotype in their minds. "He won't be interested in me then. You know how *they* look down their noses at anyone who didn't go to those fancy private schools up north. I'm from *Texas* for goodness sakes. I went to public school. Knowing my mother, she probably left that part out."

"You know she means well. And anyway, he is supposed to be real nice." She paused. "They can only inbreed so much. The circles they run in can only be so big. If one of them isn't married by twenty-five, they have to look elsewhere. They have known everyone else in their groups since they were children."

Paris wanted to laugh but Alexis was so serious it scared her. Instead, she tried to change the subject. "You do know that the camp changed to a camp for the underprivileged, right? It probably had to do something to stay in business."

"It was a smart business move, if you ask me. The Davises' daughter changed it all up when she got her hands on the reins. They say she was trying to find a way to get more state grant money or something."

"Okay, see, you are telling me this like it is gossip or something. That sounds positive to me. A good thing. Times have changed. Not many people want to send their kids to all-Black camps anymore. And folks thought that girl was too young to make good business decisions."

"Uh-huh. We are talking about the Davises. They always have some scheme cooking. But this isn't about them, remember? This man your mother wants you to meet—we can find out his vital statistics for you."

Paris let out a long sigh. She did want to be married one day, but her mother and Alexis were taking this to almost conspiracy levels. "I'm through with you. You are as bad as she is. I'm not interested, and I *really* can find my own husband. You two act like I have one leg and one eye. Things aren't that bad now."

"We never said you couldn't—"

Paris held her hand up, palm facing outward, in talk-to-the-hand fashion.

Alexis stopped talking midsentence.

"I need punch to make it through this thing. Fortification."

Paris walked away and left Alexis gaping at her. She made her way through the crowd, joining in with them as they danced to "We Are Family." Hopefully, her stepfather had been as heavy-handed with the Jack Daniel's as he always was. She was going to need an extra boost to get through this event.

Disappointment flooded over her when she got to the buffet table. The punch bowl was empty. Paris grabbed a cup, planning to stand by along with the other would-be alcoholics. It was a given that it wouldn't be empty long, not at one of Athena's parties. That wouldn't look too good, and her mother wouldn't approve of that. Paris knew from experience that her mother was a stickler for details, and she didn't expect her to change now.

Athena made eye contact with her daughter from the dance floor, her eyes narrowing. Paris could hear her voice inside her head even though her mother had not said a word to her. She motioned Paris toward the small kitchen. Paris sighed, then did as she knew her mother wanted. Helping her with the party would be better than standing around trying to figure out who the mystery man was anyway. Not to mention that she would probably get a drink faster.

A set of swinging doors separated the clubhouse room from the kitchen. Paris pushed her way through them without looking up. A group of men huddled around the punch bowl mixing various types of juices from unmarked bottles. Paris opened her mouth to speak, but changed her mind. *I really don't want to know.*

"You guys about done? There are a bunch of thirsty people out there."

"I think this will do it," one of the men said.

"You aren't trying to poison people are you? You do know that you don't put Ever Clear into punch once you are out of college, right?"

They all laughed and stepped away from the punch in acquiescence. No one answered her question directly.

Their eyes watched, then lingered as Paris's hand dropped to her hip, her fingers resting on the small bare space between her low-rise jeans and her tank top. Her fingers seemed to point to her perfectly round navel, and their eyes did, too. "I tell you what. I better not get sick, okay? No one else better either, or Athena will have your behinds. All of you." She looked at each of the men's faces, recognizing all of them as semirelatives except one. She reached out to take the punch bowl, and the man she didn't recognize stepped forward.

"Let me get that for you." He grabbed the bowl from the counter.

"I'm glad to see that my mother actually invited one gentleman."

"Athena is your mother? *You're* the one she was waiting for."

"That would be me. I'm the one that is supposed to meet some loser or something. But you know how she is." Paris waved her hand in the air as she spoke.

"Actually, I wouldn't. I don't know her that well at all. She knows my mother. Or used to know. I would shake your hand, but mine are otherwise occupied." He tilted his head toward the punch bowl he was carrying. "And I'll have you know that I am no loser. Your mother says I am quite the catch."

Paris choked on her own saliva just as they reached the buffet table. She clenched her teeth, and he put the bowl down. Her eyes drifted down to his well-rounded butt. *Two points for Mom.* She usually did her matchmaking based on the men's wallets, but this one obviously had it going on in the physique department, too.

He wiped his hand on a napkin, then extended it to Paris. "You know, I would be a little ornery, too, but I am going to let the 'loser' remark slide. My mother made me promise to come here just like yours did. I am JaBari Nolan."

"I'm sorry," Paris said as she shook his hand. It might not be so bad after all. JaBari was tall and fit-looking, reasonably handsome. Paris was mesmerized by the tone of his voice and his perfectly white teeth. For a minute, she forgot the annoyance that she felt earlier.

"And you are Paris Montague, right? My mother didn't tell me anything about you either. So we are even. But I believe it is going to be a pleasure."

"What makes you say that?"

He smiled, and Paris noticed that he had a dimple. *This one is sexy.* She let him fill a cup of punch for her.

"Well, at least you aren't ugly or anything. You could have had one leg." He chuckled and handed her the cup. "I would take it easy with this. I can't attest to what they put in it."

She put the cup down on the table instead of drinking it. "You want to dance?"

"Really?" he said. "You're not into Old School, are you?

You think you can hang with this?" He grinned at her, showing a slight gap between his extrawhite front teeth.

Paris raised her eyebrows and crossed her arms in front of her. "I tell you what, I don't consider myself exactly old, but I can shake a tail feather to anything you can dream up."

He took her hand, and they joined the dancing crowd. Paris forgot about her afternoon with Tyson for a minute as she spotted Alexis across the room. Alexis nodded and raised her glass in a mock salute. Paris was not surprised that Alexis was watching her. *This might not be so bad. What would a date or two hurt? It might even get my mother out of my hair for a while. Who knows, it might even be fun.*

Paris was going to be easy, JaBari thought. She wasn't bad-looking either. Slim hips, straight hair. Her pretty eyes were framed by extralong eyelashes. Makeup and nails in natural tones. She had an easy beauty that she seemed comfortable with. Quite a nice package. Above all that, she had the number one quality he required—access to money and lots of it.

He held her tight as they danced to the Luther Vandross song that had all the ladies swooning and felt her body surrendering to his. She was practically melting in his arms. He chuckled to himself. Who could blame her? He was hard to resist. Too bad she wasn't the right type.

The music stopped, and she pulled away, smiling.

"Let's go outside and talk," he said, grabbing her hand.

She let herself be led outside like a lamb being led to the slaughter.

The small courtyard outside the community center was

almost deserted, and as soon as the doors swung shut, the noise they left inside the room became muffled. It was dusk, and the day had just about given way to nightfall. All but a few birds were gone from the ring of cedar trees surrounding the small building.

Paris and JaBari walked over to a small landscaping wall. JaBari watched admiringly as Paris daintily perched herself on it. He licked his lips, then smoothed his thin mustache with his finger.

"I gotta tell you, when I realized I had to come to Texas, I never expected this. I thought Texas was supposed to be all brown and flat. This seems to be very nice. Very different from Houston."

Paris pursed her lips. "Was that some kind a compliment?"

JaBari could not tell if she was being facetious or not. He paused. He really just wanted to make conversation, not piss her off this early in the game.

"And I thought we were getting off to such a great start." She shook her head mockingly. "You obviously watch too much television."

JaBari released the breath he had been holding. "I guess you are going to have to show me otherwise," he said. "I wasn't necessarily talking about the scenery. From the looks of things I am going to have lots of incentive to come back here again and again."

Paris blushed.

He raised his eyebrows in surprise at her reaction as he noticed the reddening of her light skin.

"Oh, so you aren't moving here? The date Gestapo made it sound like you are new in town or something. I guess that didn't make sense anyway. When they told me you were in banking, I couldn't figure out what you were doing here. This isn't exactly a haven for the banking industry."

He liked that she had done her homework about him, too. "You see, that is where you are wrong. I'm not in banking exactly. I'm an investment analyst for the banking industry. And I dabble in government."

"You dabble? That is either code for you are a lobbyist or you are in the CIA."

He nodded, a slight smirk crossing his face. "There are several things that are happening here that I have been assigned to check out over the next couple of months. So, I could very well be moving here. Yes, I am a lobbyist, and this is the Capitol." He paused, running his hand down her arm. "I guess I could check you out, too, while I am here." He had thoroughly investigated Paris Montague and her family. They went farther back than she knew. It was obvious that she had no idea at all about how intertwined their pasts really were.

Paris cocked her head to the side and crossed her arms in front of her. "That is a coincidence," she said. "I work for a lobbying firm."

"I'm impressed. So you are a lobbyist?"

"Not exactly. Not yet anyway. But I hope to move up to being one soon. We specialize in banking, so I am not exactly a stranger to the finance world myself."

"I guess we have something in common then." He tried to look as surprised as possible, but he wasn't. He was fully aware of what Paris did for a living, a few other things, too, things she probably didn't even know herself.

JaBari stepped closer to Paris, allowing his legs to interlace with hers as she adjusted herself on the rock wall. "I guess we do."

Paris held up her hand, edging him back as she moved away. She was suddenly uncomfortable with his forwardness. Did he think that because he had her mother's blessing that she was going to just fall head over heels for him? She had things going on in her life and had no intention of being mistaken for some bimbo who was just sitting around waiting for her prince to come or something. Paris never had believed in fairy tales.

"You know, this may not seem like the South, but some things they say about Southern women are true, you know."

"Really? I would have thought you were western—" He attempted a smile.

"I'm a little bit of both actually. I like to think the best of both. And that leaves me able to appreciate a man who respects me and can takes things slow, at my pace."

JaBari paused, then stepped back. He didn't want to mess up his plan. He wanted to work his way into Paris's and the Montagues' lives. "I'm sorry if I was too forward. I didn't mean to offend you—"

Paris shook her head and then smiled. "No offense taken."

"Good. So does that mean you will allow me to take you on a proper date?"

Despite being a little annoyed, Paris nodded. "I guess no harm can come from that. We can talk about the industry."

It was JaBari's turn to smile. "Okay. If that is what you want." He took Paris's hand and led her toward the parking lot.

"So where are you staying?"

"Downtown. At the Town Lake Hyatt."

Paris nodded. She knew the hotel well. "It has a great restaurant. It's a good happy hour spot."

"I'll keep that in mind." Jabari smiled.

There was something attractive about a strong-willed woman, and Paris was definitely that. And it wouldn't hurt to let her think that she was the one in the lead, even if he did have very definite ideas about where he wanted the relationship to go.

MOVING ON UP

Eleventh Street was almost deserted by the time Paris arrived. The usual morning people walked past her office. A few waved, and Paris waved back. She unlocked the door. The office of Benton and Associates was in the middle of an otherwise residential neighborhood, occupying an old, but not quite historic, building. Her stepfather had started and built his business there, before the east side had become trendy. With the new redevelopment projects that were starting up, his modest investment had become a gold mine, and business was booming.

Paris could not help smiling every morning when she looked at the modest sign in front of the building. She had known her stepfather practically all of her life, and to this day, she had never met anyone named Benton. Her stepfather's last name, like both hers and her mother's, was Montague. She had asked her mother who Benton was once, but all she got was an extremely vague answer about an old friend and ex-partner. Now, the mystery was something else about her stepfather she had become used to.

Her nose was caressed by the smell of coffee brewing as soon as she stepped through the door. She inhaled and tried to discern what bean would be the week's favorite. Her stepfather considered himself something of a coffee connoisseur. Usually, she was the first one to arrive in the morning. She hung up her coat on the rack near the front door, then made her way down the hall. The door to her stepfather's office was open. She peered in, and he looked up, still talking into the phone that was pressed to his ear. He held his long slender finger in the air, silently telling Paris to wait until he was done.

She nodded and stepped back from his view, trying to give him the illusion of privacy although she could still hear his conversation well enough. Her stomach flip-flopped. She was anxious to hear what was so important that he called her on a Sunday afternoon to request a meeting. He never did that, so obviously he wanted to make sure that Paris made time for him first thing Monday. That could only have one meaning. He was finally ready to promote Paris from the clerical job she had been performing since she started. Paris was ready for more than being the glorified gofer she felt she was. She had spent painstaking hours and months learning all about lobbying in their industry the way he had requested, and wanted more than anything to move toward being a partner in the business. She was almost as excited about the business as her stepfather was. She had soaked up all of the reports he brought home for years, then jumped at the opportunity to work at Benton and Associates as soon as it was presented. Paris tried not to act too disappointed when she wasn't given big assignments, but it had been almost two years now. She was having a hard time being as patient as he wanted her to be. He just didn't seem to believe that she really wanted to be there. It had taken a while for Paris to convince him that she was genuinely interested and not just looking for a handout.

Paris peered around the doorjamb, immediately making eye contact with her stepfather. She could tell by the stern look on his face that he was really talking business. He was a good-looking man for his age, and although he and her mother had been married since she was about six, there was no shortage of women who found ways to call the small lobbying firm, making up excuses to talk to him. It was part of the business, he said. It was important that people liked and trusted him, and everyone always did. He wasn't exactly a politician, but he was sure good at kissing all of the babies. All the attention left her mother more than a little insecure. She often called several times a day and popped in just to discern what was going on around the place. Paris resisted her mother's repeated attempts for information as best she could, and it wasn't easy. She knew that her mother fancied her to be her own personal spy. She wanted Paris to learn as much as she possibly could about the family business, but not for the same reasons Paris wanted. She wanted to make sure that she could tell what was going on in her husband's workplace with him and his finances, at all times. She never could just get over all of the baggage that was left over from her first husband and his ways.

Paris leaned against the door to wait for Brian to finish, smiling. He smiled back at her and continued his conversation. He always handled whomever he was talking to well, be it a longtime client or a flirting neighborhood woman. His way with words was one of the main reasons that the lobbying firm had grown from just him to five full-time associates, plus Paris. Over the past two years, Paris had grown to admire the finesse he used to handle his business. He was a good leader and a great teacher. Paris was sure she knew the business inside and out, and could handle it, if he would only let her.

He placed the phone back into its cradle with his usual heavy hand. Paris cleared her throat and smoothed her conservative black skirt as she prepared to meet with her stepfather. Although he had been married to her mother for years, he still had a way of making her just a little nervous and unsure of herself, especially when it came to business. Paris sighed. If only he would have more confidence in her, trust her more. She knew she could handle any challenge he could throw her way.

His old wooden chair creaked loudly as he stood. Paris jumped and moved away from the door slightly. Brian did not believe in overspending on office furnishings, especially inside his office. The whole place, excluding the waiting room and the conference room had been furnished with old, surplus furniture purchased at government auctions at Camp Mabry, a local military installation.

Paris did not want to appear to have been listening in on his conversation, although she could have easily if she were so inclined. She hadn't been trying to hear him, but the man was no fool. Paris was sure he knew that her mother grilled her regularly about him. Given the nature of their relationship, he probably expected it. After all, he had raised her. She wanted to make sure he understood how seriously she took her job and had worked hard to reassure him that business was business. She did not want him to think that her mother's insecurities had transferred to her in any way, or that Paris would let them interfere in what was going on in the office.

"Paris?" Although he spoke softly, Paris could easily hear his deep voice without him having moved any closer to the door. She peeked into the doorway.

"Morning," she said.

He nodded, motioning her in. Her stepfather was tall and gangly. Back in college, he had been a two-sport star, excelling both in track and basketball. He never lost his love of exercise and was surprisingly fit-looking for a man well into middle age. His dark brown trousers and starched white shirt both were impeccably tailored and fit him well.

"Hear from your mother yet?"

She shook her head.

Brian raised his eyebrows. "That's a surprise. I was sure she would have called you already to find out why I came in so early." He laughed as he spoke. "You know how much she likes to protect her investment."

It was Paris's turn to be surprised. "I can't believe she told you that."

"She didn't. But I know your mother as well as I know anyone. Sometimes I know what she is going to do next before she even gets a chance to think about it."

"I am never going to understand you two." Paris shook her head. "She makes me tired sometimes."

"I understand. She makes me tired, too. But I never get tired of her. There is a difference."

Paris smiled. They had been married almost twenty-five years, and they were still romantic. That was so wonderful for her mother. "I don't understand how you two do it. I can't keep a romance going for six months."

He shrugged, then winked instead of answering her. He

opened a file cabinet that sat to the right of his desk. For a man who was so smooth and personable with clients he did not usually waste words. Paris was surprised that they had as much conversation as they did. Usually, he got straight to his point and skipped the small talk, saving it all for after hours and weekends. He had always been that way, and Paris was used to it. He saved up all his charm for business, and for her mother.

Paris could hardly contain her curiosity. When the legislature was in session, he stayed so busy, sometimes days would go by before he said much to her. He would usually send her e-mail to let her know what it was he wanted done. Requesting that she see him first thing on a Monday would certainly qualify as rare and unusual.

Brian removed a small business envelope from a file near the front of the cabinet drawer and handed it to Paris. It was all she could do to keep her hands steady as she accepted it. It felt mostly empty but was stiff at one end. She looked at him questioningly, then began to tear it open.

She ripped the end of the envelope off as neatly as possible, then removed what looked like a letter. A card slid to the floor, hitting Paris on the top of her foot. They both bent down, reaching for it at the same time.

"I hope this isn't an omen," he said. He reached the card first, then handed it to Paris. "I thought about this a long time."

Paris's hands trembled as she accepted the credit card from him. She looked at him questioningly.

"I didn't have a lot of choices here. I could hire someone else, or I could use the resources I already have." His words seemed slow and carefully measured.

Paris swallowed, trying to dispel the lump that had

formed in her throat. Brian was giving her a corporate credit card. This was certainly a major development, and she could tell it was hard for him. She had grown very close to him over the years and knew that he valued control over the business. To say he was a bit of a control freak was an understatement. In general, he was the only one who did any significant buying or traveling for the business.

"I need you to have some purchasing power coming up here," he said. "You may have to do some traveling, represent us."

"Really? Does this mean—"

He held up his hand, a smirk danced about his lips. "Don't get carried away. I know you want to be partner and all. But you have a few things to learn yet. Just think of this as one step in that direction."

Paris was both excited and anxious. It was hard to be patient. She looked down at the floor, not wanting him to see her disappointment. "Alrighty," she said. "Just tell me what you need." She tried to sound as much like her cheery self as she possibly could.

"I'll let you in on the details as we go along. Later," he said. "I needed someone to have some authority other than myself. As you may well be aware, we are coming up on a very busy time. You might have to entertain some potential clients for me. Big clients, so it might take two of us. Understand?"

Paris nodded. She was fully aware of the major changes in banking that were about to take place in Texas. Up to now, most homeowners in Texas had no access to home equity loans or lines of credit. If you bought a house with cash in the state, your money was stuck. Banks had been lobbying for years for the right to write that kind of business locally, and it looked like it was close to happening.

"That sounds exciting," she said. "Home equity legislation?"

He nodded and put one of his hands on the back of his chair, his monogrammed sleeve facing Paris. "I'm impressed," he said. "You have been doing your homework."

"Well, I try to keep abreast of things that can affect us and the industry. You always told me to keep my eyes open. But we are so small compared to some of the other firms. What client is it? And why are they choosing us?"

He clucked his teeth. "Paris, I am surprised you would ask the 'why us' question. You know how it is here. People trust people they know. And Benton and Associates is homegrown."

Paris knew exactly what he meant. Not only were they located a few blocks from the Capitol, but unlike some of the other lobbyists around town, Brian had been born and bred right here in Texas and had even graduated from the University of Texas with honors. Back then, he was one of the few African-Americans who attended the school and had made quite a name for himself in sports. Folks were still talking about some of his records. "I didn't want to assume anything," she said. "I just want to get all of the details."

"And so you will, soon enough. High limit, so guard it carefully." He winked.

Paris took the card, nodding. Brian went around the other side of his desk and once again picked up the phone. He was obviously moving on to the next thing and was clearly finished with Paris.

She exhaled heavily as she left his office. In many offices, everyone and their mother would get a corporate credit card, but at Benton and Associates, the added responsibility put her that much closer to a promotion.

Paris retreated to her own office and placed the coveted credit card in her wallet and the rest of the information that came with it into her purse. She would read the fine print later. Brian had left her a stack of paperwork to complete, and her e-mail inbox was full. She went through her usual morning tasks without giving them much thought. Other than her meeting with Brian, there was not too much that was new. Paris kept drifting off and thinking about the research she wanted to do on the new banking legislation. It was important to her and to Brian that she do a good job. She needed to show him that she genuinely loved the lobbying business and would be in it for the long haul. Her thoughts were interrupted by the ringing of her private phone line. She rubbed the back of her neck, trying to release some of the tension that she had let build up there since coming into the office. Paris knew she could be intense about things, especially about things she really wanted. Most people expected it of her. She glanced at the clock on her desk before the phone rang a third time. Only her closet friends called her on this line. That meant Alexis, Tyson, and now JaBari. She smiled, remembering giving him the number in the park last night. It looked like things would finally come together romantically for her.

"I didn't think you were going to answer. Did your party go late? For a minute I wondered if you had made it into the office at all." Tyson's voice was soft.

Paris was slightly disappointed that it was Tyson and not JaBari on the phone.

"How are you Tyson? No, it didn't go too late at all. I was in bed by ten."

"Alone? You should have come to see me."

She couldn't help smiling at his remark. How was it possible that he still had that effect on her, even though she had quite possibly met someone who could be much more suitable? "Why would I do that? I had just left you." She chose to ignore his obvious nosiness. She had been alone, but he didn't need to know that. "To what do I owe the pleasure?" she asked. "I normally wouldn't hear from you for another couple of days. At least."

"Why do you have to put it like that? It's not like I treat you like some booty call or something, only calling you when I need sex. I just try to respect a lady's privacy. I didn't want to be pushy about things. I know how you hate that."

"If you say so. What's up? I have a lot on my plate today."

"I'm sure you do. I was actually just calling to see if you were going to be free for dinner tomorrow? Maybe a celebratory one? I may have some good news to share later."

"Can I call you back and let you know?" Paris glanced at the clock again. She had a lot of information to go through before she left for the day.

"I understand if you are too busy."

Paris closed her eyes. She was supposed to be able to just walk away from Tyson, or at least that was what she told herself. How was is possible that he knew what to say to make her feel guilty? "No, it's not that. I have a lot of reading and stuff to get done—"

"Paris, I've always said you don't have to explain to me. You call me if you get free. Even if it is late, okay? What I have to say, good or bad, won't take long. And I promise you can keep your clothes on."

She cleared her throat. It was hard to tell if she had hurt his feelings, or if he really meant what he said. Tyson was so complicated sometimes.

"I'll do that. Take care."

He had already hung up.

PRETTY TOES

Tyson sighed, then looked around the Starbucks where he sat waiting for his meeting to start. It was adjacent to a Barnes & Noble bookstore and bustling with customers. There were two cashiers working, and both of them had lines leading up to the counter that were almost out the door. There were several people occupying the chairs in the small waiting area, almost all of them had computers open, taking advantage of the wireless network available to customers. Although it was clear on the other side of town from where Tyson lived, this Starbucks obviously had a lot of business going on inside it.

He promised himself that he would wait until he knew how his deal would go before he told Paris anything, but he was unable to contain himself completely. He had arrived early, and felt silly just standing around waiting. He could not resist the temptation to call Paris and share his news with her.

Tyson guessed that many of the venture capitalists that West Austin was so famous for used this very place as their favored meeting ground quite often. Since coming in, he saw more than one face he recognized from the local news or television.

Tyson rubbed his hands on his pants to try and dry off some of the sweat that was accumulating there already. He was dressed conservatively, but not in a suit. That just wasn't his style. But his dark pants and crisp shirt signaled that he was ready to be a professional. He had read somewhere that the absence of a jacket signaled to others that he was ready to get down to business and roll up his sleeves, and that was exactly the image he wanted to project. Businesslike, but approachable.

He glanced at his cell phone screen. It was almost ten in the morning. He wasn't supposed to have his meeting until ten-fifteen, but he had come early so he could get comfortable in the space. He wanted to seem as confident as possible. He didn't want to do anything that could detract from the merits of the deal he was about to propose.

He needed to be calm to convince someone to invest their hard-earned money in an unknown company, especially someone he had never met in person. He really didn't even have an idea of whom to expect. It was all so unplanned. The whole thing had come about so suddenly.

He had just finished working out and showering at his gym and dropped some papers on the way out of the locker room. A man Tyson had seen a few times at the gym had picked them up and perused them before leaving them at the front desk, with a note attached saying to give him a call. They had a wonderful conversation. It was unbelievable, like something that happened in the movies. Not only was the man interested in Tyson's idea, but he was part of a small investment group, one that was always looking for new ideas. It was all Tyson could do to keep the potential deal a secret. If it went as he thought it might, his company would be up and running in nine months, and shortly after that, he would be on his way to financial independence, and hopefully to becoming more interesting to one Miss Paris Montague.

There was something about her that was increasingly attractive, and Tyson found thoughts of Paris invading his mind more and more lately. Here he was, about to have what could, quite possibly, be the most important meeting of his life, and all he could do was think of Paris and the way she laughed, Paris and her thong, or Paris in those sexy jeans.

At first, she had been like any other random woman he met. She was pretty and well dressed. She had worn a print slip dress on their first date, with high-heeled sandals that made her legs look just that more shapely. She smelled good, but those bare, well-tanned legs that ended in perfectly manicured toes had been what caught his attention. They went out for drinks, and what started out as an occasional booty call had turned into something that meant so much more to him. He knew she didn't take him seriously, and she let it be known very early on that she had no problem with their relationship being mainly about sex, but Tyson was sure her attitude had to do with what she perceived his earning potential to be. Many women would say that what a man did for a living didn't matter, but Tyson knew that a man with means would be much more attractive to most, and he was sure that was the case for Paris. He could tell that she was used to never having to really struggle for anything. Her family might not be rich by the Forbes 400 standards, but they were most certainly better off than most Americans. They had been solidly upper middle class for at least a generation. She could talk about her grandparents going to college at Howard, where in his own family, his was the first generation to even be able to afford to attend any college, much less graduate.

Tyson's thoughts were interrupted by a tap on his shoulder. He was standing at the counter, looking out of the window into the parking lot. He had hoped to be able to spot his contacts before they spotted him, but he had apparently not done a good job. His face colored at the thought that they had the opportunity to size him up first.

"Tyson James?"

Tyson looked down and tried to hide his surprise. The person greeting him was not who he expected it to be at all. He was under the impression that all of the partners in DBA Ventures were men. And Black. Instead, a five-foot-two blond white woman was standing in front of him. "I'm sorry. Yes, that's me. You are—?"

"Obviously not who you thought I would be. I'm Sarah, I am the administrative assistant for Mr. Alves. DBA Ventures?" She looked at her watch, then smiled.

"Oh, I see. I thought I would be making a presentation to someone today. I apologize for appearing so off guard."

"That's understandable. Unfortunately, Mr. Alves had to take an emergency meeting, and the other partners are unavailable as well. They should have called you. They sent me to pick up your proposal and business plan so they could review it."

This was not what Tyson had expected at all. He had rehearsed his proposal for hours, hoping to walk away with at least a small commitment. Too much delay could really mess up his plan. Originally, he intended to look for venture capital for his idea until a certain date, then switch to more traditional financing plans, loans included. Not his first choice, but if that was what it would take to see his plans come to fruition, he would do what he needed to. He was almost at his drop-dead date, two weeks away in fact; but he believed in his idea so much, he would use his credit cards to get started if he had to. That would be a last resort, because there was no way he would get far on his measly credit limits.

He nodded. "I think it would be better if I could explain it to them myself. There is so much in here they might not understand. You know, the technical part."

Sarah smiled again, more gently this time. She reached up and put her hand on his arm. "I understand your concern. It's hard when an idea like this is in its infancy. But it will be okay. Both Alves and Bonner have technical backgrounds, years of experience in computer hardware. I know they think the time is right for your idea. They would not lead you on if it were otherwise."

"I don't mean to be rude, but I thought you said you were an administrative assistant."

She laughed. "I am. I am also the office manager and the mail room. All of the partners have other things they do. My husband and I are the 'D' in DBA Ventures. D as in Davies. I am the only full-time employee, so I'm sure we will meet again."

"I didn't mean—"

"It's okay. It happens all the time. I think it is quite amusing the way we tend to underestimate others. All of us."

Tyson could only nod. He was more than a little ashamed for having assumed that this small woman in front of him might also be small in the scheme of DBA Ventures. She probably felt the way he did when people automatically assumed something about him because he was a young, African-American man.

"You have a proposal?"

He handed her his folder.

She sensed his concern. "It will be fine. If they didn't think it was viable, they would have told you already." She turned the open edge of the folder up and flipped through its contents. "Can you come to the office on Wednesday morning?"

Tyson's heart was beating so hard that it sounded like a drum hammering in his ears. He cleared his throat. "I will make it work."

"Good. You can make your presentation then."

He nodded, then watched Sarah walk away with his baby in her hands. He swallowed. This was going to be big. He could feel it.

FIRE WALLED IN

DBA Ventures was located in North Austin, in an area that had once been a vibrant office park during the height of the tech boom. Once full of offices rented by larger companies that had long since moved to their own facilities in a small town north of the city, the buildings now housed various smaller start-up companies and think tank facilities for the University of Texas at Austin. The marquees changed almost daily as companies came and went with the changing times. People were always trying to find "the next big thing."

Walter Alves glanced up only briefly as Sarah dropped the proposal onto his desk. He glanced at his watch and stuffed the file into his bag. He had a meeting in his real office—the one that paid the bills—in less than an hour. The proposal would have to wait. The traffic going north to the computer conglomerate he worked for could be unpredictable and was often bad, even during midday. He would have a few free minutes later and could read it then.

"Thanks. Look any good?" he asked.

"Bonner was right. It has potential. If it works the way James says it will, it just might revolutionize the firewall industry."

"Really. Well it will be refreshing to see a real idea for a change instead of something harebrained and half-baked. Do you believe that last guy?"

They laughed.

"How much does he need?"

"I couldn't really tell. I didn't have time to go through it all page by page, but he is going to need several hundred thousand even to begin. You know how it is. Hardware is expensive, and this is a hardware firewall he is talking about. For servers even. Very different. The only downside I see for him is his manpower. Right now it is nonexistent."

"Well, we are really looking for a good new idea. That amount of cash shouldn't be too much of a problem."

"Thank goodness for stock options, huh?"

"Tell me about it," he said. "And thank goodness for the foresight of knowing when to sell them. Lots of people around here didn't and went from being millionaires on paper to actual paupers living paycheck to paycheck with big expenses. But they aren't going to last forever, so some good investments are key. But I am sure that Bonner has been through all of this with you before."

"Every day."

"At least you're involved. All Alexis does is spend and work out. She doesn't seem interested in this stuff at all." His cell phone began to chime, and Walter reached down to grab it from his pocket.

"She is just trying to look good for you. It's easy to get out of shape when you hit thirty. And with your impending nuptials, she has to be on her toes. No woman wants to be fat in her wedding pictures. I bet that is her on the phone right now. You talked her up."

Walter didn't answer. Instead he flipped open his small, silver phone. "Alves."

Sarah turned to leave, heading for the other room in the small, two-room office.

Walter sighed, then looked at his watch again. He knew that Sarah was right. It was about the time of day when Alexis would call him. She had always checked on him like clockwork, and now that they were engaged, it was only worse.

"I'm going to be late tonight, so don't worry about dinner for me, okay?" He cringed before he even finished the sentence. The late nights were getting to him, so he knew his hours were getting to her, too.

"Again, Walter?" she asked. Her voice became quieter. "That's fine. I'll make myself a salad or something. That isn't why I called anyway. I called to remind you about the fund-raiser for the Girl Scouts. You said you were going to go with me, remember?"

Walter rubbed the back of his neck. He was barely halfway through the day, and his stress level made him feel like it was late in the evening. He had forgotten. The Girl Scouts Capital Campaign was Alexis's chosen charity for the year. She had filled up his calendar with endless social functions. "I'm sure it is on my calendar." He lied. He wasn't sure and couldn't access his calendar from where he was. "I may have to be late though. You know it is crunch time."

"But you promised. I am the chair. How is it going to look if you aren't there? We won't look like a team—"

"Alexis. I'm doing my best. Really I am. I can't be everywhere. I have to prepare for our life together. We need to be ready for the kids to start coming once we are married. I can't expect you to rush back to the office or anything. You know how it works."

Alexis paused. Walter held his breath, hoping she didn't feel too much like arguing with him. He didn't feel like it today. He was busy, and he hadn't counted on being thrown into Alexis's pseudosocialite scene so quickly. It was so phony.

"That's fine. I understand how busy you get. But do you think you could schedule some time for me? For some sex?"

How did I know she would go there eventually? "I do my best. It is just that our schedules have been so different lately. It would help if you weren't so uptight about it." Walter regretted his word choice immediately.

"Your best? That is a sad statement. You need to manage our relationship like you manage your professional life. Maybe then *I* wouldn't be so uptight. And what exactly do you mean by lately? Try three months, because that is how long it has been since we made love. What is going to happen when we are married if this is the way we are now?"

He rubbed his brow. If she kept nagging him, they might never make it to the altar. "Look, I'm sorry. I have just been very preoccupied with things. We can discuss it when I get home okay? I gotta get back up to the office for a meeting." Walter knew that there was no way he was going to come out on top in this conversation. He would find a way to make it up to her later. After he made a deal that would ensure prosperity for them and their children.

REQUIRED MAINTENANCE

Alexis and Sarah were already waiting at the gym when Paris arrived, as she knew they would be. She hurried in and tried not to smirk as they motioned toward her. The days changed, but all else for the three of them stayed the same. The triumvirate was quite a curiosity at the Pilates studio, and Paris was sure that she was not the only one among them that knew it. It was funny to watch the other people in the studio try to listen to their conversations discreetly or check them out without the three of them noticing. It was a source of amusement for them as they watched the other exercisers try to figure them out. They had an ongoing joke about what the instructors said about them when they were done.

As usual, Sarah was dressed in all black formfitting pants and top. Paris noted that she always looked the part of a Pilates diva and was in great shape for her age. She was the eldest of the three of them by at least ten years, but you could not tell it by her body or by the way she could attack the reformer during their sessions. Her motivation for exercising was different from the other two. Sarah was doing her best to stay in shape. She had been diagnosed with breast cancer early and was surviving. Paris admired her spirit. She could not recall one day of working out that she had ever missed since they had begun over a year ago.

It was clear to Paris that Alexis was being her usual self before she even got in from the parking lot. She could see her through the large windows in the front of the studio, and although her cell phone was tightly pressed to her ear, she was laughing and moving in an animated way. This meant she was probably in rare form, and they would have a fun session.

She changed quickly and headed back out to the main part of the studio where the other two, along with the instructor, were waiting. Paris joined the group very quietly. She knew without asking that they had been talking about her. Alexis did not hesitate to take advantage of her uncharacteristically mousey approach.

"Some of us get here on time. Do they have a twelve-step program for the chronically late?"

Paris chose to ignore her remark. She could tell it would be hard to make it through the hour without having Alexis do some picking. Annoying Paris was her job.

The instructor, Brenda, chimed in. "No, it's okay. I will work you all a little faster and harder to make sure you have time to get through the entire series. You are all strong enough now." She smiled her perky-perky smile, the one all exercise instructors have in their arsenals.

Groans echoed off the walls of the studio.

"Thank you, Paris," Sarah said. "Maybe we should just move the time back some so you can get here without rushing."

"No, then we would all get home even later. I could do this during the day, you know. I have no problem moving clients around."

Paris's nostrils flared. "Don't let me stop you."

"No need to be nasty. You are the one that was late. What happened to that good mood you were in when I talked to you earlier?"

"Nothing. I'm still in it. I had a good day. I was just preparing myself mentally for the work that is ahead."

"You guys can do this on the reformers. Lie on your machines."

They all moved to their respective places as Brenda requested. They had been coming to the studio long enough to need only gentle guidance through the routine.

"See, it wouldn't matter what time I got here. Miss Brenda would still be the 'Pilatzee Nazi.'" She made a face. "We would all be just as sore tomorrow."

"But we would still all come back," Alexis said. "I am finer than I have ever been."

Sarah was silent, and Paris rolled her eyes. "Fine obviously doesn't matter. You still ain't getting none. I would be worried if I were you. Most engaged couples hit it on the regular."

Alexis slammed her machine. "How would you know?"

"Gently, ladies."

"Why did you have to go there? You have no idea what I am getting, and it really isn't your business."

"And why isn't it? You share it with us and anyone else who happens to be here, right, Sarah?"

"I am not in this. I don't talk about things like that."

Brenda cleared her throat. "Hundreds please."

"Not all of us can have a maintenance man like you do." Alexis huffed while moving her arms up and down. The exercise was getting to her.

"You don't know what I have. You are just trying, once again, to get in my business." Paris's voice was gruff but she could not help but smile at Alexis's reference to Tyson. She was right about one thing, he "maintained" her quite well.

"I still say he must be ugly or something, the way you have kept him a secret. But I guess that won't matter anymore, huh? You probably won't keep seeing him now. I saw the way you and JaBari hit it off at the barbecue. Your mother was so happy. Now that was one *fah-wine* brother."

"Would that be good?" Sarah grinned.

Alexis nodded. "Most definitely."

"I'm not discussing that with you either. I kept telling you, and you refuse to believe, that my love-slash-sex life is not your business. I don't want my stuff broadcast all over town."

Sarah laughed.

"He *was* fine though. But one has nothing to do with the other."

"Are you crazy? Not only was he fine, but he also does very well for himself. That would be enough for me right there. You can't spread your honey too thin, right, Sarah?" Alexis asked.

"I'm still not in it."

"Ha. That just means you are a coward," Paris said. "And you, Miss Thing, are as shallow as you have ever been. But we have always known that about you."

"She might be a coward, but she knows what I mean.

One woman, one man, right? Anything more, and you are asking for trouble. Why do you think men have such a hard time keeping their stuff straight?"

"Whatever. No one man can be everything a woman needs. That is ridiculous. You may choose to stay with one, but that doesn't mean you are fulfilled, especially not by the way you measure. You would choose money or large engagement rings over all else." Paris huffed, straining to keep going through the exercises. "Damn I hate this one."

"That's why they call it a 'workout.' And don't hate. You wish you had a rock like mine."

"You need to take lessons from Sarah and talk less. You have a smart remark for everything. Not everybody is as moneygrubbing as you are. I am not into that type of thing."

"No?" Alexis raised her eyebrows. "What are you into then? You have no idea what you are looking for; that is why you are perpetually single and sleeping with men you feel you have to hide from us."

Paris sucked her teeth. "I know what I want. I told you that before."

"So, tell us then."

Paris paused, amazed at how she let Alexis back her into a corner every time. "I want a man who is tall."

The room erupted in laughter. Even people in other parts of the room joined in.

Paris's face colored.

"Tall? Well no wonder you haven't found him," Sarah murmured.

"JaBari is tall."

"Isn't this where we came in? I'm not discussing it."

They did a few more repetitions in tense silence, moving

their bodies to Brenda's clicking fingers. Paris could not help glancing at the clock over the door as she worked. It seemed barely to move, mocking her. Only fifteen minutes had passed since they arrived. She was anxious to get through. There was a lot of research for her to do tonight. She had beat herself up nine thousand times already for telling Tyson she would meet him for dinner tomorrow. She could be using that time to read through some of the documents she had brought home regarding the banking legislations or to study up on the new client.

The laughter from the other women drew her back. Even Brenda had a smirk on her face.

"Okay, what did I miss?"

"Where were you?" Alexis asked.

"Thinking. You know how focused I get."

"Whatever. Sarah was telling us about this fine young man she met today picking up some documents." She turned back to Sarah. "I'm surprised at you, girl. I have never heard you talk like that before. You are so *married*."

"You are almost married, too, Alexis. Or have you forgotten?"

"*Almost* is the operative word. And I'm different. I talk about men all the time."

"Well, talk is just that. Talk, okay? You can't tell Walter I described him that way because then my husband will definitely know. You know how insecure he can be."

"Never mind that. Who was this guy?"

"It doesn't matter. Just someone the guys know. I was just telling you about him to see if Paris would share more. About the mystery man or about this JaBari guy. And what kind of a name is that, anyway?"

"Don't try and change the subject Miss-I'm-so-smart-

I-don't-have-time-to notice other men. Can we get a name?" Paris smiled along with Alexis, and curiosity danced in the usually silent Brenda's eyes.

Sarah stretched, then stood up. "No, you may not. It really doesn't matter anyway. Besides, you know I don't discuss anything that has to do with the business. That is the rule. So if I tell you, I will have to kill you. And I kind of like you all."

Alexis glanced over at Paris, still lying prone on her reformer. "I don't have to tell you how lame that is. You think that this is *Mission Impossible* or something?"

They laughed, the mood in the room suddenly lighter.

"How the guy looked isn't what I was supposed to be concerning myself with. Business, remember? Didn't I say business? Like I said I was just making conversation." She shook her head. "I guess it is *Mission Impossible* with you two. Your minds are always in the gutter."

Alexis grinned. "No better place for them to be, right?"

Paris laughed and finished her workout.

JaBari leaned forward, his elbows on the desk in his hotel suite. His head was pounding. Didn't people know what a sure thing meant anymore? It meant guaranteed, and this little investment obviously had not been. He knew that the kind of dabbling in the market he was doing might be construed as insider trading by some, but he didn't care. It happened all the time, and some of the best analysts and lobbyists did it. He had one foot in each camp, so why should he be any different?

JaBari had learned one thing for certain during his years in the business. Many people had access to information that could change their fortunes, but the difference between those who were successful at it and those who weren't was that the good ones never got caught. And if you were a high-profile person, forget it. Any little transgression would be all over the news. That is where he came in. He was virtually nobody in the game, so that left him able to make inconspicuous transactions for people who had a helluva lot more to lose. He had made a business of investing for others on the down low. People wanted to know information he overheard, and he made sure he got paid for it. He was a smart man, so who was he not to take advantage of his position? But when would he learn not to invest his own money? He rubbed his forehead, trying to prevent the usual thinking creases from settling there.

It was one thing to invest his spoils, but he must have been out of his mind when he invested his own principal. He shuddered as he glanced down at the statement in front of him. Close to fifty thousand dollars down the tubes. That was supposed to have been good seed money for something else. He promised himself he would be much more careful in the future. There was no use ending up back in the Projects or drawing the IRS's attention. He rubbed his temples. Some of the investors who had gone in with him were going to be pissed. The low balance on his statement sickened him. He was beginning to understand why his father had had a stroke so young. He had lost all his money, too.

He glanced at the clock. It was not a good time to be losing his clients' trust. There were some good deals coming up, and he could make some great extra side money by telling them where to invest if they still believed in him. He had done so well up to now, engendering trust of his clients by appearing to invest his own money, too. They didn't know that most of what he had invested had been margin, but would they still trust him if he had nothing to invest? His word would be worth nothing if he couldn't afford to appear to put his money where his mouth was.

His father used to tell him that it took money to make money. He had no idea that his margin would be called, and paying it off had left him with very little capital. He couldn't afford to make any more bad moves. JaBari had every intention of being very wealthy. His plan was to have the same people who shunned him and his mother when they were down-and-out run behind him someday, begging for a chance to kiss his ass. With all the new banking and lending legislation in Texas, he needed to drum up some more seed money to keep him going. There was money to be made here and he planned to make it, but not just for other people. He was going to make it for his father, God rest his soul. JaBari had every intention of getting what should have rightfully been his father's anyway.

He licked his lips and glanced at the clock. Time sure had gotten away from him. He meant to call Paris tonight. His mother said the Montague family was loaded. You needed money to make money, right? If she wasn't willing to come in with him, then someone around her would be. There was always someone who was hungry for more, looking for a way to increase their fortunes. Maybe it wasn't too late. A late-night call could be very sexy, and JaBari wanted to embody charm. He reached into the drawer where he had stored her number and picked up the phone.

HOT, BOTHERED, AND BATTERIES

A spritz of perfume behind the ears was the magic that Alexis was looking for. She sprayed a mist of Walter's favorite scent into the air and walked through it, shivering as the droplets landed gently on her still-damp and moisturized skin and her new silk fire-engine red merry widow. There would be no sleep for her lover tonight, at least until he gave her what she wanted.

Since they moved in together, Walter would come home and read more e-mail until the wee hours of the night. He would finally settle into bed well after she had gone to sleep. She sighed and licked her lips. It was well past the time for her to take matters into her own hands. Alexis wanted to ooze sex appeal. It would be impossible for Walter to ignore her. He would have to stroke her instead of those damn computer keys.

As if on cue, the house alarm chimed, signaling that someone had entered the house. Alexis was so busy getting ready that she had not even heard the garage door open and close. She knew it was Walter without even checking.

He was the only person that the dog did not bark at. Alexis took one last glance in the mirror and turned out the lights in her bathroom. She visually checked the room to make sure that the candle she had lit earlier was having the effect she intended, and it was. The shadows it was casting were sure to add to the seductive atmosphere. She hurried over to her perch on the edge of the sofa and sat, her body half-hidden by darkness. Alexis tried to look as nonchalant as possible. Although this was very planned, she didn't want it to look that way, if at all possible. She smiled to herself. The bed looked inviting and had been turned down strategically, and there was chocolate and champagne on the nightstand for her, and Bindi oil, slightly warm, for him. Those were normal things, right? He used to love it when she massaged him with it. She just didn't want Walter to feel pressured, but get the impression that she was the ultimate way to relieve some of the tension she knew he must be feeling. Her stomach quivered. The lack of sex had to make him tense. She sure as hell was.

A smile formed on Alexis's face as she heard the sound of his shoes on the tile floor. He stepped through the open bedroom door and half smiled in her direction. As usual, his greeting was limited as he unbuttoned his shirt and loosened his tie.

Alexis held her breath. For a minute, she thought that all of the trouble she had gone through would go unnoticed. Walter was going through his usual nighttime routine. He had not even moved to kiss her hello. Her forehead tightened as she watched him. What in the hell was he doing? She knew he saw her.

She took a deep breath and placed one leg up on the sofa seductively, leaning her body back into the cushions. "Hey, honey," she said. "Why don't you come sit over here and tell me about your day?"

Walter looked up and smiled, finally approaching her. "Is this all for me?" He smiled as he leaned down and pressed his lips into hers.

Alexis turned her face upward, allowing herself to sink fully into his kiss. He smelled slightly of sweat. Alexis tasted the salt on his lips, savoring the flavor of his full workday. There was something about the way he dedicated himself to his job that was sexy, even if it did keep him too busy. "You know it is. I missed you."

Walter ran his hand down his wife-to-be's beautifully smooth shoulder, then down her side, finally resting it on her firm backside. She was small, but Alexis had a nice ass. Damn beautiful, but he was more exhausted than he was aroused. "Is it the weekend?" he asked, then kissed her again.

Alexis stiffened. "Funny man. I wasn't aware it had to be."

"Not really. It's just that I have so much work to do tonight. Tons to read." He stretched, reaching one hand toward the ceiling.

Alexis stood up and pulled her body into his. "That is your mind talking. What is your body saying? Can you read me instead?" She breathed into his ear. They had been together long enough for her to know that it was his weak spot.

"I'm surprised you would still be up."

"Not sleepy tonight."

Alexis did not want there to be any excuses. She smiled and rubbed his back as she continued to probe his ear with her tongue.

Walter enjoyed the feel of her moist tongue in his ear. It felt as good as she looked. But he had to stay focused. If they made love, he would be done for the night. He was already exhausted. "My body is just as tired. I'm sorry honey. Maybe this weekend—"

Alexis felt as if he had punched her in her stomach. What was happening? Walter never used to be able to reject her like that. "But it has been so long. I need you."

"It hasn't been that long, Alexis. It is hard, you have to understand that. I work very hard to try and provide. I want us to be set up the right way. Not to mention that expensive honeymoon and wedding we have planned."

"But I need you to provide for my body, too." Her eyes stung with tears. She was young, sexy, and being rejected by the man who professed to love her.

"I know you do, and I promise I will. But just not tonight." He kissed her on her forehead. "I just need to get through this next hump."

"But I need you to hump me." Alexis didn't want to whine but couldn't help it.

Walter laughed, then walked into the bathroom. "Always a comedian, girl. That's why I'm going to marry you."

Alexis was still standing where he had left her, openmouthed, when he came out two minutes later.

He smiled, then reached under the bed and pulled out his laptop computer from its storage place. "Thanks for being so understanding," he said. "I'll make it up to you. I promise."

Alexis did not have time to answer him before he was out of the door and on the way to his den on the other side of the house. He seemed to spend all of the hours that he was home in there lately. She knew that if she was lucky, he might finish early and not bring the computer to bed. *Am I that bad?* Her feelings of hurt melted into anger.

The idea of not finding a release for her sexual tension was not appealing to Alexis. Wasn't regular sex in her marriage vows somewhere? If it wasn't, it sure needed to be. What were things going to be like later if they weren't getting any now? There would be no bed for her, at least not yet. She walked back into the bedroom and opened a drawer on her vanity. It was jumbled, full of various discarded potions and powders. She moved most of them aside and pulled out a small plastic box. She smiled. Just what she needed.

Alexis placed the box on her vanity and peeled off the lingerie she had so carefully put on not a half hour before. *Oh well,* she thought. *Too bad lingerie doesn't come with some kind of guarantee, because this stuff was obviously a flop.* Walter had ignored her. She got a better response in sweatpants. A relaxing bath would be just what she needed.

She unscrewed the top on the jar on her favorite bubble bath crème and scooped it out, enjoying the feel of the silky smooth crème between her fingers. Calmer now, she savored the feeling as she rubbed her fingertips together under the running water, watching the luxurious bubble foam appear. It had a warm earthy scent that she loved.

The bathroom began to heat up immediately as the hot water filled the Jacuzzi-style tub. The sound of the falling water was calming. Alexis felt her heartbeat start to slow down.

It only took a minute for her to relocate the aromatherapy candles she planned to use to set the mood with Walter to the ledge near the tub. There was no reason why she couldn't create a calming and sensual atmosphere just for herself. She turned off the lights and flipped open the top on her plastic box. A smile crossed her lips. Hopefully, the batteries were still good. She had been using them a lot lately.

She stepped into the water and eased her body gently into the water, trying hard not to disturb the foam that filled the basin. She wanted it to cover her completely once the tub was full. She closed her eyes and sank back, inhaling deeply. The smell, the foam, and the water would eventually relax her and help her to release some of the frustrations. It had been almost three months since she and Walter were intimate with each other. Her skin yearned to be touched. Why had it gone from feast to famine between them?

Alexis stretched out in the tub and tried to touch the end of it with her neatly manicured toes. This tub was extra large, big enough for two. They used to use it a lot when she first bought the house. Then working became more and more important to Walter, and he started to take less time for himself, for them. She believed that commitment was a good thing, but she found herself increasingly envious of Paris and her secret boyfriend. Alexis sighed. At least one of them was having regular sex. And to make matters worse, Paris never wanted to tell her anything. *Why did it always seem like Paris had the perfect life?* Alexis lifted her hand from beneath the water, cupping a handful of foam. She rubbed it on herself, first by running her hand down her arm, then up her legs. Her thighs and calves were slightly sore from her Pilates session, so she massaged them gently at first, then with more force. It wasn't as nice as having someone else do it, but it felt pretty good.

Alexis smiled. She removed her vibrator from the box and turned it on. The humming sent a chill down her spine, and she shivered, despite the warm water. Sometimes, a girl just had to do things for herself. And that was exactly what she planned to do.

DELICIOUSLY DANGEROUS

The restaurant that Paris and JaBari agreed to meet in was one of Paris's favorites. Normally, she would meet Alexis and Sarah at Cuba Libre for drinks, but it was as good a place as any for this impromptu dinner with JaBari. She really had not expected him to call so soon.

Paris navigated the downtown streets with ease. She knew exactly which streets to avoid so she would not get tied up in traffic.

She slid her car to a stop in front of the valet-parking podium, stopping right behind one of the horse-drawn carriages that frequented the area right off Sixth Street. She opened the door and swiveled in her seat, letting her feet hang out of the car and touch the uneven cobblestone street. She pursed her lips and hoped that the extra-high heels she had chosen to wear would not make her trip on the way to the restaurant. Her dress was form-fitting and very cute, but not so cute that it wouldn't look ridiculous if she busted her behind and ended up sprawled out in the middle of the street.

Her cell phone chimed, and she answered it quickly, without thinking.

"This is Paris."

"You aren't at work anymore. You can just say hello."

Paris sucked in her breath. It was Tyson. "You are right about that. Sorry. How are you?" Hearing Tyson's voice brought on a flood of mixed emotions. She had forgotten about him, and now she was double-booked.

"I'm fine. I just need to know where we are going to meet for coffee. Crescent City Beignets stays open until eleven or so. They have the best café au lait. Not to mention the beignets."

Leave it to him to remember that she loved a good café au lait with a passion. This was going to be harder than she imagined. Three times that evening, Paris picked up the phone to dial Tyson's number, then put it back in the cradle. She bit her lip. It was not like her to change her mind, but he would understand. "Oh, I can't meet you. I forgot. I have other plans. I'm sorry."

Tyson was silent for a minute. "Other plans?" He caught himself. No use in pressuring her. "Well, I guess we can meet some other time. I have some news I want to share."

"Well, I'm down here waiting for the valet. I have a minute I guess."

"No, that isn't what I had in mind. I want to tell you about it in person. But you let me know what works for you, okay?"

"Is this an excuse for us to get together, because if that is what you want, all you have to do is ask."

"I wouldn't mind seeing you either, but I need to *talk* with you this time."

Two people approached Paris's car. She stood up, still holding the phone to her ear just as JaBari reached her side. He smiled at her. He was stylishly clad in a very fashionable and very expensive-looking gray suit. Paris let her eyes drink him in. The man was obviously no stranger to the tailor either. He was even better-looking than she remembered.

The valet attendant was right behind JaBari. Alexis accepted the claim ticket he gave her and moved aside so he could get into her car.

"Um, okay. I will give you a call when I am in the office tomorrow and can check my calendar. My appointment is here, okay?"

It wasn't what Tyson hoped for, but it would have to do. He could sense that Paris was in a hurry. "That's fine. Are you going to dinner or something?" he asked.

"We can discuss it tomorrow. I promise." She smiled at JaBari and held up the "just a minute" finger.

JaBari licked his lips, then took a long look at Paris. He enjoyed her with his eyes, taking his time. It was a shame she was so good-looking. He would have to be careful so he wouldn't get too emotionally involved with her. He took his hand and placed it on her elbow, guiding her toward the sidewalk, then put his other arm around her waist, holding her tight.

With the cell phone still held tightly to her ear, Paris inhaled. JaBari smelled delicious. His cologne was manly, but not overpowering. It was difficult for her to concentrate on her conversation with Tyson.

"There's that Montague mystery again." Tyson chuckled. "But I like that about you. Try to make time for me in your busy schedule, Miss Paris."

"I will." Paris felt a twinge of guilt as she closed her phone. If she didn't want to be with Tyson, why was it that she felt as if she were cheating by going to dinner? They didn't exactly have an agreement that they would not see other people, although she wasn't sure if this simple dinner classified as that.

"Everything okay?" JaBari's deep voice carried easily over the sounds of the busy street around them. It was already teeming with people although it was early.

Paris nodded, then smiled up at him.

"Boyfriend?"

Paris's heart raced. "What makes you ask that?"

"Nothing really. Other than you referring to me as an appointment. I couldn't help but hear you."

"Oh, that. No, not really a boyfriend. I don't think I have one of those, not in the old-fashioned sense of the term anyway. The person just did not need to know my business, that's all."

"I see." JaBari paused a minute. "That is not what the guilt that is written all over your face is saying, but I understand. Sometimes it is hard to move on from relationships, even platonic ones. One person always ends up more involved than the other, even if they don't want to admit it. But if the arrangement no longer serves the purpose I want, I just like to wash my hands of it and move on. Know what I mean?"

Paris looked down at the ground as they walked but didn't answer. Immediately on guard, she missed the part where she had asked him for advice. Was that what he planned to do with her, too? Dismiss her when he was done? And just what did he mean by "no longer serves a purpose"? Tyson served a purpose. Up to then, he had always made her feel good when they were together. A twinge of annoyance hit her. "And what *purpose* do you plan to serve in my life?"

"That remains to be seen, doesn't it?"

JaBari was oblivious to her reaction and continued talking. "Personally, I try never to waste my time on feeling guilty for my actions. It is just energy that I could expend in a more useful direction."

Before she could answer, they reached the hostess stand at Cuba Libre and were led to their table. Paris was not entirely comfortable with JaBari's views, but decided to let it slide until later. She could bring it up during small talk. There was something alluring about JaBari, in a dangerous kind of way. He seemed to have a little roughneck hidden beneath his fine suit, and that was more than a little sexy. Although he had managed to annoy her in less than the two minutes they had been together, Paris was willing to put up with him a while longer, at least for the duration of dinner.

The hostess seated them quickly. Paris picked up her menu just as a waiter came over, bringing them a bottle of wine.

"I didn't order wine."

"I did. I told them when I made my reservation. It's one of my favorites, and I wanted to share it with you." He smiled, revealing a dimple so deep that Paris wanted to put her tongue in it.

She paused, openmouthed. This was not starting off as she had expected. She let the waiter fill her glass. "I'm not used to men who take over like this."

"I'm sorry. I didn't think I was taking over. I thought I was being thoughtful. Please forgive me if I have offended you." His voice was suddenly full of warmth. "I'll send it back if you would like something else."

Paris could not help melting a little as she looked into his eyes. He seemed so sincere. She raised her glass to her lips. "It's fine."

"I'm just so used to being in control of things. It's hard to stop sometimes." It was hard enough to let her taste the wine.

"I can relate to that. I'm a bit of a control freak myself." She smiled. "We should be good together then," she said facetiously.

"You seem like you are pretty much running things yourself. Maybe that's why folks thought we would be such a good match."

"You think? I would think we were in for a pretty rocky relationship if we even decided to go there. I mean, you are used to having your way, I'm used to having mine. That could get tough."

"I suppose it could. If we let it. But it could also be challenging, in an interesting way." JaBari put his drink down. "I think I turned into such a control person after my father died. I couldn't control that and what happened to my mother at all, so I think I compensated for it by overcontrolling the things that I could." He rubbed his forehead. "But that shouldn't concern you. You just let me know if it gets out of hand or if I step on your toes, okay?"

Paris was surprised at his admission. "I think I can handle that."

He nodded, then reached over and placed his hand on top of Paris's. His fingers did not really move, instead they suggested a caress.

Paris's face flushed. She moved her hand away quickly and picked up her menu. "Have you been here before?"

"Once. When I visited town before. Is there something on the menu you would suggest?"

She cleared her throat. "I love this place. Everything is good."

"Yes, everything here is good."

Paris looked down at her menu. She could not tell if she was flustered, or uneasy with JaBari's self-assured manner. Why was he trying so hard to pour on the charm? He was bordering on overdoing it.

"Speaking of recommendations, I have some for you. You do remember that I told you I was here because of big things happening in the industry, right?"

"You mean in banking?" Relief flooded over Paris. She was glad that the conversation was turning back to less personal things. "I am well aware of the happenings. Your visit wouldn't have anything to do with pending home equity legislation, would it?"

"Yes, actually, it would. But I also happen to know of other things that are happening in the banking and home mortgage arena. And because I like you, I can make sure you know about them, too." JaBari picked up his wineglass, twirled the stem in his fingers, then sipped carefully. He swallowed hard, hoping he did not seem too eager.

"Why would you do that, and what good would it do me?" Paris tensed. She felt as if he were about to give her a pyramid scheme pitch. "I have so much going on at my office right now I don't have time to take in any worthless watercooler information."

JaBari chuckled, lowering his voice. "But this wouldn't

be worthless to you. I could do for you what I do for some of my clients. Help you put money in some places that would really work for you. A few thousand dollars can grow really fast if you know where to put it."

Paris's brain clicked. What was he talking about? "What makes you think that I can't handle my own investing or that I would need help from you? I do just fine, thank you very much. Besides, you didn't say you were an investment advisor. You said you were an investment analyst and I thought we were on a date, not in a business meeting."

"I am, and we are. But I know things, and I like to see people benefit from them. Consider it free advice."

Paris could not believe her ears. What exactly was he suggesting? More like free ticket to jail. "So you like me so much that you want me to be a party to something that sounds amazingly like insider trading—"

"That is such a nasty term. It's not exactly that. But I understand if you are not interested." He lowered his voice. "Other lobbyists benefit from their positions of knowledge all the time." He cleared his throat. "Let's order." JaBari changed the subject. He had obviously brought it up too quickly. Paris was not ready and had more integrity than he had thought. He was going to have to forgo the direct route this time. It did not appear that she was about to just hand over any money to him, so he would have to think of something else.

Paris stared at her menu, but couldn't concentrate on it. She could not believe that she had given up a nice, comfortable coffee with Tyson for dinner with this man. He was attractive, but he definitely had a dark side. Did her mother know any of this about him? She was going to have to keep the conversation away from business, or he was surely going to piss her off. They would never get to romance this way. Her mother's words echoed in her head. *It is just as easy to love a rich man as a poor man*. How about a man who thought you were stupid? If he wanted to get to know her, then he was going to have to work on that.

Cuba Libre was just getting started by the time Paris left. The lights were low, and soft Caribbean music played in the background. JaBari was not in a hurry to go anywhere, so he moved to the bar so he could finish devising his plan.

Paris didn't bite as he thought she would. He didn't even have the chance to tell her anything that would make her whip out her checkbook or offer to help him out at all. He was going to have to come up with a more creative way to get some cash and fast, before people started asking questions.

He smiled at the bartender. He was young and handsome, with Tom Cruise good looks. In another life, he might have liked him a little bit, but JaBari had figured out that being with men didn't pay in his business.

"Dirty martini, please."

He needed something stronger than the wine he had shared with Paris over dinner, something that could get his creative juices flowing. The more he thought about it, he realized that he had probably approached Paris the wrong way. An older women would have been easier, they usually were more needy and soaked up the attention he would pour on them like a sponge. In the past he had chosen the older, divorced women first. He could have them writing checks in no time. But then his mother told him about

Paris. He barely remembered her, but as more details were filled in, it seemed like opportunity was knocking for him. He shook his head and accepted his drink from the bartender. He had underestimated her, that was clear.

At first, he thought that Paris was just another spoiled kid who took it for granted that she would one day own her parent's assets, including the family business; but he knew better now. She obviously had a good head on her shoulders and knew her way around the banking industry. Her stepfather had taught her well. He smiled. That would not necessarily make his job harder, just different. He was going to have to release an extra dose of his charm on her to get what he wanted. He lifted his glass to no one is particular.

"The game is on." He downed his martini in one gulp and slammed the empty glass down on the bar.

DINNER, EVERYONE

Paris could barely get her key in the lock after she stumbled home. She didn't bother to turn on the lights, instead she hit the on button on her CD player, intent on listening to some relaxing music. Norah Jones flooded the room, and she started to relax as she hummed along. She poured herself a glass of wine and plopped down on the couch. Her day had been packed full from the minute she stepped into the office that morning.

Her back, shoulders, and feet hurt worse than she imagined they ever could. Brian had dropped a bombshell on her. At first she was excited when he told her that she had to set up a meeting as soon as possible with the bank people, but now she was just tired from being so tense all day. If she did a good job, there was no way he could avoid promoting her to lobbyist.

She had read every piece of paper in the file, and researched the bank and its history at the library and on the Internet. She wanted to be as well prepared as possible for the meeting. The task had seemed daunting at first, but she had done it. By the time the meeting had rolled around, Paris was able to talk about and to the client as if she had been working on their file from the very beginning. No one would have ever suspected that she had given herself the most thorough crash course in business development history.

Paris took a sip of wine and kicked off her shoes, freeing her overtired feet. She had not had the chance to return any personal phone calls or e-mail all day, but now she wished she had. She was sure that Tyson had called her several times. He would have gladly massaged her feet and anything else that needed attention, she was sure of that. Out of the corner of her eye, Paris could see that her message light was blinking. She stretched over and pressed the button, trying hard not to have to get up from the comfortable spot on her sofa. Just as she had suspected, Tyson had called here, too. He had only left two messages, on the third, he'd just hung up. Paris frowned. That was unusual. They usually talked at least once a week, but Tyson seemed more anxious to get in touch with her than usual. They had just talked yesterday. Too bad, she thought. He really was tripping out about her reiterating that she had no interest in living together. What more did they have to discuss? The whole thing was hard to understand. She thought that they had the ideal relationship, or at least one that most men would relish. Good sex, with minimal complications and expectations. Besides, she couldn't afford to get sidetracked by someone who had such different life goals. She had been raised to succeed, and Tyson seemed too laid-back about his career.

The fourth message was from her mother. Paris almost cringed as Athena's husky voice boomed through the answering machine speaker, sounding as authoritative as it ever did.

"Paris. This is your mother." As if she didn't know. Athena's voice was certainly distinctive. "Don't forget family dinner this weekend. Dress nicely."

Once a month, the Montague family had Sunday dinner together, just as they had every Sunday since Paris could remember. Her mother always called her, like clockwork, to remind her to be there. She was annoyed. As if she could forget. Paris took another sip of her wine. It wasn't as if she had ever missed a dinner. That wasn't allowed. Her mother would probably have a heart attack if she did. Athena already claimed that Paris had single-handedly been responsible for the demise of her mental health, so there was no way she was going to give her any excuse whatsoever to blame any other ailment on her. Not on purpose anyway.

Her mother continued. "Call me when you get this. I want you to fill me in on the date Alexis told me you had with JaBari."

Paris shook her head. Leave it to Alexis to be unable to keep her mouth shut. She probably enjoyed telling that little bit, too.

For the third time, Alexis pressed the select button on her TIVO remote. They had a trillion satellite channels, yet she knew there would be nothing new that would interest her. She sighed. She was in for another late night. Her fiancé had already called and told her that he would be working late. *Something better come of his little company soon*, she thought. She was losing her patience, and his late hours were affecting her sex life. Didn't he know that her sex drive was at its peak? What happened to the days when he used to chase her around the bathroom with a hard-on poking through his underwear? He moved in, and now it seemed as if sex was the furthest thing from his mind. The only thing he seemed to care about nowadays was work, work, and more work. She understood his desire to make sure they had a secure future, but what about the here and now? What good was all that money if their quality of life was terrible?

Alexis stopped herself from dwelling on it. Walter would say that she was watching too much of the Lifetime Channel anyway. He was right about one thing, there were much better ways to expend energy than to sit around and whine about things. She stood up and stretched. It was not dark yet. A brisk walk was what she needed to take her mind off things. She grabbed her keys from their spot near the door. She left a voice message for Walter on the security system.

"I'm going for a run at the lake, back soon." Not that she expected him to come in or anything, but it wouldn't hurt.

It took less than ten minutes for Alexis to get downtown, to Town Lake Hike and Bike Trail. It was a popular place for Austin's many fitness enthusiasts, and even as late in the evening as it was, the trail was still teeming with runners, walkers, and bikers. She pulled her car into a parking lot of the Town Lake Hyatt. It backed up to the trail and would be well lit when she completed her walk. She reached under her seat and grabbed her headphones. She wasn't really dressed for a run, so she was going to take it easy. Alexis planned to take a short stroll by the waterfront while she listened to her favorite music. She put the ear buds on, and headed for the trail.

The trail was made of packed dirt and rimmed by trees on both sides. The water was peaceful, and most people kept to themselves. It was dusk, and the sky glowed with shades of red and blue as the sun began its descent. Alexis concentrated on the crunch of the ground under her feet, and she walked to keep pace with the music. She wasn't exactly running, but it did not take long for her to begin panting and break a light sweat. She relaxed as the rhythm of her walk and the music began to wash away her stress.

After the third song, Alexis felt much better. She had been in a funk all afternoon, and it was almost as if a weight had been lifted from her shoulders. She glanced at her watch. It was later than she thought. Where in the hell was Walter? He usually called her if she wasn't home when he arrived. He should be home by now, tucking her into bed.

Still walking in time to the music, Alexis spun around to head back in the direction she had come from. The trail was slightly uneven, and she looked down at her feet as she turned. It would not be a good thing if she ruined the good mood she had created by falling. She smiled as she turned, amused at the almost military-like spin. Just as she lifted her head, Alexis walked directly into a man who had been coming her way. They collided, and Alexis's face smashed into the bridge of his nose. Her teeth bit into her lip, and Alexis grabbed her mouth and tasted her own blood seeping into her mouth.

Alexis was knocked off-balance, and the man reached out and grabbed her arm in an attempt to steady her. He removed his own headphones at the same time.

"I am so sorry. I should have been paying better attention," he said.

She pulled away from his grasp. "Yes, you should have. I'm going to have a fat lip tomorrow." Alexis snapped at him. She was back to her normal, irritated self. A bruised face would make her look very competent to her clients. Not that it mattered. Divorce law was not rocket science.

"I'm sorry, but you weren't exactly looking where you were going either. This time of day, it's hard to see things and people. You could have been hurt. Are you okay?" His voice softened.

Alexis looked up, then frowned. She knew this man. JaBari Nolan was certainly unforgettable, if nothing else.

"As fine as you are, you should be more careful. I'm surprised there isn't a whole line of men running behind you." He smiled and lifted one eyebrow. "Can I buy you a drink or something? For your trouble?"

"Aren't you JaBari Nolan?" she asked. "I know you."

He took a step back. "Uhm—"

"You just went out on a date with my cousin, Paris Montague. I was at Athena's party, too, but I didn't have the pleasure of meeting you formally. She didn't tell me you were so smooth." Alexis put her hands on her hips. "And I know you ain't trying to hit on me. I'm practically a married woman."

JaBari cleared his throat. "I think I remember you now. And how could I not? Looks sure run in your family." He smiled. "You know, a much easier way to have met me would have been to introduce yourself at the party. Running into me like you did was a bit dramatic."

Alexis's face felt warm. "Very funny. And you ran into me." She hated to admit it, but his flattery was welcomed. The way Walter was practically ignoring her, it felt nice to be reminded that she was still desirable.

"You sure you don't want to get a drink? I'm staying at the Hyatt, right over there."

A part of her wanted to, but was not about to say it. "Don't be silly. I'm engaged, and my family would kill me. I'm sure you have realized by now that you are supposed to be for Paris."

"Am I?" Amusement played about JaBari's lips. He raised his eyebrows and stepped back.

"Yes, you are. I have to get home anyway. But I am parked over at your hotel. The least you could do is walk me to my car." Paris was right about one thing. JaBari was as fine as they came. Alexis felt like a schoolgirl. The way she saw it, she deserved a little good feeling, the kind that came from a good-looking man paying a girl a little positive attention. She might be in a committed relationship, but she wasn't dead.

"I can do that." He held out his arm, and Alexis took it.

They made it back to the parking lot quicker than Alexis wanted. She had forgotten how good romantic attention felt as she ignored the little voice screaming at her in her head.

They walked slowly to the car. The air was filled with an awkward silence.

"You know," she said, "you ought to be more careful running down at the lake so late. There are some pretty scary places down there. It could be dangerous."

"Yes, I could run into people like I did you."

"That's not what I mean. You could run into far worse people than me. This isn't the safest place in the whole world. I'm surprised they didn't tell you that at the hotel."

"Really? And it was dangerous for me and not you? Thank you for your concern. They did tell me to be careful, but I can take care of myself, I assure you. I don't know if you noticed, but I am a big man." He smiled and opened her door.

Alexis felt her heart flip. It should be against the law for him to be so good-looking. He was a big man alright. Paris had better jump on him before someone else did. And chivalrous. He would fit right in with the family. "You know, you should come to dinner."

JaBari smiled slyly. "I thought you said you were engaged?"

Alexis chuckled. "That isn't what I meant. I am not that kind of woman." She hit him on the shoulder playfully, enjoying the hard rock feel of his muscles. "I meant come to dinner on Sunday. Our *family* dinner. Paris will be there, and I'm sure she will be glad to see you again. It'll be great."

JaBari paused. Paris hadn't seemed too happy when they parted. They had not had a chance to talk yet, so he couldn't gauge how annoyed she had been. A dinner would be a good way to see her again, and with her family around, it would be more neutral territory. "You sure? That sure sounds a helluva lot more appealing than room service. I don't want to intrude though."

"Trust me. You won't. Dinner is at Paris's mother's house. It is a very social affair." She reached into her car and scribbled the address on a scrap of paper. "At this address. Think you can find it? There will be lots of family there."

He nodded and took the paper from Alexis. His fingers brushed over the back of her hand, and he lingered just a little too long. "I'll find it. I appreciate the offer." He smiled and ran the tip of his tongue over his lips.

Alexis got into her car and closed the door. She waved as she pulled away.

JaBari stood in the almost deserted parking lot and watched her leave, remembering the way her fancy sweatpants clung to her athletic thighs. Paris's cousin seemed a lot more willing and friendly than Paris had been. She probably had some money of her own, too. Her fiancé was a small matter, even an asset. There was nothing easier to manipulate than a frustrated girlfriend or housewife. He could butter her up and make her feel sorry for him. The best part was, she wouldn't be able to tell anyone a thing. Didn't his mother always say there was more than one road to the square? Maybe she should have told him there was more than one cousin that could show him the money. Their money. If Paris didn't work out, Alexis could be plan B.

POKING, PRODDING, AND PRYING

A light rain was falling. Unusual for the time of year, yet Paris was used to Texas weather. Either they experienced horrible drought when everything was burned brown from the sun, and fire danger was high, or torrential downpours that filled the levees so cars washed away as easily as small animals. Her hair would be a wreck, but this rain was pleasant. She welcomed the feel of the light mist on her face the same way the thirsty wildflowers would.

She opened the door to Alexis's SUV and hopped in, immediately reaching for the radio. She pressed the CD button on the touch screen. Hopefully she would be able to get Alexis into the music early and keep the conversation light during the twenty-minute ride to her parents' house.

"Good thing I like you. I normally require my dates to come to the door to greet me when we go out."

Alexis grimaced. "Very funny. Walter had a meeting, so he is going to catch up to me there. I just didn't want to drive by myself. Those roads home from the Lake are dark at night, not to mention the rain is going to make the roads slick. I appreciate you letting me pick you up."

"Whatever. You are the one that had to drive out of your way to get me. And you don't have to act crazy with me. I know that you just like to enjoy the wine Brian is always pouring out so liberally at dinner. Drinking and driving has a high penalty around here." She snapped her fingers in time with the music. "You're a lawyer. You know that sheriff would love to have a chicken like you locked up and wearing those designer prison duds."

Alexis was oblivious to anything Paris was saying. As always, she seemed to have shown up with an agenda. "You have been a little scarce the past couple of days. What has been going on? I missed our girl talk."

Paris rolled her eyes. What that really meant was she had no one's business to meddle in. "You just saw me when we exercised. I have been so swamped with work. I think I am finally going to make it to lobbyist. I had some good meetings, and I think we landed a major new client, thanks to my efforts. A really big name. Brian is going to have to move me up instead of treating me like his personal assistant."

"Well, that's good. But you know that isn't what I mean. I don't care about all that business stuff. What I want to know is have you seen your sex toy lately or are you done with him?"

Paris sucked her teeth. All chances she had of keeping Alexis from at least attempting to discuss her business were gone now. "You *should* be interested in business. Maybe if you had an intelligent conversation with your other half about what he did, he would spend more time with you. You may be cute, but you still have to make an effort, you know. And you better ask somebody. You need to know what you are marrying."

"Did I ask you that? I know exactly what I am getting myself into. Walter and I are very open when it comes to his business."

"Yes, but did you get it? I would want to know about *my* husband's business. How will you know what you have if you don't participate? What if something happens to him?"

"Nice try. And nothing is going to happen to him anytime soon. I'm not completely ignorant. But we aren't talking about me. I want to know if you have had any clandestine meetings with the mystery man since the last one you told me about."

"Why? How many times have I told you—"

"—that your sex life is not my business? I know. But you know I live vicariously through you. I want to know how to get that glow you have. You telling it is better than a steamy novel."

They laughed.

"Not happening, sweetie. My glow is about me, not a man. I haven't seen him, okay? I haven't even had time to talk to him on the phone, I have been so busy."

"Busy with JaBari?" A sly smile crept onto the corners of Alexis's mouth.

"Oh, I see. You just have to know *all* my business, but we can't even begin to discuss yours. Is that it? Can't I keep anything to myself?"

"I thought, you know, since you were telling—"

"I'm not telling, but if I were, I would tell you that one thing has absolutely nothing to do with the other."

"And I would disagree. I told you that you can't spread yourself too thin, right?"

Paris sighed. "I got it, Miss Perfect. I have good sense, okay? When something happens with JaBari, I will let you know."

"So, you are not even going to let a sister know how the date went, huh? I *need* to know if you liked him. What is the deal?"

"Since when do you *need* to know my business? I can't believe you are even asking me about this." She looked out of the window. Paris was not sure how she felt about her meeting with JaBari. He was attractive enough, but there were no bells ringing. He didn't move her the way Tyson did when they were together. And there was still that something else that she couldn't put her finger on.

"He's alright. I might go out with him again."

Alexis bounced up and down in her seat. "I knew you liked him. Tell the truth, you said yourself that the only requirement was that he be tall. And he has that covered."

"You don't have to get so excited. I said he was alright. That is not exactly a precursor to planning a wedding or anything."

"I know, but that is a start. Did you make another date?" Alexis was excited for Paris, but part of her felt bad. She had to admit that she liked the way JaBari had flirted with her, but she didn't want to. Not if her cousin liked him.

"Not really," she said. "He is a little strange. He seemed almost desperate. I wanted to go on a date, and he had to bring business into it. I felt like I was out with someone trying to get me into some kind of multilevel marketing scheme or something."

Alexis opened her mouth, then closed it. "Don't tell me he is into one of those health food or legal pyramid schemes? He isn't selling anything, is he? 'Cause I couldn't stand that."

"No, I didn't get that. I didn't really let him finish. He caught me at a bad time. But it was almost like he was trying to talk down to me or something. Offering investment advice." She sucked her teeth. "Do I look like I need investment advice?"

"He better ask somebody. Now you know why he is unmarried. I would never have guessed that he was the overbearing type. But you can overlook a lot of things."

Alexis pulled the car into her aunt's driveway. There were already several cars there. She turned off the ignition, and they both got out of the car and slammed their doors.

Paris stood up and straightened her skirt with one hand. "You mean *you* can overlook a lot of things. You are sounding like my mother again. Deep pockets don't make up for everything, you know. Well, I don't know what it is with JaBari, but the verdict is still out on the two of us."

JaBari stirred something in her, but Paris didn't want to tell Alexis that. He seemed to have a cloud of danger hanging over him. That made him even more sexy. Paris's stomach quivered a little as she thought about it. She didn't comment further as they approached the door, but Paris could not help but wonder what it was that her cousin was overlooking in her relationship with Walter. True, some things you could take, the small stuff. Leaving the toilet seat up. Chewing with your mouth open. But not everything was about money, right?

She didn't get a chance to ask her. The oversized front door swung open to reveal Athena Montague standing there. She had a wineglass in her hand, and she was smiling from ear to ear. Her smile was just a little crooked. Paris could tell that she was already feeling the effects of the wine.

She yelled out to Paris and Alexis. Her voice was unnecessarily loud. "C'mon in here. Let's see if you two can settle this argument." Athena left the door open and waved them in. She disappeared back into the house.

Paris shook her head. Her mother had some kind of radar for people approaching the front door. A knack for sweeping people into the house and into the middle of whatever argument or discussion was going on. Usually, it was something that no one would remember tomorrow.

They didn't fight it. They both knew it was useless to resist.

Paris followed her mother in, then hugged her tentatively. She skillfully avoided the wine that was sloshing about in her mother's glass. Athena was tipsy enough not to notice or at least not to care.

"Hello, Mother," she said. "Let me get inside and say hello first." Paris tensed as Athena hugged her a little too tightly, then did the same to Alexis. She wiped her feet on the mat that was always just inside the door. Then dropped her bag inside the front hallway closet as she always did.

Paris glanced around the room. As full as the house was, it looked like her mother was having a party rather than a simple family dinner. People were divided the way they usual were. Women were in the kitchen whether they were helping or not. Men were in various spots, away from the kitchen, talking. Everyone had a glass of something in hand.

Paris headed for the kitchen with Alexis behind her. Each of them grabbed a wineglass from the counter. Someone reached over and filled them. If she didn't know better she would think that her mother and Brian surrounded themselves with nothing but alcoholics. As always, there would be no real sit-down dinner. Once the food was ready, people would eat wherever they could, then stay for several hours. A few more might show up for dessert, then the games would begin.

There would be several games of Spades being played, along with the requisite trash talking. It would stay peaceful if no one got drunk. Paris hoped to be gone by then. She sipped her wine. The trash talking was the worst. No subject was taboo, as long as it was talked about in jest. Lately, she had been the subject of too many of the jokes. Old maid jokes. Single jokes. Jokes about being childless in old age. It was fast becoming unfunny.

Other than the chance to talk with her stepfather and see if he approved of her work, Paris was beginning to wonder why she had come. There was not much about these Sunday dinners that had changed lately. No one new came, even the food stayed the same. It seemed almost as if the rest of her family, her mother and Alexis included, were stuck in their ways and beliefs.

Paris wandered into the den. As usual, that room was darker than the rest.

Most of the house had been updated, but this room was the sole place where her stepfather had complete control. Renovating houses seemed to be her mother's favorite pastime, and this house was the third one they'd purchased since Paris had been out on her own. It was evident from this room that this was an old house. Low ceilings still made Paris feel as if she wanted to duck when she entered. Flagstone floors echoed when she walked across them.

Three of the walls were covered in late-sixties dark wood paneling. There was a large stone fireplace with a giant hearth, and although they had only been there a short while, the room already smelled like Brian. Some of the other rooms seemed cold and almost ultramodern, by comparison, but this room had a warmth to it that was rivaled only by the kitchen. Like the kitchen, Brian's den was a favorite among guests. They flocked here whenever they could, and today was no exception.

Voices wafted from the room. Paris stiffened. Men talking business. Their tone said they were trying hard to impress one another. She shook her head. Maybe she should think twice about going in there. Nothing much was worse than a roomful of men with puffed-up chests, but even that would most certainly be better than the questions that would greet her in the kitchen.

She plastered a smile to her lips and plunged in. She didn't really want to take part in any heavy discussions today, but did want to get some feedback from Brian about landing the new client.

Brian was talking to two other men, family members. They stood facing the sliding glass doors, overlooking the lake. They didn't notice her at first.

She cleared her throat. They stopped talking midsentence and turned around to face her.

Brian swung around. "Hey. The woman of the hour." He kissed her cheek lightly, then hugged her. A smile similar to her mother's was plastered to his face, except he managed not to look drunk or at all goofy, just distinguished as always. Paris hugged him back just as warmly.

Paris nodded and accepted the customary hugs from her

cousins. They had both been at the last family dinner, and Paris was sure they had been at every one before that, at least for the past year. For the life of her, she couldn't figure out how they were related to each other, but that was her mother and Brian's way. Someone could be a fifteenth cousin, twice removed, and that would be family enough to get invited to dinner, as long as you brought some wine along with you.

Sweat rose to Paris's palms, and she rubbed her fingers together. *Why am I nervous?* "What are you men doing in here?" She grinned. "Beating your chests again acting like Tarzan?"

Brian rolled his eyes. "Actually, we were discussing an investment opportunity—"

"—that Miss Paris let me know, quite clearly, she wasn't interested in." JaBari strode into the small circle.

Paris sensed a challenge in his voice. The smoothness of it irked her, but she bit her lip to stifle the urge to take him up on his unspoken challenge. Brian and the others did not speak. No need to be drawn in, too. Her mother would make sure he was in on things soon enough, Paris was positive of that. There would be time enough to give them reasons to be nosey.

"What are you doing here?"

"Well, I was using the bathroom." He motioned toward the small powder room in the corner. He smiled, and her defenses melted away. A faint glint twinkled in his light brown eyes. "But you don't have to act so glad to see me."

Brian looked from Paris to JaBari. He sensed tension between them. He just couldn't tell which kind.

"That's not what I meant." She wanted to be angry with

him for being a smart-ass, but couldn't. The most she could muster was mild annoyance. JaBari smelled as good as he looked. Paris ran her eyes over him. She was nervous again, but this time it was because of JaBari. His sapphire blue shirt was crisp and obviously freshly ironed. The expertly tailored garment hugged the curvature of his muscular chest, making her acutely conscious of his athleticism. She blushed.

Brian stepped in. "JaBari was just telling us about an investment idea he had. This young man has some ideas that can make some people a lot of money. But I don't know about the risk. It just seems so huge."

Alarms went off inside Paris's head. "Risk?" She looked from Brian to JaBari.

"Let me explain," JaBari said. His voice took on a more hushed tone. "Most of the information I have is highly privileged. Only the best investors know about it. Because I am right there, I happen to know, too. No more risky than the stock market, really, just with a little extra something—something on the side, know what I mean?" He paused, then cleared his throat. "But you know what? We can talk about something else. It's Sunday, and this is supposed to be a social occasion. We can talk about this stuff during the week, right?" JaBari turned to Paris. "Can I get you something to drink?"

Paris looked at the floor, measuring her words. Was JaBari hiding something? He seemed to be dismissing her again. She studied him intently. Just what was he up to?

"You know what? How about I get you something to drink this time?" He had managed to make her feel like an outsider in her own parents' house, for goodness sakes.

No one in the room spoke as she and JaBari stared at each other.

He licked his lips, and, although a warning bell was going off in her head, Paris's stomach fluttered. She was torn by conflicting emotions. Why was he so disarming?

Paris could feel the four men staring after her as she left the room. Their conversation began again, just as she reached the door. Their voices were more hushed than before. She struggled to keep herself from looking back.

In the hallway, the air seemed somehow lighter, easier to breathe. Paris headed back to the kitchen. She turned the corner and tripped on nothing in the carpeted hallway. Did JaBari have her so flustered that she couldn't walk? She chuckled to herself and shook her head, just as Alexis came around the corner.

"Don't tell me you are drunk already?" Alexis asked. "Having a little trouble walking? I was counting on you—"

Paris didn't stop to take the bait. "You will never guess who is in the den talking with my stepfather." She paused. "JaBari."

Alexis wasn't as surprised as Paris thought she would be.

"He's here already? I'm surprised he came so early." She hesitated as she spoke.

"You knew he was coming?" Paris stepped back and placed on hand on her hip.

"Knew?" Alexis pushed her on her shoulder. "Girl, I invited him. Of course I wasn't sure that he would actually come, if you know what I mean. Does he look as good as he did the other day?"

"Does he look as good?" Paris narrowed her eyes. What

was she sensing about Alexis and JaBari? "What do you mean? What happened that I don't know about, and how dare you invite him without asking me. How could you be so sure that I wanted to see him again?"

"I wasn't. But I ran into him down at the lake the other night and thought that dinner with us would be better than dinner at the hotel. And you didn't really say you didn't want to see him again. If I recall, you weren't sure. Besides, as fine as he is, I thought someone here would be glad to see him even if you weren't." She peered around Paris and down the hall.

"Wait. I know that look. You got the hots for JaBari, right?" Her eyes flashed with a twinge of jealousy. "You should be ashamed of yourself, Alexis. You are virtually a married woman. And I never said I wasn't interested. You are my cousin, and I thought you were my best friend."

"You can keep your voice down. I *am* your best friend." She laughed and smoothed her hair. "I can't say someone is attractive now? I just want the best for you, that's all. We all do. I thought it would be better if he were here, because the rate you are going, you need all the help you can get. And just because I am almost married doesn't mean I am dead. How many times do I have to tell you that? He is charming, and nothing makes a girl feel as special as a little flattery every now and then."

Paris's nose flared. When did JaBari have the chance to flatter her? "You are unbelievably selfish sometimes. I can't believe you would invite him here without asking me first. Everyone seems so ready to get me married off to the first bidder."

"Calm down, girl, It's not like that at all. If I offended you, I apologize, but it seems to me that all this reaction over nothing means that you care more than you are willing to admit. Or am I detecting a little jealousy?"

"You are unbelievable." There was a heavy dose of annoyance in her voice, but Paris was not surprised by Alexis's nerve.

"Maybe. But let me go say hello."

Alexis left Paris standing there and headed toward the den. She shook her head. She *was* a little jealous, but wasn't about to admit it to Alexis. Just what had JaBari said to Alexis that left her all hot and bothered? It really didn't matter, because Walter would arrive soon. Hopefully his presence would be enough to put a stop to any flattering, flirting, or unapproved hanky-panky that Alexis had planned. Paris headed back to the kitchen and talked with all of the other people in the room. She tried hard to get her feelings together and avoided thinking about Alexis in the room with JaBari and the other men in the den. She was most certainly in there flirting uncontrollably. That girl was impossible sometimes. She would give them about ten minutes, then she would go break up their party. She nursed her drink and had about enough of the conversation around her when the doorbell rang.

She looked up at her mother, who stood on the side of the split kitchen stirring her pot. Athena nodded at her. No one else moved, so Paris knew exactly what was expected of her. She set her glass down on the counter and headed toward the front door. Athena's radar must have been on the blink for this one. This would be the first person all night that she didn't personally greet.

Paris glanced at her watch. It was probably Walter, along with his partner and Sarah. Since dinner was just about ready, they were due to make their entrance.

She pulled on the heavy door and it swung open. Paris stumbled backward, then caught herself, just as Walter stepped through the door. He grabbed her elbow to help steady her.

"Take it easy," he said. He was smiling ear to ear. "I have someone I want you to meet."

Walter stepped to the side of the hallway, and Paris looked up. She had expected to find Sarah and her husband behind him, but instead she looked into Tyson's face.

Her mouth dropped open. What was he doing here? Their eyes met.

His smile was nervous, uneasy.

Paris felt her stomach jump.

"This is Tyson James. Our company is seriously considering investing in his idea." He flashed a smile.

"We've met." Paris's voice was hushed. Her throat was suddenly dry.

"Really? Austin is such a small town. How do you two know each other?" Walter looked from Paris to Tyson. Amusement danced in his eyes.

They stepped in, and Paris closed the door behind them. She cleared her throat and swallowed hard as she tried to manage a feeble answer. "We're friends."

The very thing she thought she had been keeping to herself was staring her in the face.

Tyson inhaled loud enough for her to hear. He wasn't comfortable with her answer, that was clear.

Walter looked from Paris, then back to Tyson again. His eyes narrowed suspiciously. "Okay then. Tyson, come on in and let me introduce you to some of the folks that you *don't* know. If your ideas are half as good as they looked after our initial meeting, you will be seeing a lot of these folks. We are sort of a close-knit group of friends and family."

Tyson nodded, all the time keeping his eyes locked on Paris's. There was a lump in his throat. Although the awkwardness hung heavy in the air, he was glad to see her. If she had been avoiding him, it would be hard to do that now.

Walter guided Tyson into the house, leaving Paris standing by the door openmouthed and full of disbelief.

Why had she not known what was going on? Sarah must have known about this. How could she not have put two and two together? Now that Paris thought about it, Sarah had described Tyson so thoroughly she should have caught on, but as usual, she had been so preoccupied with work, she had let it slip by her. Paris shook her head and headed back toward the kitchen. It might not be a bad idea for her to hide there all night.

Paris spent her time avoiding Alexis, Tyson, and JaBari. Wanting to stay away from them all, she hung around with the other female family members, holed up in the kitchen. She feigned interest in their conversations as much as possible, but her thoughts kept drifting back to the two unexpected guests in the house.

Athena leaned against the wall with her, martini glass in hand. The sweet smell of her perfume caught Paris's nose. She glanced over to find her mother watching her intently.

"What?"

"Why don't you tell me?" She raised her eyebrows. "You seem to be somewhere else when you need to be up in there with JaBari, being charming and all." She sipped her drink, then swallowed. "So, you gonna tell your mama or what? He is a fine one. I don't know why I should have to guess about your date and things."

The conversation in the kitchen paused as everyone tried to listen in.

Heat prickled Paris's face.

"Mother, there was one date, and that was it."

"You have to do better than that. I know there is more, chicken. I like him for you. Your stepfather does, too. He is what the family wants for you."

"What about what I want?"

"If you knew what you wanted, you would be married already."

There was a chorus of nods and grunts of acknowledgment.

"Tccch." Paris grabbed her drink. "I don't want to talk about this. I don't know why everyone thinks I have to be married right away. Don't my wants and likes count for anything?" She looked at the faces around her. "You would believe we are living in the Dark Ages or something the way you people are trying to push us together."

Everyone in the kitchen was speechless. Paris felt closed-in. She just wanted to get away from them. All of the excitement she had felt about her accomplishments at work was now gone. No one seemed concerned with the things that made her happy. They just focused on one thing—her love life.

She looked at her mother's shocked expression. She turned and headed toward the patio, leaving the women standing there staring after her.

Tyson finally cornered her there as she stood watching

the sunset. She watched the light as it changed the sky from blue-gray, then to a dusky amber.

"They have an incredible view here." He came up behind her. His voice was slow and sounded as smooth as her drink felt.

Paris jumped, then collected herself. She continued to look out over the horizon so she would not have to look into Tyson's eyes. Why did he have to be here today? She had not decided if she should be angry, confused, or happy about all the uninvited guests at dinner.

"Why haven't you ever introduced me to your family, Paris? It feels weird having to meet them this way."

She turned slightly. "Don't get me wrong. I like being with you, but I never thought we had that type of relationship. Not that it matters, you have met them all now. Why didn't you tell me that it was my Walter, my cousin's fiancé, that was considering investing in your business?" Her nostrils flared. "All this time, I thought you were just blowing smoke about things getting ready to take off for you."

"How would I have known that? Would it have mattered?" he asked. "Would that have made you want to be with me more or go out in public? And how was I supposed to know you are related to half the town? You never really told me anything about yourself. It isn't like we talk much when we're together. You have spent so much time hiding me, being ashamed, what was I supposed to think, anyway?" His tone was velvety and low, yet edged with steel. After talking with her family, it was clear to him what she thought they expected of her. Paris was clearly running from him and looking for love in all the wrong pocketbooks. She talked a good game, but her actions made it clear what her priorities were. He was not going to be cast aside that easily.

"I'm not ashamed."

"No?" He held up his hand. "Look at me in my eyes and say that. You think I don't know that you feel that I am not good enough for you?" He paused. "I'll tell you what, Paris. I'm tired of being toyed with. Either you want to be with me, or you don't. I may not be as well-off as you would like me to be, but I will get there."

Her heart beat loudly in her ears. "Why does everything have to be an ultimatum with you? Can't we just enjoy each other the way we have been?" Her mind refused to register the significance of his words. What was he saying?

"You mean why can't we just enjoy an occasional booty call and that's it?" He put his hand on her shoulder, almost in a possessive way. "You need to make up your mind. We are too old for this kinda shit anyway. I'm ready to be a grown-up about things.

"If I wanted to just have a roll in the hay, I could have had that, with someone far less interesting than you. But you have to let me be a part of your life. It is obvious to me that none of these people here knew anything about our relationship at all." Tyson searched Paris's face for a response. "You have to have something outside of work, you know. I tried to call you to fill you in on what was going on with my company, and you stood me up. I could tell when we talked on the phone that you were with someone else. You wouldn't even call me back because in your mind it is all about sex. If that is what you want, then say so, instead of jerking me around all the time and expecting me just to understand what it is you want. I won't be your gigolo, Paris."

Paris didn't respond. Instead, she looked away as tears filled her eyes. What happened to a relationship without ties and complications?

"I will move on, if that is what you truly want. But don't come calling me up when you need a piece of ass. I'm not looking for that."

A cloud came over Paris's face as anger began to well up in her. She pushed his hand from her shoulder. "I'm sorry if that is not good enough. Look, you need to take what I can give you."

The two of them had been so intense in their discussion that they did not notice the door open. JaBari stood across the patio watching her. He watched as Paris spat her words at Tyson. He cleared his throat loudly.

"Excuse me. Is there a problem?" he asked. His voice was stern.

They whipped around.

Paris's face colored. How long had he been standing there?

Tyson exhaled, puffing up his chest. "No, there is no problem."

"Good." JaBari said. "Seems like Paris is done talking."

"You should mind your business. She can tell me when she is done. Paris, is this the reason you avoid me so much? Is this the *boyfriend*? I heard them talking about your date in the den. Is he the *family-approved* candidate?" Tyson's voice dripped with sarcasm.

"I don't know you," JaBari said. "But it seems to me it is not your business. Paris is a big girl, and I'm sure she knows her mind. And it doesn't look like she is interested in whatever it was you were offering her."

The patio was silent and tense for a moment as Paris

looked from Tyson, to JaBari, then back again. Her face burned, and she was at a loss for words. For the first time, she realized how attached she really was to Tyson.

Tyson's breath was loud as he waited for an answer from Paris. He was annoyed at JaBari's intrusion. Who was he anyway? If Paris was really interested in him, she would be quicker to tell him to leave, but she wasn't telling him that. Instead, although her mouth was saying that she wouldn't be pressured, her body was still reacting to him in a way that said she was very interested.

"Okay," Tyson said. His voice was softer now, and he rubbed his palms together. "Paris, you call me when you are ready to discuss this." He walked to the door that led back into the house. He turned and made eye contact with Paris just long enough to see the indecision and anger in her eyes. He smiled to himself. That was enough for him. She needed some prodding, and he was glad to give it to her.

Brian closed the front door and relief flooded over him. He was exhausted, and his body felt heavy. The last guest had finally left. He was getting too old for these marathon Sunday dinners that went on and on, but Athena seemed to enjoy them so much, he didn't have the heart to tell her any different. He made his way to the bedroom. Just as he thought, Athena was already getting ready for bed. He sidled up behind her in the bathroom and hugged her from behind.

She grabbed the arms that enveloped her and let them hold her. She leaned back into her husband, enjoying his embrace. Their eyes met in the mirror over the sink in front of them.

He kissed her on the curve of her ear. "Once again, you give a fabulous dinner party," he said.

She smiled. "How about we give a fabulous dinner party, although I wouldn't exactly call it a party."

Brian admired the way his wife threw herself into everything she did. And over the years, she had become masterful at it. "If you say so. Do you really think it is a good idea to be meddling in Paris's life so much?"

Athena pried his arms loose and turned around to face him. "What do you mean?" Her eyes held a suggestion of annoyance.

Brian knew he had to be careful. Athena had never been one to let him get away with too much criticism. "Well, I mean, if it were any more obvious that you were pushing her and JaBari together, it would be on the evening news. She seems happy, why not leave her alone? Every time you try to get involved she gets all tense."

She grabbed her brush. "Look, haven't we been married a long time, longer than most other couples we know?"

He nodded.

"That's right. So I must know what I am doing. Paris might be grown, but I am her mother. I know her better than she knows herself. Besides, I have my reasons for thinking they would be good together." Her words were short and clipped. She brushed at her thick, dyed black hair so hard that it made Brian flinch every time the brush made contact with her head.

He sighed. "If you say so, honey." He was too tired for an argument tonight. Besides, one of the reasons they had been married so long was that he knew when to leave well enough alone.

POSSESSION

Alexis opened the door from the garage to her house. Walter watched, still sitting in the car, his eyes boring into the back of her head.

Her fingers fumbled on the wall in search of the light switch. She flicked it on. Cotton mouth was already beginning to set in, and it was bad. Her bag hit the kitchen table with a thud just as she pulled on the door to the large, stainless-steel refrigerator. It always took more muscle than she anticipated, but it finally swung open. She grabbed a bottle of water from her bottom shelf, unscrewed the top, and had drunk half of the sixteen ounces before she noticed that Walter was standing in front of her.

"What?" she asked.

His face was full of disgust. "I don't believe you."

"Maybe I can fill you in if you would just tell me what I did."

"I shouldn't have to explain it. It should be as obvious to you as it was to everybody else." Walter loosened his tie.

"You are drunk. I had to drive you home. Paris had to get a ride home. Doesn't it bother you a little bit that you can't be trusted to be the designated driver?"

She sat her bottle on the table. "Now, you look here. First of all, I am not drunk. A little tipsy, maybe, but not drunk. I enjoyed dinner along with everyone else. And I wouldn't have been driving Paris at all if *you* had been around to ride with me. But as usual work was more important." Alexis's nose flared as she spoke. She walked through their kitchen and out the other end.

Walter followed close behind her. "We are not talking about me right now, Alexis. We are talking about you. I can't believe you would embarrass me like you did."

They had reached the doorway to their bedroom. Alexis spun around. "Embarrass you? How did I do that? This wasn't a bunch of business associates, this was MY family. They know me. And I didn't have any more to drink than I always have. There were quite a few people there who drank more. My uncle Brian included."

"But it was his house. I just can't have my fiancée running around in public acting like some kind of drunkard." He unbuttoned his shirt as he talked and threw it on the clothes horse.

"I'm not your wife yet."

Alexis flicked on a few more lights as traces of a headache started to creep into her head. Walter's concern was amusing at first, but now he was becoming annoying.

"If anyone was embarrassing anyone else, you were embarrassing me. You were holed up in the den the whole damn time talking business. You had your head so far up Brian's ass that it was ridiculous. Can't you ever leave business at the office? It was supposed to be a family dinner, where we all get together and let our hair down and things—"

He cut her ranting short. "I'm not an ordinary man, Alexis. That is why you want to marry me. You knew that from the get-go. It takes an extraordinarily thorough and hardworking man to produce the life that women like you require." It was his turn to smirk. "How many times do I have to tell you that I do what I do so that I can ensure our future? Our children's future, too. I know you don't want them ever to have to worry about anything. I'm trying to build a lifestyle for them, even if you don't appreciate it now."

Alexis felt tears welling up in her eyes. Why did he have to go and spoil a perfectly good mood?

"How can you plan a life for children who aren't even here yet? What about me?" She sat on the edge of the tub and turned the knobs. "There won't be a future if you don't tend to the here and now."

Walter loosened his belt and stepped out of his pants. "I'm sorry I was so harsh on you." His voice was softer now. "You deserve to have a little fun with your family." He walked back out to their bedroom and hung his pants with his shirt. "You forgive me?"

Alexis nodded, although her feelings were still hurt. She scooped her favorite bubble bath into the tub without looking up.

"What do you know about that JaBari guy? He seemed to have some good investment ideas. He had everyone's ear almost all night."

"Did he?" She tensed, but did not want Walter to see her reaction. Why was it that her otherwise nonattentive boyfriend seemed to have radar where other men were concerned? "He tried to talk to me about it some, but it all went over my head."

"Really? He did seem to be talking to you a lot while you were over there in that corner with him. He must have been interesting."

Alexis sat up straight. "Are you fishing for something, Walter? Just say what you mean to."

"I said what I meant to. He was new, that's all. And he talked about money a lot and spent a lot of time with my woman. My two favorite things. I think I have a right to ask some questions, don't you? I mean, he *is* a very handsome man."

"What does that have to do with his ideas about money?"

"Nothing at all. But it has a lot to do with you. I'm not blind. You think I didn't notice that you were all up in his face, cheesing and smiling? He must have refilled your wineglass three times."

Alexis let her clothes drop to the floor. Her back was turned away from Walter, and she couldn't help but smirk. He was jealous. "That is not true. I wasn't *cheesing*," she said.

He shrugged. "Maybe not. But it looked that way to me. I mean, I can't blame him. He seemed like an intelligent enough man. Something would be wrong with him if he wasn't attracted to you. Any man would be, as fine as you are."

A chuckle escaped her lips. "I'm attractive now? So anything that was happening was my fault? Is that what you are saying?"

Alexis was not used to Walter being jealous, but it felt strangely good, sexy even. She felt a tingle in her loins as she lingered, sitting on the edge of the now full tub. She dropped her hand into the warm water and rubbed some of the luxuriously silky suds between her fingertips.

"No, I'm not saying that."

"Well, what are you saying, then?" She swung around and placed her feet inside the king-sized tub. Goose pimples immediately rose all over her body. The sudden heat from the water caused her to shiver, and her nipples suddenly perked up.

Walter moved to the edge of the tub. "I'm not saying anything."

Alexis laughed again and slid fully into the water. It was now filled to the brim with bubbles. She smiled as they enveloped her.

"Yes, you are. You were jealous." She paused. "Don't worry, honey, you have nothing to worry about. I'll admit, he is an attractive man, but I have more restraint than that." Walter didn't need to know that he was right, she had enjoyed the attention. She had needed it even.

He sighed. "I know that, Alexis. I wasn't suggesting—"

"Uh-huh."

"I know that I haven't been as attentive as I should have been the last few months. It's so easy to get caught up in life. And you are a woman with needs like everybody else. I know that attention feels nice, and he was definitely *attentive.*"

"You can stop worrying. He is for Paris. Handpicked by Athena. You met him at the barbecue the other day, remember?"

"Actually I didn't meet him. I don't exactly rate with your family. I'm not even an in-law yet." He made imaginary quotes in the air with his fingers. "I only saw him from across the room." The worry that had been dancing about his eyes had melted away. He rubbed his hand gently on his forehead. "That would explain why they left together."

"That and you had everyone convinced that I was too inebriated to drive her home. He was the next obvious candidate."

He grabbed her bath sponge and sat on the edge of the tub. He smiled down at her warmly.

"Can I wash your back?"

Alexis leaned forward so he could reach her. She drew up her knees, then closed her eyes so she could languish in the feel of the slightly rough sponge on her wet skin. It had been too long since they'd taken the time to have a decent conversation. It felt good.

"Uhm, nice."

Walter smiled. It was too bad they didn't have more moments like this one.

"So, are we investing in Tyson's company? I was surprised that you brought him along with you. You never mentioned him before. Where did you find him?"

"Maybe. We like the idea a lot. So much, we might want to even buy him out." He paused. "I thought you knew him. He and Paris seemed to know each other."

Alexis shrugged in the water. "She never mentioned him. I'm surprised, because he was a good-looking one, too. And, contrary to what you might believe, she and I are not joined at the hip."

"Is that all you woman talk about?" Walter gently rubbed his fiancée's shoulders with the loofah. "I have to say it was a little strange when she opened the door. She seemed shocked to see him. They just stared at each other like they had seen a ghost or something."

"Hmm. Maybe she had. I have to remember to ask her about it. You know I have no problem getting in her business."

"I think everybody knows that." He chuckled. Alexis was so obviously nosey and didn't care who knew it. "Poor Paris, the whole family is on her case. No one would ever believe she was a grown woman."

Walter let his wide hands slip downward. He cupped Alexis's breast gently, then touched his lips to her neck.

She gasped, and her lips parted in surprise. Her nipples stood at attention. "If I had known that gossip would make you frisky, I would have tried it sooner." She leaned into his touch. There was anticipation between them that she had not felt in months. "Will you be joining me?"

He whispered, his breath hot against her ear. "I'm already wet up to my elbows." Walter released her, then stood up and let his silk boxer shorts drop. He stepped out of them, leaving them where they lay. His gray-green eyes smoldered.

Alexis felt her pulse quicken at the thought of him joining her in the bath, another something he hadn't done in a while. She scooted forward in the tub as he stepped toward her, making room for him in the back of the oversized basin.

Without speaking, Walter stepped into the bath, making the water level rise. Trickling sounds whispered as the water flowed into the emergency drain. He sank behind her and wrapped his long, toned legs around Alexis. He savored the feeling of her soft curves against him.

She leaned back into him and closed her eyes again. His

fingers lingered as they trailed softly down the front of her body. It had been too long since they touched each other this way. She exhaled heavily and caressed his calves. A delightful shiver ran through her, reminding her of how she felt back when they first started dating. His breath was uneven against her cheek.

He held her snugly and probed between her thighs with his fingers.

Her legs parted. His strokes sent jolts of pleasure through her. A part of Alexis sensed that this was really about possession, but she did not care. His touch felt good to her, and she planned to enjoy every bit of it.

"Bath time is over," he said. His voice was hushed and husky.

They leaned forward as he reached around her and opened the drain. Alexis let him grab her hand and pull her to her feet. His mouth covered hers hungrily. Water sloshed onto the floor.

"My new bath mat—"

"We can buy another." Walter pushed Alexis's head back around to face him, kissing her again.

Alexis's breath came in gasps. She was enjoying the game of cat and mouse they had been playing. The prolonged anticipation was almost too much for her.

Walter slid his hands down and around her thighs. He guided her to wrap her legs around him and lifted her bodily. Water splashed around their calves as he turned her around, then backed her up against the wall behind the tub. He grazed the top of her shoulder with his teeth, then in a sheer act of possession, he lifted Alexis up and brought her down, slowly, until he had completely entered her. He grunted.

Alexis let out a sound that was half moan, half sigh, then wrapped her legs around him tighter, drawing him deeper inside. She welcomed his desire, even though she could tell that it was motivated by his insecurity. It was what she needed, too. At that moment, she didn't care.

UNFINISHED BUSINESS

Bittersweet. That was the only word Tyson could think of to describe how he felt. He sat in the center of his leather sofa, alone. He had not bothered to turn on a light. As soon as he returned from the dinner, he grabbed a beer and sat down to think things through.

He had wanted to celebrate his possible business success with someone he liked very much, but instead he ended up fighting with Paris. If it wasn't a fight, the atmosphere between them was certainly more tense than it had been. He wasn't sure what had happened. He had not been prepared to see her. He shook his head in disbelief. How small a town was Austin?

The way she treated him took him by surprise, too, acting like he had committed some kind of crime by coming to her parents' house. Had he somehow soiled the premises by his presence? His nostrils flared. His feelings oscillated between anger and remorse.

He admitted that he had reacted rather strongly when he overheard the famed Alexis talking about Paris and that

JaBari guy. But he had been too sure of himself. It was disgusting. His reaction was, too. It was becoming clear that his feelings for Paris had long ago crossed the line from just casual sex. Unfortunately, it didn't look like she had crossed that line with him.

There was no way that he could have known that dinner with his future business partners would end as it had. They hadn't written anything down yet, but it looked like the partners were going to invest a substantial sum into his company. At least enough to get him through a year. The only things missing were their signatures on the dotted line. That and Paris.

He was on his way. He should be happy, ecstatic even, but he wasn't. The first person he wanted to tell was Paris, and he hadn't even gotten the chance to do that. He hit the sofa with his fist. Dammit. He had tried to tell her, that day on the phone. It was clear now that she was with someone else when he called. Probably on that date with JaBari. Tyson supposed that he was probably doing very well for himself, something that made him an acceptable candidate for Paris.

The night had brought some clarity to his latest conversation with Paris. She liked to be with him in the bedroom, but when she said they were in different places, what she really meant was his pockets weren't deep enough, or he didn't have a fancy education. Tyson shook his head. He never thought he would be the kind of guy you slept with but didn't bring home to mother. Paris was so busy letting her family dictate who Mr. Right would be that she was running away from something that could be real and lasting, and she didn't even realize it.

He drained his beer can and half chuckled to himself.

She probably already knew about his potential success, considering that the investors were her own flesh and blood. She had not mentioned a thing. The more he thought about it, the more he realized how little he really knew about Paris. He was still indescribably drawn to her though. It was becoming harder and harder to get Paris out of his head.

The more aloof she was, the more she tried to push him away, the more attractive she became. And when she talked about banking and finance the way she did, that just did it for him. Talk about sexy. Tyson took a swig of his beer and smiled. She was so damn intelligent—and there was something about that smarts that made him hard as a rock every time he thought about it.

Tyson had a sudden urge to talk to Paris, to see her. He picked up the phone, then put it back in its cradle. She was angry with him. He had to take care of that first, send her something that said what he felt. And he needed to find out about JaBari. Was she really interested in him? Where had he come from? It was as clear to him as it had ever been that Paris was the one for him, even if she didn't know it yet. But if he was going to win her over, he had to do his homework first and come to the table armed.

The lobby was deserted by the time JaBari arrived. He was glad. The night clerk had been trying to make conversation with him since he had checked in. He didn't feel like talking tonight. His agenda had no room on it to waste with people that were beneath him. And the way he saw it, that clerk couldn't do anything to help him, so he was most definitely a waste of time.

JaBari glanced at his watch. It wasn't quite midnight. It

was late, but not so late that his client wouldn't be glad to hear from him. He had good news. Hopefully it was good enough that he would not have his knees broken or whatever it was they planned on doing to him. He didn't know and didn't plan to find out.

The elevator seemed to take too long to come. As soon as he got to the privacy of his room, he flipped open his cell phone and dialed the number he knew by heart now.

"Yes." The voice was groggy.

"Sorry to call so late, but I thought you might want to hear good news."

"It's not that late here. We are two hours earlier than you. It better be good news."

JaBari sighed. "It is. I have some money for you." Sweat beads rose on his forehead. He wiped them away with his hand.

"Some? How much is some? You owe me a couple of hundred thousand dollars. I took a big hit because of you. I have no idea what possessed me to listen to your scheme."

"That is behind us now. And it wasn't a scheme. People make money doing things like that every day, Wesley. I'm trying my best to get you your money back. And it was a legitimate idea. That movie company had money flowing through the bank like water through a faucet, and all their other movies were hits. I had no idea that the one they were looking for financing for was going to be a big flop. If you were anybody else, the loss you took would be on your shoulders, not mine. But since we go so far back—"

Wesley and JaBari did go far back. After JaBari's father died, they worked together in a supermarket in Queens, New York, where they were both from. They remained friends ever since. It was Wesley who introduced him to the seedier side of life. Wesley had taught him that sometimes you had to use less-than-scrupulous ways to get what you wanted, or you would get stepped on. It was the way of the world.

His voice deepened and took on a threatening tone. "Don't give me that, you asshole. We are not supermarket checkout kids anymore. We are all grown-up, and this is real shit. You worked as hard as I have for what we got, and you know that money doesn't grow on trees. I trusted you, and you fucked it up. I want my money JaBari. You know I know people, and I can reach far—"

He cleared his throat. The elation he felt earlier was quickly dissipating as he began to lose his patience. Who the hell did Wesley think he was ranting at anyway? "Don't forget you are not part of the Chivers clan anymore. Not since that wife of yours left you."

He was sorry as soon as he had spoken the words. Wesley's wife had divorced him and had him fired from the company her father owned after a family scandal not too long ago.

"You stupid motherfucker. Don't think I won't kill you then come cry at your funeral." He paused. "I am going to let that slide because you said you had my money. I have my own connections, don't worry. Just like I was smart enough to make sure I had my own money. Let's get to business."

JaBari toyed with the envelope in his hand. "I gotta make a deposit tomorrow. Then I'll wire you some funds in a day or two."

"What does *some funds* mean?"

"I think you will be happy. I have to take it slow because I didn't want to move too much at one time. You know Uncle Sam is always watching."

"I don't give a fuck who is watching. You better just do the right thing."

Wesley didn't wait for him to answer.

The phone clicked in JaBari's ear, and it took him a second to realize that he had been hung up on. *The right thing for whom?*

He glanced over at the nightstand. It was too late to call Paris. That could wait until tomorrow. He wanted to stay on her good side. He had to. Miss Montague had lots of things he needed, and she had no idea. This was going to be the most *right* thing he had done in a long while.

CRUNCH TIME

The rain was relentless. What had begun as a drizzle on Sunday had given way to what seemed like a torrential downpour on Monday. Paris's skin crawled; by the time she made it to the office, she was soaked through to the skin and sniffling. She wiped around her eyes with her fingertips, trying to leave the remnants of her eye makeup in place. Her head ached from the aftereffects of too much wine at dinner the previous night, but she sat down to her desk right away and started reading the refinancing file.

"I didn't hear you come in." Brian poked his head through her door.

Paris jumped. She had been immediately drawn into what she was doing and tuned out the office sounds around her.

He pushed the door open and stepped into Paris's small office without an invitation. His forehead was furrowed, and he rubbed it with his hand.

Paris stood up to greet him and looked at him questioningly. "You okay? Don't tell me you had too much to drink last night, too? You and my mother always outdo yourselves with your events."

He shook his head. "It wasn't an event. It was dinner. I have one of my migraines, that's all. I can handle it. But that isn't what I came here to discuss." He paused. "American Bank has called another meeting. I want you to go with me this time. I'll be your backup. This one is important. It could make or break us. We should know by the end of the meeting whether we will be representing their interests or not."

Paris stomach jumped. This was her chance. "Wow."

"Is that uncertainty I hear? 'Cause I don't have room for that."

"No," she said. "I can do it. I'm ready. I have practically memorized this file."

He sat down. "Let's hear it. Why should our firm be their lobbyist of choice?"

"Now?" Paris's eyes opened wide in surprise. Sweat trickled down the inside of her forearm.

Brian nodded.

Paris cleared her throat. "Well, I want them to know about the equity that they could have access to here on the east side in these historic homes. There's lots of room for them to make loans here, and I think it is a good angle to use when we are trying to convince people to support the new legislation." She paused again, searching for a reaction from Brian. "You know, chance to revitalize an otherwise underprivileged area."

He was slow to respond. "What else you got?"

"Don't you want to hear the idea out?"

"I'm sure it is a great one, but you can bring it up after you have won their business. I'm sure there will be someone you talk to that will want to know about how this is all going to help the less advantaged side of Austin. But these people want to know how we can help them sway the legislature in a direction that will benefit them so they can make big money. They are not asking us to help them find a market. I'm sure they are aware of 'untapped areas' in many Texas cities, not just Austin. If they don't, they will soon, but it is not our concern."

Paris opened her mouth to speak but was interrupted by the buzz of her phone. She glanced at the caller ID screen.

"Mom."

Brian stood up to go.

"Wait." She held up her hand. "I'm not going to take that. Let's talk this through.

"No, you talk to your mother. If you don't, she will just call me next anyway. But I know you can come up with what the client needs to hear. I'll be there with you. Just jot down your highlights and get it to me by two, okay? The meeting is in a day or so." He walked out of the room.

Paris was fuming. She grabbed the phone off the hook. "Yes."

"Is that how you answer your phone? Paris, it's your mother." She paused. "Is everything okay?"

"I'm sorry. If you call being shot down before I even get started okay, then I am fine. I'm really busy, Mom."

"I understand. I'm not going to keep you. I need a favor. Can you remind your stepfather that he has a doctor's appointment this afternoon? He keeps canceling. We need to make it to this one."

"He okay? He's not sick, is he?"

"No, nothing like that. It's just his yearly physical. But we aren't getting any younger. He works too hard and needs to take better care of himself."

"Okay, I'll remind him. But I have to get to work. He just gave me a two o'clock deadline."

"You'll be fine. But he is going to have to change that until tomorrow because I doubt he will be back by then. Physicals take a while." She paused.

Paris breathed just a little easier. She might have a full twenty-four hours to come up with a new plan of attack and rewrite the entire presentation.

"And just remember that he is so hard on you because he wants you to be the best. You are all we have."

Paris nodded to the empty room. *Just pour on the pressure, why don't you?* "You're right, Mom. I know that." She rubbed the space between her eyes with her forefinger. At this rate, her headache would last forever.

"Oh, and speaking of that, I hope you plan on going out with JaBari again. I need some grandbabies soon, while I can still enjoy them. I was so glad that Alexis invited him to dinner. He is quite the gentleman."

"I hope you want me to get married first." Paris was surprised it took her as long as she did to mention her date. And she had just reminded her that she owed Miss Meddling Alexis a tongue-lashing at the very least.

"I would prefer that." She chuckled. "You better hurry up though. Someone else might snatch him up. He sure was charming all the ladies."

"Mom, I got this, okay? It is under control, I promise. I have to get to work. I'll put a reminder on Brian's calendar."

"That sounds fine."

Paris hung up the phone and shook her head. Her mother meant well, but she sure was annoying. As if her stepfather trashing her perfectly good idea and not letting her finish wasn't enough. Her mother was pressuring her and making her feel as if she were the last hope for the family business and the family bloodline.

Lunchtime slid by without notice as Paris worked diligently on her assignment. She turned the ringer off on both her office and cell phones and disabled the bell on her e-mail program. She expected Brian to summon her to his office to hear what she had come up with. Paris would not at all be surprised if he called her in early. He was like that. If they weren't related, she would say he was tough to work for.

After several hours, Paris was convinced she was ready. She prepared her presentation in PowerPoint. It was laid out in pretty much the standard format. And it was boring. But if that was what he wanted, she would give it to him, although she was not quite confident that the same old run-of-the-mill approach would win them the business. American Bank was part of a big conglomerate. Benton and Associates needed to look like they could represent their interests at the Capitol now and on other issues, too. She still had a week. She knew from experience that in order to get him to listen to her ideas, she first had to give him what he wanted to hear.

Exhausted, Paris finally stood up to stretch her back. She was as close to finished as she was ever going to be. And had done a damn good job, too, considering that she had redone a week's worth of work in a few hours. She glanced at the time on her computer screen and frowned. It was well past two o'clock. She expected Brian to have been beating her door by now. Being late was unusual for him, especially when he gave someone a deadline. She expected him to at least want to take her notes with him to the doctor.

His phone line was not lit up, so she buzzed him on the intercom.

"Brian?"

He didn't respond. She held the button down and listened, but couldn't make out any discernible sound. There was not even the sound of his hard drive whirring or his fingers clicking on the keyboard. That was unusual. At any given time, Brian's office was generally buzzing with activity.

He was probably around the office working with one of the other associates. American Bank was not the only client that was active right now.

Paris gathered up her papers and tried to smooth some of the sitting creases that had appeared in her skirt. She didn't want him to think that she was not capable of getting the job done in a pinch. She pulled her office door open. For the middle of the afternoon, the office was unusually quiet. By now, the other associates would be back at the office after their morning meetings writing reports or at the very least, gossiping about who said what and where.

Paris's headache returned, stronger than ever, as she listened to her heels click along the wooden hallway. What was going on? This was an important time, and the office did not seem busy at all. Brian's door was open. As usual, she listened first. She plastered a smile on her face, then poked her head in.

He wasn't there. She stepped inside, balancing her presentation in one hand. His chair was pushed under his desk, the computer was off, and his desk was neat. Maybe she got the time wrong. Her computer clock was not the most accurate timepiece in the world. She walked around behind his desk and picked up the small, old-fashioned clock on his credenza. Her mother had given it to him on Father's Day. The time read three-thirty. What in the hell was going on? Brian must not have been as concerned with that deadline as she thought he was.

Paris took a deep breath and made her way back down the hallway. She spotted one of the associates and called out to him.

"Hey." She tried her best to hide her frustration. "You know where Brian is? I have his report ready."

"He left a few hours ago. Said something about a doctor's appointment."

"Oh. You know if he is coming back?" How could she forget about that appointment? She was the one who had checked his calendar. She was so engrossed with this whole project that she was losing touch with reality.

"He didn't say, but you never know. Try his cell." He put his head back down and continued what he was doing.

Brian was usually the catalyst for all of the activity in the office. His absence would explain why it was so quiet. He was not there to crack the whip. Since he was gone, she could catch up on some e-mails, then make her Pilates class. Might as well. She needed relaxation more than anything else right then.

"Thanks."

He didn't look up. "Oh, a package came for you. You

had your do not disturb light on so we put it on the front hallway table."

She nodded. She could pick it up on the way out. And, just in case Brian came back, she was going to leave a copy of her presentation on his desk.

ALLIED FORCES

Tyson couldn't help it. He was fidgeting under the table. The meeting had gone well so far, and it was all he could do to contain his excitement. After two years of talking about his idea, it looked like it was finally getting off the ground.

DBA Ventures were a formidable trio. As soon as he had come into the room, they lit into him with a barrage of questions. He was prepared, though, and made his presentation effortlessly. His palms didn't start to sweat until he took his seat. He had to kept rubbing them on his pant legs to keep them dry. He glanced down as he rubbed them again, hoping he wasn't making an ugly sweat spot.

"Your idea sounds great." Walter spoke, and Tyson was glad that what he had to say was positive. Up to that point, it had been hard for him to read any of the other partners' expressions. They sat there with faces of stone, not reacting to anything he said or to any questions he answered with anything more than a noncommittal nod.

"Thanks. I think technology is ready for this. And as far

as I can tell, no one has come up with a similar or as effective an idea. At least not one they have publicized on any level or that could be so affordable to adopt. Everything that we heard about before was almost cost prohibitive for potential customers."

Barry Davies nodded. "I agree. But that window will close soon, I'm sure of it." They all nodded, agreeing with him.

This was the first time Tyson had met Barry, the one the other partners referred to as Davies. He knew he was married to Sarah, the lady he met that day in Starbucks. As far as Tyson could tell, the husband and wife were a team. Although she played the part of office manager for the small company, she seemed to have as much say in what went on as he did. Sarah was sitting behind them now, facing Tyson, taking notes. He made eye contact and smiled at her. She had not really commented on anything he said to that point, but had nodded along with the rest of them. Tyson noticed that she tapped her husband on the shoulder twice during their short meeting, passing him notes each time. She seemed to be the warmer of the two. While her husband had remained stoic, her warm blue eyes appeared to agree with virtually everything Tyson said. She smiled back at him now. It was good to see a little positive reaction from someone.

Walter spoke up again. "The only thing I think we need more clarification on is repayment of our note. It isn't clear to me how the DBA Ventures will get its money back if we decide to underwrite your company's initial project. We discussed it, and we would like to see you draft a plan that would provide some equity in the company combined with some cash repayment. Have you considered issuing your own bonds? Some options maybe?"

Tyson measured his words carefully. "Well, I hadn't planned to sell the company or the idea outright, if that is what you are suggesting." He licked his lips and paused. He had sensed this coming. "I would still want to maintain majority ownership in the company."

Davies held up his hand. "And we are not suggesting otherwise. We are just saying that we think we like your idea so much we want to invest in it in a major way. Our money and our skills. We want a piece of the pie, if you are willing. With us as part owner, I think we can get you the rest of the financial support you need, if the deal is right." He rubbed his pointed chin with his fingers.

Tyson looked at the faces of the partners. They were all smiling at him.

Sarah winked.

His dream was happening for him. What would the naysayers say now? He nodded. "I can work on it."

They all stood, signaling that the meeting was over. "Good. Let's shake on it then. We are counting on hearing from you so we can get going. We should let our lawyers work out the specifics?"

Tyson nodded. The meeting had been intense, but his mood suddenly felt buoyant. They shook hands all around, then gathered their things to leave. He was relieved. A deal had almost been struck, but there was one other thing he had come for.

Tyson made eye contact with Sarah and motioned to her as the other men started toward the door.

"You have a minute? I have some things to ask you."

She nodded, then said something to her husband that he could not hear.

"What can I do for you?" She moved around the room

and immediately began straightening the chairs, returning them to where they had been when they first came in.

"Nothing really." He shifted his weight from foot to foot, impatiently. "I was wondering if you could help me with something."

"Me?" She paused, head cocked to the side. She had a questioning smirk on her face.

"Well, I have a few questions, not to do with business or anything."

"Let me guess. I got your e-mail. I just didn't have time to answer it. Paris, right?"

Tyson blushed, thankful for the shadows that the afternoon light was casting in the conference room. "I'm not trying to get into her personal business. But JaBari Nolan doesn't seem—"

"I heard that you and Paris knew each other. Walter said it was strange at the Montagues'. You must be the mystery man, right?" She chuckled. "That girl. I don't think you have too much to worry about where he is concerned." Sarah remembered Paris talking about JaBari.

"I never said I was worried. I can hold my own, now."

"I never said you couldn't. I get where you are coming from. I don't get good vibes from him either."

"I'm glad I'm not the only one."

"I'll keep an ear out. But you better make a move soon. That mother of hers wants her to carry on the line, push out some kiddos, if you know what I mean. That family is full of old-fashioned ideas. They are a little odd."

"Paris never struck me that way."

Sarah moved toward the door, and Tyson walked with her. "No, I don't think she is. Miss Paris *is* sort of a rebel. But I have known her a long time, and her family is important to her. On the one hand, she has her own mind, but on the other, she wants them to approve of her actions. Especially her mother."

Tyson held the large glass door to the conference room open for Sarah to pass through.

"I'm glad you're a gentleman. That should work in your favor." She paused. "Tyson, I like you. You seem to be an honest, hardworking person. And with ideas like yours, you will be very rich." She paused. "Trust me when I tell you adding wealth will work in your favor, too." Sarah had to reach up to put her hand on his shoulder. "Because I like you, I'll let you drop me a line every now and then. I don't know what I have to tell you, or even if I do, if what I have to say will help."

He looked down at her but did not speak.

Her eyes were full of mischief. "But the rest is up to you." She paused. "You have to understand, though, that Paris is my friend. That is where my loyalty lies."

Tyson nodded as he took in the full meaning of what she was saying, then extended his hand.

Sarah took it, and they shook hands. Paris would kill her if she even thought she was meddling in her business. But some things were too good to let pass by.

INTERROGATION

Pilates 360 was quieter than usual. Paris listened to the hum of the ceiling fans as she mounted her machine. She lay back on the pulley bed and waited for the others to arrive. She inhaled as the scent of eucalyptus filled her nose, and a sense of peace drifted over her. She smiled as she thought about how surprised the others were going to be. She was actually early for a change.

Brenda smiled down at her as she looked through the banister on her way down the steps. She descended the wooden stairway almost soundlessly, humming as she came.

"You're really early," she said. Brenda smiled warmly as she walked over to the desk and grabbed Paris's folder.

"I needed to work off some steam." She closed her eyes and took several deep breaths, preparing herself for the exercise to come. Her day had left her tense and edgy.

"Steam or stress?"

"Are they different?"

Brenda paused. "Maybe not with you." She moved to the

foot of her reformer, then glanced at her watch. Almost as if on cue, Alexis and Sarah came though the door. The noise of their arrival filled the small studio with a buzz, and Paris felt the sense of peace flit away. She tensed again. Whatever they were talking about was exciting to them. They were chattering away, and Paris sensed a conspiratorial air about them.

"Could you two hurry? I think you are a few minutes late. You are on my time now."

They paused, mouths agape. Neither one of them answered her. Instead, they looked at each other, then back at Paris. Alexis cleared her throat as the two women first placed their bags in holding cubicles, then lay next to Paris on their respective exercise machines.

Brenda rubbed her hands together, then began to direct the exercise. The three women were silent. They were all very familiar with the routine. The rhythmic sounds of their breathing filled the air.

As they finished the first exercise, Paris could hear the muffled sound of her cell phone ringing. She grinned at Brenda sheepishly.

"Sorry."

Brenda waved her comment away, then continued counting. The sound of her voice combined with the whirring of the ceiling fan blades.

Paris found herself sinking deep into her thoughts. She pondered her report, which she knew was good. Her mind kept drifting to thoughts of Tyson. She'd overreacted with him, and she had not intended to. Now she regretted it. She missed him. Paris realized that she made the mistake of letting her momentary anger over JaBari being at her mother's place get displaced onto Tyson. He didn't deserve all that.

She was the one who had kept her family life closed off to him. His questions were legitimate.

Alexis sucked her teeth. "You should have put that on silent."

The here and now crushed in on Paris's thoughts. She jumped, slamming her machine to the resting position. "Huh? I'm sorry. I didn't hear what you said."

"Well, that's obvious. But your phone is ringing again. It is a little distracting. You should get it."

Paris shook her head. "Whoever it is can wait. I need this time."

"We need the time, too," Sarah's lips were pursed into a tight, thin line. "At least put it on silent."

They paused as Paris sheepishly moved to where her purse lay. She reached inside and turned her phone to silent. "I'm sorry."

"Maybe it's your *man* calling."

Both Alexis and Sarah broke into fit of laughter.

"He can wait, too." She paused. "I never said I had a man anyway."

"We know. It looked like you had two at dinner," Alexis said.

Paris returned to her re-former and stretched out again. "You two have something you want to ask me?"

Brenda cleared her throat, trying to appear as if she was not listening. Alexis and Sarah shook their heads. They answered her in unison. "Nope."

"You don't lie well. Before we get to your questions, I want to ask mine. Alexis, do you mind telling me what made you think I wanted JaBari to come to dinner at my family's house? You could have at least warned me."

"I wasn't aware that extra guests warranted permission.

Besides, Athena didn't mind. You know your mother better than anyone."

"And it never occurred to you that I might mind?" She paused, waiting for a reaction from Alexis that she knew would never come. "You just can't help meddling. At least Sarah minds her own business. I know you want to ask me what happened with JaBari. I wouldn't want you to kill yourselves with curiosity." She paused again, then took several deep breaths as she moved the way Brenda indicated. Both Alexis and Sarah appeared to be waiting too eagerly for what she had to say. She wasn't surprised, but that did not stop her from being annoyed with them.

"Let me help you with that. Abso-fucking-lutely nothing happened, okay? He was a perfect gentleman. A good driver, too. Unlike *some* of us who are supposed to be the designated driver, but then can't fulfill our duties because we are too sloshed—"

"I wasn't sloshed," Alexis chimed in.

Sarah laughed.

"Got a guilty conscience then? I didn't mention your name or anything." Paris rolled her eyes and continued. "Anyway, he drove me home, I got out of the car, said good night and thanks for the ride."

"What is wrong with you? That's all? You didn't invite him in?"

"No, I didn't. I was in a bit of a bad mood."

"And why was that? As fine as he is—"

"Alexis, how many times do I have to tell you that not everything is about looks? Did you ever stop to think that the two of us are just not compatible?" The conversation was getting intense, making her feel backed into a corner. Paris wanted to shout at them.

Alexis waved her hand in the air, dismissing Paris's remarks as they all moved to a sitting position. "Uh-huh. I'm just saying. Some of us would have used that opportunity to get us a little somm'un somm'un."

"Some of us are not that desperate." There was nothing worse than a horny woman in a committed relationship. Is that what they wanted her to become?

Sarah cleared her throat. "So you are saying that you aren't attracted to JaBari, then?"

"No, I'm not saying that. He is attractive enough." Paris smiled. "Sexy. He has a roughness to him that is intriguing. But I have not had the opportunity to be in a romantic setting with him yet. And I'm not sure he is really interested in me that way. He seemed more interested in helping me make money." They didn't need to know that he made her nipples stand at attention when he was around.

"But you have, right? Didn't you go on a date?"

Paris sighed. "Let's just say no bells have rung yet, okay?"

"Okay." She paused. "And what about that Tyson guy? Now he is good-looking. And a gentleman. And I hear he was just so charming at dinner. Does *he* ring any bells for you? Walter said you two knew each other."

Paris stiffened, then cleared her throat. "Sarah, if I didn't know better, I would think that you were trying to get in my business, too. *Please* don't tell me that Alexis is rubbing off on you." JaBari might make her nipples stand at attention, but Tyson was another story. Her whole body reacted to him. She hated to admit it, but he scared her.

"I'm not being nosey. You know that is not my style. We are just talking about attractive men, that's all." Sarah glanced over at Alexis. She licked her lips. It would not be good for Paris to stop trusting her now.

Paris's nose flared. She decided to take the safe road. "Tyson and I know each other."

"And that means—?"

"That we know each other." Paris wiped the imaginary sweat from her brow. She could recognize an interrogation when she saw one, no matter how casual it was. Exercising was supposed to be relaxing; instead, all the discussion was making her feel like she was under an even bigger microscope than the one her mother usually used to dissect her private life.

Paris looked over at Alexis. She was unusually silent, but she was grinning from ear to ear. Whatever was going on, they were in it together. She was sure of that.

"I don't believe you two."

Brenda cleared her throat, reminding them to keep their peace. They were nearing the more strenuous part of the workout.

"So, in other words, it is not our business." There was the strong glow of curiosity in Alexis's eyes as she spoke, and it only served to incense Paris more.

It wasn't their business, not really. She had been saying this since the beginning, but that didn't seem to stop anybody from prying. She held her lips tightly together. She didn't want the anger welling inside her to cause her to say the wrong thing.

"You know what? I think I'm done for the day." She stood up and reached for her bag. Her face was stoic. She would not play their game.

Brenda glanced at her watch. "But we haven't even been here a half an hour."

Paris nodded. "I know, but my heart isn't in it. I can't concentrate. I just have to go. I have work."

The three women watched, mouths agape, as Paris gathered her things and left the studio. The wooden door slammed shut behind her, then Paris started her car without hesitation and drove away.

She listened as the pavement passed under her car. The sound was hypnotizing. It did not take long for her to get lost in her thoughts again. Paris wanted to relax at the end of her day, not get more stressed. She rubbed her temples, then the spot between her eyes. A headache was trying to find its home there. Her plan, now new and improved, called for her to go home, turn on some Janet Jackson, and soak in a tub while she drank her favorite Riesling. She reached up and pressed the button that opened the sun roof. The cool evening air fluttered across her face. The road she was driving on toward her apartment was densely lined with trees. Most of them were in full bloom. The overwhelming scent of blooming mountain laurels filled her car. This was more like it. She exhaled and let her body lean more toward the relaxation she needed and tried to shrug off the nagging she had gotten from her so-called friends.

Unsynchronized stoplights interrupted her flow. She stepped on the brake, and her car rolled to a halt. Paris glanced over into the car in the lane beside her. The woman in the car gabbed away on her cell phone, seemingly without a care in the world. She threw her head back, laughing. Paris remembered her phone ringing earlier and reached over to grab it.

Six messages. You would think she had been exercising several hours rather than just a few minutes. Paris had a feeling that not one of them would make her laugh like the lady in the other car had done. Brian was probably calling her about the report. It was so unlike him to leave after he set up a meeting. He had never done that before. She recognized most of the numbers. Tyson. The hotel where JaBari was staying. Her mother's cell. And a hospital.

Her chest tightened.

She pressed the small phone to her ear. It was worse than she thought. Paris cringed as she listened to the full message. Her mother was normally composed in most situations, gliding through even the toughest spots with grace. On the surface, her message sounded just as calm as always, but Paris could hear the strain peeking through her voice. Something was very wrong.

BAD DAYS

Hospitals made her cringe. Paris could not remember a happy occasion when she had been summoned to one. The doors swished open, and she recoiled as the disinfectant-laced smell of the building greeted her nose after only one step inside the door.

Paris paused a minute and took a deep breath in order to get herself together. She steadied herself on the steel handrail that appeared to run the length of the long corridor she faced. She had to at least have the appearance of strength, no matter what her mother was going to say.

The woman at the information desk pointed her to the elevators. Paris made her way to the fifth floor, as her mother instructed, but was still bewildered as to what was going on. She wasn't even sure who was in the hospital yet. Was her mother having some problem they hadn't discussed or was Brian? Her mother's message had been vague. Thoughts of the worst things imaginable ran through her head on the slow elevator ascent. She fought back the tears that kept attempting to sting her eyes.

The elevator doors opened, just in time to keep Paris from bawling. She dabbed at the corners of her eyes with her fingertips. Her imagination was getting the best of her. It was only tests, right?

A reception desk guarded the entry onto the floor. The woman sitting behind it glanced up from her book briefly, appearing to size Paris up. They made eye contact for a moment, then Paris let her eyes trail to the sign above her head. Cardiac Care. Her stomach turned over again. This was worse than she thought. She turned the corner, heading toward the room number her mother gave her in her message, and stared at the floor. She did not want to make eye contact with any of the other people in the hallway. It might give away her confusion or, worse yet, start her tears really flying. Paris swallowed as she walked, not sure if she was trying to keep the lump in her throat or make it go away. It was annoying, but on the other hand, she was sure that it was acting like a dam that was already strained and bulging, holding back the waterworks she knew would help no one. Crying wouldn't even make *her* feel better, especially since she wasn't clear what she should be crying about.

Someone cleared her throat, and Paris looked up to find her mother standing almost directly in front of her. She had been concentrating so hard on putting one foot in front of the other that she had not even heard her come down the hall to meet her. She looked into her mother's eyes. Her face once again clouded with confusion. What could be so urgent that could leave Athena looking so calm? Her mother looked as calm and composed as always. Strong. Paris swallowed.

Her mother put her hand on Paris's shoulder.

"Mom?" Her face was full of questions.

"It's Brian."

For a moment, Paris registered a hint of panic in her mother's otherwise composed face.

"I thought he had a physical—"

"He did. They made him do that stress test thing, like always. He seemed to be doing fine. Then they stopped the test after two minutes." A look of seriousness came over Athena's face. "I don't want you to panic, okay, Paris? You know how emotional you can be." She rubbed her arm calmingly.

Paris nodded. "But didn't he have a physical last year? What could have changed so much? Can I see him?"

"You have to not look so afraid, dear. You look like a deer caught in headlights of some truck or something." She attempted a wan smile. "Brian is going to have a bypass in the morning. The arteries leading to his heart are clogged. They said if he hadn't come in, he might have had a heart attack. Dropped dead on the street."

Her words stung. Paris swallowed again. What was her mother saying? Brian was young. In good shape, right? "Did you get a second opinion? What did Brian say about this? He never complained about anything more than a headache. I don't understand."

"Paris," she said, "you have got to be calm. You are not to upset him. Do you understand me? This is all God's will. It is a good thing we found this out now. Think of the bright side, okay?"

The bright side. "God's will?" She could not help the alarm in her voice. What was that? When had Athena become religious? Paris inhaled, then exhaled heavily.

Her mother glared at her in warning.

Paris's eyes darted around the hallway. This was not the time for arguing. She would have to speak with the doctor herself. That was obvious.

Her stomach cramped. The smell of the hospital was sickening her. "Can I see him?"

Her mother followed her to Brian's room. He was lying in the bed, TV remote in his hand. Paris swallowed hard. He looked older than he had that morning and somehow shrunken. The slightly graying temples that made him look distinguished and handsome before, now just made him look old. For the first time, Paris noticed how her stepfather had aged.

He glanced over at her, smiling. "You think they would have cable in here, as much as it costs a night. Room service, too."

How could he possibly make jokes?

"Don't look at me like that, Paris. I'm not dead or anything. I just need a little tune-up."

Paris relaxed a little and walked over to the lone chair beside his bed. "What do you need?"

He cleared his throat. "I haven't heard the final verdict from the doctor yet, but it looks like I am going to be in here for a bit." He paused, searching her face. "Not sure how long yet.

Paris nodded. Now was not the time to panic. What in the world was she going to do?

"You are going to have to meet with the bank on your own."

"Why? You said 'a bit'? You can't be in here more than a week, right? Besides you didn't even get a chance to read my presentation—"

He waved his hand as if dismissing her words. "You got

it under control. I don't think you will have any problem handling things. Just stick to our core business, okay? Keep the office going for a couple of days. You will present to them the day after tomorrow."

"The office?" What was he saying?

"Yes. I'll be here to help you. You can always call me if there are any questions or problems. There is nothing wrong with my head, thank God. Get me some water, will you? I'm under doctor's orders not to get up."

The sound of a pair of rubber-soled shoes shuffling at the doorway interrupted them. A nurse, clad in standard hospital white, interrupted them. Her smile was immediately annoying to Paris.

"I need to get some vitals. Is this your daughter?" She paused, but didn't really wait for an answer. She closed in on the bed. "She is a pretty one. But she is going to have to step outside. I recommend that she let you get some rest. You and your family are going to have a long day tomorrow." She pushed the button to raise the head of Brian's hospital bed.

Paris opened her mouth to speak. Her stepfather held up his hand to stop her.

"It's okay, Paris. You go on home. If you get a chance, go into my Outlook at the office. You will see the tasks that I planned on doing the next couple of days. Take care of as many of them as you can. I am counting on you, okay?"

Again. They were counting on her, again. What was she going to do? She nodded.

"And send your mother in. I have some other things to discuss with her before they make me go to sleep."

The nurse was already wrapping the sphygmomanometer cuff around his arm. Paris cleared her throat, then backed out of the room. Her head was pounding again. She was overwhelmed. Waves of emotion washed over her. She couldn't breathe. She headed straight for the elevator.

Paris got in her car and drove. Tears stung her eyes as she sped back down the highway toward her house. Everything around her was a blur until she spotted flashing lights in her rearview mirror. She swore under her breath. Was she speeding? She was so deep in thought she had been driving on automatic. A ticket would be just what she needed to put the icing on her day.

She pulled her car onto the shoulder and waited. She deserved whatever it was she got. It didn't seem like the forces that be were on her side today anyway, so she expected the worse. Alexis had been merciless, then Brian, now this.

She waited for the policeman to knock on her window before she opened it. His lips were drawn into a thin line. She had made him mad, that was obvious.

"In a hurry?" He pulled out his pad. "You have any idea how fast you were going??"

Paris shook her head slowly. "I'm sorry, Officer. I just had a really bad day. I—"

"Did I ask you about your day? A bad day does not make it okay to break the law."

Tears welled up in her eyes again. The cop looked away.

"I need to see your license and registration."

"How fast was I going?" she asked.

"Fast enough where you won't be dismissing this one with defensive driving. License and registration, please."

There was no use arguing. Paris didn't have the strength

for it anyway, even if she could make a case for herself. This one had balls of steel, and it was obvious he lacked a heart. Probably did not want to hear her sob story. She nodded. What kind of superiority complex made someone want to do this job?

Her bucket-type purse was perched on the passenger seat. As usual, it had flopped over to the side. She looked at the officer to make sure he could see what she intended and scooped the wayward contents back in and picked it up. A lipstick rolled out of her reach and fell down beside the passenger door. She cringed as she listened to it clank against the car door.

The officer glared at her while he waited for her to comply with his request. Paris sifted through her purse look for her wallet. She could get the lipstick later.

The wallet was long and thin, the kind that had room for everything, including a checkbook. It took up a lot of room and should have been easy to find inside her bag. Paris fished inside the bag. It seemed cavernous and ridiculous now. Her fingers kept coming up empty. Where in the hell was her wallet? This was just great.

Now that she thought about it, her usually full-feeling bag felt sort of empty. She dumped the contents back out onto the seat and smiled thinly up at the officer.

"Just a minute, Officer."

From the corner of her eye, Paris could see that he glanced at his watch, then pulled his sunglasses down over his eyes from the top of his head where they had been resting. She ran her hand through her things. She couldn't remember taking the wallet out of her purse. Where had she seen it last? She ran through it in her mind. The date with JaBari, when she paid the valet parking attendant.

Her stomach tensed further. Did they take you to jail in Texas for driving without a license? She put both her hands on the steering wheel.

"Officer, you are not going to believe this—"

"Try me." He removed his glasses again.

Paris smiled nervously. "I think I left my wallet at home or something. At least I hope I did. I'm sorry. I don't know what happened to it."

The officer paused. "I am going to have to give you another ticket for that. Tell me your name. I can have them look you up in the computer. Your address, too. You do have insurance, right? Current?"

She gave him the information he asked for. "Unfortunately, my registration is usually in my wallet, too."

"Um-huh." He looked at her quizzically, his mouth turned into a smirk of disbelief. "Just wait here." He walked to the patrol car parked behind her. He appeared to move in slow motion as Paris watched him through her rearview mirror.

Her breath quickened. Going to jail would certainly be a new experience for her.

INSTANT GRATIFICATION

Appearances were everything. JaBari wanted to exude self-confidence, knowing that as long as he acted like he was supposed to be doing what he was about to do, there were few people that would dare question him. He was six-foot-four, handsome, and impeccably dressed. The years had taught him how to use that to his advantage. How to be imposing. Most people would cower in his presence.

The bank was almost empty. Just like he wanted it. He had counted on midday being the time when the branch would be least busy. The bank was furnished exactly how he expected. Standard, nondescript furnishings with cheap upholstery and muted colors. He was greeted immediately by a young man, smiling ear to ear. Jabari looked him straight in the eye but did not smile in response. Why anyone would want to do this job was beyond him.

Bank cameras off to the left were aimed directly at the tellers. Just as he thought they would be. He nodded, then made a note of the young man's name. "James, I need to make a deposit."

"Certainly. Would you mind signing in on our log here?"

"Actually I would. I'm in a hurry. I have a business meeting I would hate to be late for." He glanced at his watch for emphasis.

James nodded. "I can take care of it for you then. No need to stand in line." He turned to the small table near him and picked up a pen.

"That would be fine." JaBari placed the two checks he was holding down on the table, turned them over, and signed them. He tapped his foot as he waited for the young man to note the amounts and write it on the deposit slip he was now writing on. "Here's my account number."

James took the number and wrote it on the deposit slip, too. He finished filling it out and handed a receipt to JaBari.

"And these will show up in my account today? I have to write some checks against them."

"As long as you are a regular customer in good standing, I don't anticipate any problems with that." He smiled his bank smile. "Two are drawn on a local account, and the other is an institutional check. Is there anything else I an help you with, sir?"

"That will do it. Thanks." JaBari turned and left the bank. A smirk spread onto his face. Too easy.

The shades were drawn and the apartment was warm. Tyson was almost done with the finishing touches on the plan that the partners had asked for. They were going to be pleasantly surprised. At least he hoped they would be.

He glanced down at his computer clock. Where had the time gone? Just a minute ago it had been a gloomy, rainy morning, and now it was suddenly the middle of the afternoon. It was really a good thing; the rain had forced him to concentrate on the task at hand. It took all the willpower he had not to call Paris more than the two times he already had. But enough time had passed.

He started up his instant messenger service and sent Sarah a happy face. Hopefully she would not mind the intrusion too much.

SARAH1: Tyson?

TYSN: I hope I am not bothering you. Any news?

SARAH1: Aren't you the persistent one? I told you I would let you know what I found out.

TYSN: And?

SARAH1: Nothing. She did not seem to be in a very good mood. She left our exercise session early because Paris was bugging her about JaBari.

TYSN: Thanks. I hope you don't think I am overly aggressive or anything.

SARAH1: No, I don't think that. I think you are a man that goes for what he wants. People appreciate that.

TYSN: The only one I want to appreciate it is Paris.

SARAH1: And she will. Give her time and keep charming her. Just so you know, Alexis's prying really offended her.

TYSN: That's a good thing. And how do I charm her? She seems to be blinded by the dollar signs. Many of the women I meet are that way. Folks can't look past that to see what a person really has to offer.

SARAH1: Not true. Yes, some people are impressed by money, but many women just want to be with someone who loves them. I don't think JaBari is that person for Paris.

TYSN: Yeah, but what does she think?

SARAH1: She said no bells were going off with him, but her family is very important to her. You better get on it before she softens up to him.

TYSN: Thanks for looking out. Ciao.

Tyson turned off his computer and rested his face in his hands. He better get on it, she said. Did she know more than she was letting on? It was time for their relationship to come out of the dark. He picked up the phone and dialed Paris's home number. Again.

HOT TIPS

Darkness was good for her. Soothing. Paris dropped her keys on her counter and sighed. As bad as her day had been, she definitely needed some soothing for a change. No need to bother with lights. She flopped down on the couch and sat in the darkness, thinking. What was happening to her? What had she done to warrant such bad karma? Her world was falling apart.

Her mother seemed to be handling things well on the surface. Whatever was happening to Brian didn't appear to be affecting her too much. That was just a facade, Paris knew that. All that calmness was just a cover-up. That was Athena's way. Over the years, she had become so practiced at making things look easy that it was now automatic. She was so used to making sure that appearances were just right, so there was no telling how she was *really* feeling.

Paris sighed. She never felt as strong as her mother. She was never able to keep a stone face and hide her troubles as well as Athena could. And the idea of something happening to Brian terrified her. He was the only father she had ever really known. Her stomach was tied in knots, almost as if this thing was happening to her, not to him. Like punishment for something. Tears flowed freely down her cheeks.

A knock at the door interrupted her thoughts. She glanced at her watch and tried to remove the evidence of her tears with her fingers. Who could that be at this hour? She stood up. Her head swam unexpectedly. Paris steadied herself on the edge of her couch.

"Just a minute." She shouted, then closed her eyes and opened them again. It took a second for her vision to clear. Paris sniffled, then opened her door. It was JaBari. She was momentarily speechless. What was he doing here?

He spoke first, his mouth turned into a smirk. "Most people say hello."

Paris looked down at the floor. "I'm sorry. I wasn't expecting anyone. How did you know where I live?"

"I dropped you off at the corner, remember? And the exact address was in your wallet." He held her missing wallet in the air and moved it back and forth. "Not too hard to figure out."

Paris's mouth dropped open, then her eyes narrowed. "How—?" She could not help being immediately suspicious.

"You left it in my car. The other day, when I drove you home. These other papers were there, too. I thought I would bring them over. You might need them for something."

Relief spread over Paris. Her suspicion faded away. It was obvious she needed a new purse, one that closed like it was supposed to. "I thought I was going to have to cancel all my credit cards. I'm so glad you found them." She took her wallet from him, along with the envelope. It was the information that came along with the new corporate credit card. How could she have not missed that? It was a good thing he found it. She hadn't even realized that was missing. She would never live it down if she screwed up.

Paris's head swam again, and she felt light-headed. She closed her eyes and opened them again, leaning on the doorjamb for support.

JaBari reached out and put his hand on her elbow, steadying her. "You okay? Maybe you ought to sit."

"I'm okay. I just forgot to eat I think. Plus I am exhausted. I can't even begin to tell you. I'll be okay." Paris let him guide her into her apartment and over to the sofa.

"You know, we all should eat every day." He smirked again. "Can I get you something?"

"I see. A smart-ass. I had a very hectic day. It just got away from me." They paused awkwardly. "Thanks for my wallet though. I appreciate it."

He nodded, studying her. Her face was streaked, and her eyes were puffy. It was obvious that she'd been crying. Whatever was going on must be bad, he thought. She didn't strike him as the crying type. "I tell you what. Can I feed you? I mean, I feel like we didn't exactly start out on the right foot. It would give me a chance to start over."

She shook her head. "I'm really not up to going out. I have a ton of work to do, and I have to get up early in the morning. I have to get to the hospital." Tears welled up in her eyes again.

He smoothed her hair possessively, and his voice softened. There was no way he was going to pass up the opportunity that was right in front of him. "Look, we can stay here. You have to have something in your kitchen that I can cook." He smiled.

Paris was acutely aware of his tall, athletic physique. She dabbed at her eyes again. "I'm sorry. I—"

"You don't have to talk about it if you don't want to. But sometimes, it is just so much better to have another person around. Take your mind off the things." He paused. "And I make a mean grilled cheese."

JaBari had an air of authority about him. One that made Paris want to say yes. He may have been annoying before, but this was better, much better than before. And she certainly would prefer not be alone. He was right about that. She nodded.

"Grilled cheese sounds great. I think I am craving some carbs right now anyway." She stood up. "I'll show you my kitchen."

He stood, too, and followed behind her. He looked around the duplex apartment as they walked through it. It was immaculate. Either Paris was a neat freak, or she had one hell of a housekeeper. And good taste. All of the furnishings were perfectly coordinated. "Nice place. I would have pictured you as a house kind of girl though."

"My mother did most of the decorating. She likes that kind of thing. It's not exactly a big house or anything, but I do own it. It's a condo. I didn't need much else in terms of space. It's just me." She paused. "Here's the kitchen. I'm not used to men cooking for me. This is going to be a treat."

"I did say grilled cheese, right? I wouldn't exactly call that cooking."

JaBari started walking around the kitchen, helping himself to what he needed.

Paris leaned on the counter, looking through into the kitchen. She pointed out where things were even though he didn't ask her to. "You could have just called me. You didn't have to come all the way up here from downtown."

"I tried. I didn't get an answer. I left two messages on your cell."

Paris remembered the messages she didn't get a chance to listen to. "Oh. I'm sorry. I got some disturbing news before I got a chance to get all the way through my messages. I didn't even know that my wallet was missing until I got pulled over by the cops and needed it."

JaBari grimaced. "I hope that wasn't too bad. Were you speeding?" He turned the knob on the stove to light the flame and placed a small skillet on top of it.

She nodded. "Terribly. I was upset." Her voice cracked.

"I got that." He paused. "I hope you have real butter and not margarine." JaBari opened the refrigerator and feigned searching for ingredients. He felt a twinge of guilt and did not want to look into her face just yet.

The phone rang before she could comment. Paris glanced at the caller ID. It was Tyson. She frowned. It was her turn to feel guilty. Based on his last encounter with JaBari, she knew that talking to him now would not be a good idea. She didn't want to lie to him, and he just didn't need to know that JaBari was there now. Besides, she wasn't in the mood to argue.

JaBari noticed that she didn't move. "Your phone—"

"It can wait."

"Your choice. I wouldn't want to talk to anyone either if my day was half as hard as you said yours was. I need a top for this pan—"

She pointed at a spot underneath her counter. The calmness of his voice was surprising. They didn't speak as they waited for him to finish cooking. Paris felt her stomach rumble, and the smell of the cooking butter he put in the pan filled the kitchen. She was suddenly ravenous and could not remember having anything since that morning; and then it had only been coffee. Paris was flattered by JaBari's unexpected caring. He could have just dropped the wallet off and left. Maybe she had misjudged him. Perhaps all the pressure from work was clouding her judgment more than she realized.

Paris watched as JaBari slid the warm sandwich onto a plate and pushed it across the counter toward her. They made eye contact, and she smiled. His eyes studied her face as their gazes met. Paris reached for the plate, and their fingers touched. She blushed and looked away, embarrassed. She was tentative as she bit into the sandwich.

"I had no idea how hungry I was. Thank you." Suddenly self-conscious, she dabbed at the corners of her mouth with a paper napkin.

He laughed. "No problem. I have lots of talents."

It was Paris's turn to smile. "Do you now?"

He leaned across the counter and brushed his lips softly across her forehead.

Paris cleared her throat. Her stomach fluttered.

"You should let me show them to you sometime."

"I have to tell you, you surprise me." A familiar tingling started in her groin. She pressed her knees together as she sat perched on the stool. She was surprising herself, too.

"I'm hoping that is a good thing. I didn't get that you were too excited at the end of our date at Cuba Libre. In fact, I thought I had made you angry. So I was surprised that you let me take you home Sunday, even if you did make me drop you off at the corner."

"A girl can't be too careful."

"But I came with high recommendations. Your own mother is the one that set us up."

Paris paused, then nodded. "Maybe that is the problem. In case you haven't figured this out, a mother-endorsed setup isn't always the best deal. And a girl can't be too cautious. Besides, you were kind of forceful yourself. You started in talking about money and investments so quickly. Kind of—"

"Pushy?"

Her mouth dropped open. "I wasn't going to say that."

He held up his hand. "It's okay. I get kind of excited when I am onto something." His voice became more hushed. "Plus I feel like I have known you forever. I just wanted to share. I apologize if I offended you. I hope you will let me make it up to you."

She took another bite of her sandwich. The momentary silence between them was awkward. Loud. She chewed slowly. The simple sandwich was hitting the spot for her. It reminded her of the ones her mother used to make when she was little. "Nothing to make up for. And this more than did it."

He nodded. "I'm glad. But I can do more than make you a grilled cheese sandwich." He rubbed his hand up and down her arm. "Maybe you will take a chance and go out to dinner with me again." He paused, his hand still resting on her arm. "I tell you, when your mother makes as much money as I think she will, that should help you be nice to me, too."

Paris stiffened. "My mother? What do you mean?"

"She didn't tell you? I gave her a hot tip. It did fabulously for her in only one day."

"I don't understand. She didn't mention anything to me. You told her where to put some money, and she did it? She isn't really a short-term investor. And at her age, she shouldn't be. She and Brian really need to be conservative."

He nodded, his face suddenly became more serious. "I'm well aware that they can't really afford too many risks as close as they might be to retirement. I took care of it for her so—"

"So, let me get this straight. You took money from my mother to invest heaven knows where? Sounds to me like you were trying to take advantage of a gullible older woman." Paris's eyes flashed with anger. Her face felt hot. Alexis had mentioned how charming he was. Apparently so much so that no one noticed that he was charming the money out of all her relatives. And his visit was probably only a ploy to get into her pockets, too.

"Your mother is a smart woman. She thought it was a good idea, great even." He paused, searching her face. "Perhaps if you listened to me, you could get some good returns, too."

"Listen to you? What the hell does that mean?" She slammed her hand on the counter, and the plate jumped in response. "You don't know me well enough to know a thing about my investment goals at all, or even if I have any money to invest. Surely you know even less about my mother." She jumped off the stool. "And I didn't hear anyone say that you were qualified as an investment advisor, either. What kind of shit are you trying to pull?"

JaBari's mouth hung open. "I had no idea that you were this pigheaded. I was only trying to help. Why won't you let me?"

"I never asked for any help. Not from you. I think you should go."

JaBari nodded. "If that is what you want. Fine."

Paris marched toward the door. He followed.

She opened the door for him and he paused. "Not everything is about money. Next time, run it past me before you ask any of my relatives for anything, okay? And don't bring it up again, not if you want us to become friends. I'm not interested." She glared at JaBari. "Oh, and thanks for my wallet." She had thought he was being nice by bringing it back, but his ulterior motives were clear now. JaBari wasn't doing a good deed, he was leveraging an opportunity.

JaBari stepped outside and Paris closed her door. He stood there for a moment, a smirk on his face. Money was obviously a sore spot for Paris. How unfortunate for her. And she was mistaken. Everything *was* about money, even if she didn't see it yet. He shook his head. It was okay though, he wouldn't ask her again. Not directly. He didn't have to. He had already taken what he needed.

PUSHED AWAY

Morning came before she knew it. Her head had been buried in her files from work. Paris ached from exhaustion. Her body was tired, but her mind would not rest. She hadn't slept a wink. Her mind had raced all night, alternating between thoughts of Brian, JaBari, and her new client to be.

Under normal circumstances, she would be prepared for the upcoming meeting, but now this thing with Brian added further stress to the equation. Not good. She was going to have to prioritize and get herself together. He would be counting on her more than ever now, and she would have plenty of time to confront her mother about her investment shenanigans with JaBari soon enough. First she needed to go and be by Athena's for Brian's surgery. Paris knew that her mother was a proud woman and would never ask her to come; but on the other hand, if she were not there, she would never be able to live it down. And she wanted to be there. He meant a lot to her, too.

There was a no-sleep zombie on her back, and only a

cold shower would help to get rid of it. Paris let the water hit her directly in the face. She shivered as it cascaded over her and delighted in the goose bumps that rose on her skin.

She pulled on her favorite jeans. They were comforting and familiar, just what she needed. She grabbed a cup of coffee and headed out the door. Any other day, she would have taken a deep breath and enjoyed the smell left behind in the aftermath of a heavy rain. Today she was just glad that the rain had finally stopped. Things changed quickly in twenty-four hours. She had taken a lot of things for granted before they found out that Brian was sick. He might not be there tomorrow.

She needed to stay as calm as possible. It would be too easy for her to get all worked up if anything bad happened, and none of them needed that. Paris took a deep breath. Things were going to be tense enough, even if her mother put on a happy face. She didn't need to add to it with any histrionics of her own. She smiled at her use of her mother's favorite description of what Paris resorted to if she got worked up over things. They were not cut from the same cloth where stress was concerned.

Her mind was occupied for the entire drive. Before Paris knew it, she had pulled into the parking structure across from the hospital. The click of her shoes on the paved walkway echoed in her head. Her limbs were heavy as she moved in the semidarkness, automatically, toward the waiting area she knew she would find her mother in. A sense of dread crept over her the closer she got. Paris tried to think happy thoughts, but a shadow kept invading her brain.

Sliding glass doors whooshed open as she approached. Paris glanced at the clock just inside the doorway. Brian would already be on his way to being prepped for surgery. She took a deep breath and walked into the waiting area.

Athena looked up. She had her game face on. Paris was confused for a minute. Her mother did not look upset at all and was as carefully made up as any other day. It was almost impossible to tell that she had spent the entire night in the hospital.

She stood and walked toward her daughter. No words were exchanged, and the only signal Paris got that something was amiss was a slight quiver in her mother's bottom lip. She took her hands, holding them tightly in what she thought was a comforting embrace. Paris wanted to hug her, needed to in fact, but decided to pass on it. Her mother was not exactly the hugging type. She searched her mother's face, trying to make out how she was feeling. Paris felt irritated. She had never been able to read her mother and was not able to now.

"He is already being prepped for surgery. I got to talk to him a little this morning. He is fine." She nodded. "Grateful."

"Did you see the doctor?"

Athena shook his head. "Last night. He was busy this morning when I got here. They said he would see us afterward."

Paris rubbed her hand on her mother's back. "I'm sure it will be fine. If I could just get a minute with the doctor. I have some questions myself. I still don't understand, how, if he had a physical last year, things could be this bad."

"What good is asking those questions going to do? This is where we are now Paris, and this is what we need to be focusing on. His future. Not the past."

She didn't answer. Tears stung her eyes. Someone who

did not know her mother as well as she did might mistake her coolness for callousness, but Paris knew better. This was Athena's way of coping.

"Don't start. I know how you are. You have to be in control, find someone to blame. It is no one's fault. And you can't control everything, no matter how hard you try."

"Oh, so you are going to get religion on me now? Is that it?"

Athena clenched her teeth and counted to three. "Don't take that tone of voice with me. I'm still your mother." Her voice was hushed, but her whisper still resounded across the small room.

Paris held her breath. Her mother's words stung her as effectively as if she had slapped her. "I don't understand how you can be so calm."

"I never said I was calm, Paris. I am controlled. There is a difference, and it would behoove you to learn it." She paused. "I have learned, over the years that you have to pick your battles. It makes no sense to me to waste energy and emotions on things you cannot control."

Paris gazed at her mother, seeing her differently than she ever had before. "And just when did you realize this about yourself? Where has this whole, new, rational woman come from? I always remember you being the one who was in control of everything in my life. People always do what you want, Mother."

"Not true. The people who are close to me respect my opinion. I'm getting old, they should. They give me the courtesy that most families give to their matriarch, which, if you haven't noticed, I am. And if they don't agree with me, then they humor me anyway. And Paris, I have always been a rational woman. As your mother, it was my job to control or guide what went on in your life when you were younger. I haven't done that for you in a while."

"Excuse me? You do so. You might not realize it—"

Athena held up her finger. "No, wait. I *suggest* things to you. It has always been up to you to listen to me or not."

"Really? I would have never thought it. Most of those so called suggestions come across as orders or demands. Just as if I was still a little girl. Sometimes I feel like if I don't do things the way you want them, then I am going to be punished, or spanked like I am five years old. Not over thirty."

"Then that is on you. It comes from you, not me. We never talk about it or impose demands, not really." She paused. "You are harder on yourself than any of us could ever be. But we don't expect you to be perfect. You do that yourself. You have always been that way."

Paris shifted her weight from foot to foot. She ran her fingers around her collar. It suddenly felt hot in the room. She didn't want to think about it now. "Okay, so we can talk about me later, Mother. I didn't come for therapy."

"Suit yourself." She shrugged. "I thought we were just talking. We don't do that often enough."

Athena might be "just talking," but her words were making Paris very tense. "Can we go back to your being a rational person, Mother?"

She nodded.

Paris tried to keep her voice as calm as possible. She moved closer to her mother. "How good of an idea was it for you to give JaBari, whom you barely know, money to invest for you? And why didn't you tell me about it?"

"Not that what I do with my money is any of your business, but your father and I thought it was a good idea."

"Brian knew about this, too? And he agreed to it? He is

the last person I expected to take part in any harebrained scheme."

"Who is being judgmental now? I wasn't aware that you were such the expert on money now. Is 'harebrained' your professional opinion?" She rolled her eyes. "We are adults, you know. You might not believe this, but we can take care of ourselves and have been doing it for years."

"I can't believe you. You two aren't getting any younger, you can't just be throwing money around—"

"Hold your horses. I'm not going to discuss this with you. You are the child, no matter how grown you think you are."

Paris paused. Athena sounded about ready to give her the Black-mother-I-brought-you-in-I'll-take-you-out speech. She cringed.

"We have been handling ourselves just fine for years. And we may be getting gray around the temples, but we are not dead or feeble yet." Athena flashed her eyes at her daughter. She had some nerve. "I'm not discussing this. Not now."

They sat in silence. Paris had not wanted to upset her mother. She cleared her throat.

Legs crossed at the ankle, Athena shook her leg constantly, but her face was still the picture of calmness. She was the one to break the awkward silence between them.

This was neither the time nor the place for them to discuss things like money. They should be focusing on Brian. Paris's presence was not calming at all. In fact, she was having the opposite effect. Athena felt a familiar burning in the pit of her stomach intensify.

"You know what I need you to do for me?" She glanced at her watch, then up at the large white face of the institutional looking clock opposite her. Paris had only just arrived, and it felt as if she had been there for hours. "I will probably be here for a while. Several hours until they are done, then a few more till he wakes up. I have some things that need to get done, and I am sure you probably need to go into the office." She paused. When had Paris grown up to be just like her?

Paris started to shake her head, but her mother put her hand on her leg, stopping her.

"Brian would want you to at least make an appearance. Keep things seminormal there. And I was about to pay the bills and things when this all happened." She opened her handbag and pulled out her keys. "Go to the house. In the office, everything is all lined up. I'm going to need you to take care of it. Mail what needs to be mailed. Call people. Water the plants. You'll know what to do."

"But I want to stay here, Mother. With you. You shouldn't be here alone. What if something happens?" She searched her mother's face. "You need me here."

"Nothing is going to happen. And I can handle this." She lowered her voice. "I don't want you to take this the wrong way, but I don't want you to be here now, Paris. I don't want to fight with you. I prefer to be alone right now. I need to be."

Paris's feelings were hurt for the second time that morning. She swallowed, then took the keys from her mother's outstretched hand. "If that is what you want."

Athena smiled at her daughter. "It is. Thank you. Just make sure you enter everything into my check register."

The temptation to argue with her mother was hard to resist. Of course she would do things the right way. Be extra careful even. Paris chewed on her lip and fought back her feelings of anger and annoyance. Not only was her mother treating her like a child, but she was pushing her away, almost as if she didn't have a right to be at the hospital. Athena was far too skilled at making her feel scolded.

She would save it for later. She, too, was learning to pick her battles. She nodded, then pushed through the swinging door and left the room.

HAUNTED BY HISTORY

He answered his cell phone on the first ring. The annoying ring resonated through the halls of the Capitol. JaBari's face flushed. He did not want the attention he imagined he was attracting. He didn't have to even glance at the caller ID to know it was Wesley. Ever since the wire transfer, Wesley had been calling regularly. He thought they were through with each other. What could he want now?

"Yes." JaBari's voice had an edge to it that he was unable to mask.

"Don't sound so glad to hear from me." Wesley chuckled.

A sense of foreboding took over JaBari. He was beginning to feel as if he would never be rid of Wesley, no matter how much he paid him back. "I will get you more money soon. I have stuck to my schedule so far, haven't I?"

"You have. But that is not why I am calling. Word has it that your little girlfriend is about to close the deal with her client. I need you to have your eyes and ears open."

"I never said I would help you with anything else. I am supposed to just be getting you your money back so we could go back to the way we were before. Just friends who know each other from childhood and shared a few good times."

"Uh-uh. I helped you by investing in your little plan. I thought one hand washed the other."

JaBari blew out his breath. His nostrils flared, and he glanced around the corridor to see who was around him. Things were overheard all the time in his business. "I never knew we were like that. I never agreed—"

"You didn't have to. Our earlier deal was an unspoken contract. Besides, help me, and I may be inclined to forget some of the money you lost for me." He waited for JaBari's answer.

JaBari hesitated. "I'm not sure how I can help you out. I'm not even in on what is going on. And you might say that things with Paris Montague aren't the best."

"You aren't cut out for this, are you?" He laughed again. "I'm not saying you have to marry the girl, just find out what is going on with the banking legislation, how fast it is moving. My partners aren't for this home equity stuff. If it is really going to happen, I want to know. You know we make a lot of cash bailing homeowners out. Making loans, so to speak." His chuckle was sinister. "If those people have ready access to another source of cash, they have less of a reason to come to us."

"There will always be people who can't go to a bank, Wesley. People will have bad credit even if they can get cash out of their property the traditional way. I doubt if you will ever have a shortage of customers."

"I don't have to explain this to you. We just don't want our market narrowed. Right now, customers come to us because we are the only way to go. We lend money at high rates, and we have a lot of customers. We are not too keen on them having a cheaper way to get funds."

JaBari paused as two men walked past him talking. He ducked into a hallway and paused behind a flight of stairs. He lowered his voice. "Look, I don't think there is much you can do at this point. I'm not sure there is much I can do. This is just one bank and one small lobbying firm we are talking about. There are a lot of people who want this, and I don't think you can stop it. No offense to you, but I think you are overestimating your importance in the scheme of things."

"And you are overestimating yours. You could be gone in the blink of an eye, my friend. You should have been when our deal went bad. But since we have history—"

"What do you want, Wesley? I'm short on time."

"That bank has the most to gain when and if this happens. We fully realize that we can't stop this. But I think we can slow it down. Cause a little trouble. We need to buy some time."

"And?"

"I think you can help us. Do whatever you have to in order to make some waves around your little girlfriend and her client. Our salespeople need to bring in some more loans. Get some more of the folks tied up in long-term obligations. High-interest ones."

JaBari's mind whirred. In the beginning, he just wanted to make things even for himself. How in the hell did he get involved in something with consequences so far-reaching for all of these people? He licked his lips. "And my choice is?"

"Choice? I'm not aware you have one."

BUSINESS AS USUAL

No news was good news. Alexis sat up in bed and looked around her room. Paris had not returned her call. All night, her mind would not be settled. Every time she found a deep sleep, she bolted awake. The nightmares were fresh in her mind, and sweat covered her brow. Tornado dreams. Falling dreams. Every kind of bad dream one could imagine. She was worried and scared. It was a good thing she didn't believe in symbolism or anything. She would be running for the hills if she did. Or at the very least, she would be telling Paris to.

After all that had happened over the past few days, Paris still called and planned a dinner for them, to celebrate her impending successful meeting. She was sure she would deliver her proposal well, even with Brian still in the hospital. Alexis was happy for her, but it was weird, and Paris sounded strange. It didn't seem as if they should be celebrating anything at all in the light of Brian's sickness.

Alexis shrugged. Paris was closer to him than anyone. If she was okay about dinner, then who was Alexis to second-guess or judge her? She could do with some good old-fashioned girl time herself. And Paris had been working so hard lately they rarely had any time to talk.

Paris was under a lot of stress. That was obvious given how she had reacted to their questions at Pilates gym the other day. They were used to her being harder on herself than the average person, that was her way. But their teasing was a normal part of their relationship. Nothing new. They did it all the time to each other, and it had never been a big deal before. Her storming out like she had was uncalled for. Even Sarah thought so. And the news about Brian was like icing on the cake for Paris. Bad icing.

Alexis glanced over at Walter. He was sleeping like a baby, although he had also tossed and turned all night. He was lying on his side, his back to her. Alexis had barely glanced at the clock when he slipped into bed the night before. She wasn't sure what time it had been, but the test pattern on the television set in their bedroom told her that it had been late. Very late. She sighed, then reached over and shook him.

"Walter, it's time to get up. You are going to be late." He grunted, then turned over again. Alexis took a sip of the bottle of water she kept on her nightstand. She stretched, then slipped her feet into her slippers and padded toward the bathroom.

That man slept like a zombie. It was a wonder he got anywhere on time. Alexis swore that he had a sleep disorder. She turned on her water in the shower, then walked into her closet to choose her underwear. She opened drawer after drawer to make her decision. She ran her fingers across the silk and satin in each one, enjoying the feel of the soft fabric. This was her favorite part of dressing every day. The nice fabric, close to her skin, always made her feel good. She sighed as the remnants of her bad night's sleep began to fade away. She finally settled on a pale blue silk thong with a matching Victoria's Secret bra.

Alexis stepped back into the bedroom just as Walter opened the clear shower door and stepped into the large shower stall.

"Good morning to you, too." She placed her bra and panties on the vanity and stared at him. She couldn't even really be angry at him for getting there first. It was her own fault that he preempted her shower. She had taken longer than necessary in the closet. But she should be used to it by now. He did that to her a lot.

"I'm running late." He mouthed at her through the clear shower door.

"You are *always* late. Do you realize that those are the first words you say to me every morning?"

"You are making stuff up again." He rubbed soap on his shoulders and half smiled at Alexis.

Alexis felt a familiar tingling in her spine. They had been together a long time, and he still looked good to her. She pulled her satin nightdress off over her head. It was a good thing the shower was a big one, one of the original charms of the house. "Can I join you?" Her voice was sultry.

Walter shook his head. "No time. I have to get to the office. My day is jam-packed. I have meetings all day, then have a special meeting set up with the partners midday." He paused, rubbing soap over his hard body as he spoke. "You won't want to get in here anyway. Trust me, all you would be doing is washing."

"I could wash you."

"No can do, Alexis. I'm serious. I gotta get out of here.

What time is it anyway? I can't believe you are thinking about sex again."

"Again, what are you talking about? Don't tell me you plan on having us go another three months—"

"We can talk about this tonight. When I get home." He turned to face the wall, his back toward his her.

They were obviously back to normal again. Alexis touched her cheeks. Her face was flushed and hot. "I apologize for being so damn annoying to you then. Taking care of your future wife is such a burden for you, isn't it?"

"You are being silly. Nothing like that. My mind is already halfway into my day. If this deal with Tyson goes through and works out half as good as I think, I will have much more time for you, I promise. I will be able to quit my regular job, and we will be making money hand over fist. Now if that isn't a turn-on, I don't know what is."

Alexis paused, stunned. She could not believe what she was hearing. "So, you are saying that a couple of dead presidents are sexier than I am? I don't see why I bust my ass to look good for you. You only pay attention when the checkbook is healthy. Or if you think you might have some competition."

He reached behind him and abruptly turned off the shower. "You are being childish. What is that comment supposed to mean? Instead of worrying about all that and arguing with me over nothing, you should be concentrating that energy on helping your family. Any news on Brian? Last you mentioned, he hadn't woken up after surgery."

She shook her head. "How am I supposed to help them? They don't need my help. They have Paris." She paused. "I'm having dinner with Paris tonight though. She should have some news by then." Alexis looked at the floor. She felt pushed aside. Again.

Walter toweled off, his back to the room. "You let me know what is going on."

"How? I can't ever reach you during the day."

"Alexis. Stop. Let's not. I'll be busy today, too. But you know I'll be home. It'll be late though. We'll talk then. If there is an emergency, tell my secretary. She can always reach me."

She knew his words were supposed to be comforting, but Alexis found herself seething with anger instead. Once again, he had put her and her family last. "I'm glad someone can."

Walter pulled on first one sock, then the other. Her tune would change when they were rich. She would see. He could feel her staring at him as he pushed his feet into his shoes. He didn't want to argue with her. He hadn't even had his cup of coffee yet. He took one last look in the mirror, grabbed his keys from the counter, and left.

SURPRISE, SURPRISE

Paris unlocked the door to her parents' house and let herself in. She stood in the entryway and listened hard to the sounds of the house. Everything was still, except for the ticking of the grandfather clock that had guarded entry to every house they had ever lived in for years. She surveyed the house as she made her way to the office. Everything looked to be in its place as far as she could tell. Not that she would expect any different from her mother. She kept house well. God forbid she not be ready for company, expected or otherwise.

The door to the office was ajar. Paris pushed it open and walked around the massive desk. She slid into the black leather chair and could not resist the urge to rock in it. When she was a child she often found her way to the office, sometimes falling asleep on the floor while Brian worked. The room smelled of his cologne mixed with her mother's scent. A pang of sadness came over her. Although she referred to Brian as her stepfather, he was as much her father as anyone had ever been. More than that, he respected her, and in the time she had worked in the office, he had become her friend.

Paris's vision clouded as tears welled up in her eyes. She swiveled the chair and grabbed a tissue from the box that sat on the credenza behind her and dabbed at her face. Her mother's voice resonated in her head. She shook her head and sniffled. Her mother was right. She was being overly dramatic about things. Brian was not out of the woods yet, but he wasn't dead.

The clock that sat on the edge of the desk caught her attention. She had better hurry if she was going to meet Alexis tonight. Although she was the one who had invited Alexis, she almost didn't want to go. Originally, their ladies' night was going to be a celebratory one. Her presentation had gone well and as far as she could tell, she had landed American Bank as a new client. But her happiness had been weighed down by the her sadness about Brian. She couldn't even really share the news with him yet. He had slipped into a coma after his surgery yesterday. A night out might be what she needed to relieve some of the stress she was feeling. Paris sighed, then picked up her pen and turned her attention to the matter at hand.

Her mother was as organized as ever, so everything that needed to be taken care of had already been laid out. Paris glanced through the bills. She had quite a few checks to write for her mother plus a few things to mail.

Just as she had been told, the checkbook was in the top drawer. She found it without too much trouble. Paris lined up all of the bills, grabbed a pen, and started writing checks. She felt only a momentary twinge of annoyance as she remembered her mother's comments about checkbook register.

Her phone rang, and she jumped. Paris answered while she put the finishing touches on the last check.

"Hello?" She opened the desk drawer and took out the check register. Her mother had always kept that separate from the checkbook for some reason. *Probably from years of hiding questionable investments from her husband.*

"I hope I'm not bothering you. How have you been? Sarah told me about Brian."

Paris cringed. She should have checked the caller ID first. It was Tyson. She should have known that one of her friends would not pass up the opportunity to tell her business, good or bad. She was slightly annoyed at the interruption, but his silky smooth voice was refreshing. She flipped through pages of the check register and stared at the last page. "I'm fine."

"Are you busy? You sound distracted."

"Not really. I'm taking care of some things for my mother so she can stay at the hospital."

Paris flipped the pages of the check register back and forth. She must be reading something wrong. It looked as if her mother had written a check for twenty thousand dollars. There was less than two thousand dollars in the checking account.

"That is one of the things I admire about you, Paris. You take care of the things and people. I won't keep you long. I was hoping you could meet me for dinner later."

Paris rubbed her forehead as if she were trying to erase a memory. "What?"

"Dinner. You still have to eat, right?"

"I'm sorry, Tyson. It's not a good time. I already have plans anyway."

Tyson was silent.

The only sound in the room was that of Paris flipping the pages on the check register and scratching numbers down on the page in front of her. Her mother had surely made a mistake. Maybe she had added an extra zero or something.

"Are you avoiding me? I used to feel as if you were ashamed to be seen with me. They all know about me now, so I'm a little confused."

"You know what Tyson? It's not about you, you know. It's true, you have met most of my family now, but they don't know about *us*. There are some things that are going on that I need to take care of. And I am not thinking about *dating anyone*, really. I need to get my head together and figure out what it is I want." She paused, flipping pages again. "I can't talk about this right now."

Paris struggled to keep her voice calm as the reality of what she was seeing hit her. She didn't want to jump to conclusions, and she was not ready for another disagreement with Tyson.

He cleared his throat. "Fair enough. I will give you a call later then."

Paris hung up her phone, and although she was distracted, she got the feeling that there was more that Tyson wanted to say to her. She just wasn't ready to hear it yet. Not when she had to deal with her parents and JaBari, who despite his bad boy allure, was turning out to be a bigger villain than she had ever thought. What had her mother gotten them into?

She did the math two more times, and her stomach sank from the dread. Not only had her mother given him twenty thousand dollars to invest in heaven knows what, but it appeared that that was the bulk of their savings. She opened the drawers and found where they kept the bank statements. Her worst fears were confirmed. She could find no significant evidence of any other cash. Paris grabbed her purse and the handful of bills. Perhaps there was something she just was not seeing. She needed to talk with her mother right away.

DOUBLE-DIPPING

Tyson smiled and waved at Sarah as she came through the spotless glass doors of Starbucks. He let her get close to the table before he sat down.

"Thanks for coming," he said.

She waved her hand in the air, dismissing his comment. "No problem. But what is so urgent that we couldn't cover it in our next meeting?"

"Nothing urgent. I just really want to make sure that I structure the rest of this proposal correctly and understand thoroughly what the partners want." He picked up the sheet of paper in front of him. "So let me get this straight. What they are proposing is that I become president of this new company and two of the three become officers? Sounds to me like they are trying to buy me out before I get started."

Sarah sighed. "More like they are trying to buy their way in. As advisors. But you didn't have a problem with any of this earlier. Matter of fact, you were all for it." Her eyes narrowed. "What is this really about?"

A sheepish grin overcame Tyson as Sarah searched his face. He cleared his throat. "I talked with Paris a little while ago."

"Really." Sarah raised her eye brows.

"Well, sort of. She seemed distracted."

"I'm not surprised. You know about her stepfather, right?"

"Vague details. She didn't mention much."

"She wouldn't. But she was left to run that office all by herself. From what I understand, she met with some very important clients alone. Did a good job, too." She reached over and put her hand over his. "I'm sure you know that they are very close. She *should* be stressed."

"I understand about all that. But I still feel as if she is pushing me away. Maybe she really does like this JaBari guy."

"Stop whining." Sarah chuckled. "I don't think she is pushing you away." She paused. "She is running from you. But I have known her a long time, and whether she sees it or not, he is not her type. Alexis is the only one that is pushing them together. And her mother."

"I hope not. I did some checking, and he is bad news. Word is that he has had his fair share of trouble. As far as reputations go, he is a sleazy one. Lately he has been involved in a whole slew of deals gone bad."

Sarah's eyes became slits. "How do you know all this?"

"Just because I don't have any money to speak of, doesn't meant I am not connected. My cousin works at the Capitol. Mr. JaBari has been double-dipping, so to speak. No place is private in that building. Someone is always listening." He took a drink from his coffee. "Apparently he has been investing his money and other people's in shady deals. He is like a gambler at the racetrack, only his horses are speculative corporate deals and things. Overheard things." He leaned back in his chair, lowering his voice. "He seems to be real good at talking people out of their hard-earned cash."

"Is that so? Well, I guess we better keep an eye on him, then. But I don't think you have anything to worry about with Paris. He won't get any money out of her, if that is what he is looking for. She is pretty shrewd about things like that. And I didn't see any special glint in her eye when we were talking about him. Matter of fact, she was sort of negative." She leaned back in her chair. "You just work your charm on her. You a playa, right?"

Tyson blinked. If his eyes were closed, he would think that Sarah was a sista girl instead of a blond, waiflike white woman.

"She is under a lot of stress right now. And from what I can tell, she does care for you, or she would not be bothered at all."

Sarah stood up, and Tyson followed suit.

"I hope you are right."

"I'm rarely wrong. I have a sixth sense about these things. But in the meantime, the rest of the family seems to think that JaBari is the greatest thing since sliced bread. I think it's time someone looked a little closer."

GHETTO FABULOUS

The elevator could not reach the floor quickly enough. Paris punched the buttons repeatedly, in the hopes that she could make it move faster. She tapped her foot impatiently while she waited. The doors finally opened, and she made a beeline for the waiting area.

What had her mother been thinking? They barely had enough money left in their checking account to make ends meet. Aside from her giving money to JaBari, where was their money? The reality she found in their checkbook register was not exactly what she expected it to be. *What in the hell was going on?*

"Paris."

"Oh, Mom. I thought you would be in with Brian." Athena was sitting in the hallway outside his room.

"I hardly figured he would miss me." She gestured toward Brian's room. "He is still asleep." A weak smile played across her lips. "It gets a little intense in there, with all the beeps and lights. I take a break out here every now and then."

"What did the doctor say?"

She shook her head. "No, change, like I told you before. But they are still saying that everything went fine. They claim it is normal after surgery for him to sleep a while. I'm only allowed in five minutes per hour."

"Still? It's been days. Are they calling it sleep now instead of comatose?"

Athena shrugged. "I was trying to use a nicer term."

Paris nodded and licked her lips. She was upset, but she knew that she had to approach her mother with kid gloves.

"What are you doing here anyway?"

"Well, I was at your house, paying the bills as you asked, and I had a question." She paused. "There was an entry I didn't quite understand." Paris reached into her handbag and pulled out the checkbook register.

Athena raised her eyebrows. Her face hardened.

Paris sighed. It didn't look like her mother was going to make it easy for her. "It seemed like your checkbook balance was awfully low, so I only looked back because I thought it was some kind of adding mistake—"

"I don't make mistakes."

"Okay then. I had a question about one entry. For twenty thousand dollars?"

"What about it? I wrote that check."

"You wrote it to JaBari? What is going on?"

"First off, I told you before it is not your business. I decided to invest in an idea he had. It is no concern of yours. And I didn't give you power of attorney to freely rummage through our things. You were just supposed to pay the bills."

Paris looked at her mother in disbelief. "Why did you have to write the check directly to him? That didn't seem strange to you?" She lowered her voice. "Do you think that was wise? What did Brian say?"

Athena looked away and cleared her throat.

"Wait. He doesn't know, does he? Mom, what were you thinking? What are you going to live on?"

Athena seemed to shrink. She folded back into the chairs that lined the hallway. Tears ran down her cheeks.

Paris was shocked. They seemed to be moving in slow motion. She could not remember the last time she had seen her mother display any sort of weakness, let alone cry.

"I was going to tell him, then this happened. I didn't want to upset him or anything. He is going to be so pissed at me."

Paris handed her mother a tissue.

"I just hope this works out. Brian means well. He works so hard at that damn business, but over the past few years we have been putting more money into it than we have been getting out. I was just so tired of living ghetto fabulous."

The truth came rushing at Paris like a ton of bricks. "It doesn't look like there is much left. I don't understand. I thought you two were so well-off—"

"Well-off? Paris, Brian is a good provider, no question about that. That is one of the things that made him so attractive to me. His *potential*. He always was a hard worker. But we are very far from rich. There is a big difference between being wealthy and being rich. Brian makes a lot of money when things are good. And our lifestyle takes a lot to maintain. We have a fancy address, and we have fancy expenses to go with it."

"I don't understand. That goes against everything you ever told me, Mom."

She shook her head. "What I told you was that it was just as easy to love a rich man as it was to love a poor one. I never said *we* were rich. Sure, we have *things*, but we just get by like most other Americans. Rich is different. I still balance the checkbook to the penny."

"So, I don't understand why you would make a risky investment."

"Paris, investments are like gambling. You make them and hope they pan out. But if you don't take any risks, you don't make any gains. I never imagined that Brian would be sick like this." She paused. "I'm just glad you signed that new client. We need the income now more than ever."

Paris stood up. "I'll see what I can do to trim some fat, as Brian would say. But I wish you would not keep me in the dark so much like you have been doing. Maybe I could have helped. I do know a few things, you know."

Athena nodded. Her brows drew together. Paris could clearly see the agony that was stretched across her mother's face, as if it were extremely painful for her to discuss her finances with her daughter.

She had always seemed almost larger than life to Paris. She looked up to her mother, no matter how much she annoyed her. She looked as if she had shrunk several inches over the past few days. "So what do you want me to do, Mom?'

"Pay the bills like I asked you to. Run the business. I will take care of the rest." She sighed. "And right now I am going to go hold my husband's hand. Let him know that I am here."

Paris looked at the floor. Ashamed. She realized that through the whole ordeal, she had only been thinking of herself. Her mother was having a harder time than she thought. She was just a helluva lot better at hiding it than Paris was.

Athena stood up again and wiped her face. "Paris, I really do believe that JaBari is a good young man. He is ambitious, and he has that drive to succeed. Don't discount him."

Sudden anger lit Paris's eyes, then quickly melted into confusion. "I don't know what to think about him. The verdict is still out." On one hand, he was attractive and alluring, on the other, he was pushy. And there was still that something that she couldn't put her finger on.

Athena nodded. "I realize that you have to make your own decision about your life. Like you said, you are a grown woman. But give him a chance."

Paris nodded but didn't answer as her mother walked away. A knot formed in the pit of her stomach. It was true that her mother had trusted JaBari, but she was still uncomfortable and angry. She could not help but feel that he had taken advantage of her parents.

And she meant to tell him so.

JUST DESERTS

The hotel bar was in the center of the building with no external windows. It was reminiscent of speakeasy days, with its dim lights and darkly colored walls. Alexis glanced around as she entered. It was empty for the early afternoon, just a few other people. As it was downtown, she was not surprised. Many downtowners would have gone home already, and she was early for the dinner crowd.

Most of the patrons were sitting back in corners, like they were hiding from something. Alexis smirked. This was the perfect affair bar, if there was such a thing. Always fairly dark, even if it were still light outside, and a little out of the way for most people. She took a seat at the bar. She didn't recognize anyone and didn't care if anyone recognized her. She had nothing to hide, which was probably more than most of them could say. She was there to meet her cousin, not a lover as she surmised more than one of them was.

She glanced at her watch. Early. Paris would probably be

late so that meant she had quite a bit of time to kill before their celebratory girls' dinner. The dinner would help to take Paris's mind off her stepfather, too, cheer her up a bit. He was still in the hospital, and although the doctors said he would be alright, a quadruple bypass followed by a coma was serious business.

Alexis played with her napkin and did not notice the bartender standing in front of her until the woman cleared her throat. Alexis looked up. A bottle blond with fried hair. At one point she had been pretty, Alexis supposed. She smiled, showing her yellowed teeth.

"Vodka martini, please. Dirty." Alexis ignored the woman's raised eyebrows. In some people's world, it might be too early for martinis, but Alexis was feeling neglected and needed something to take the edge off.

She was tired of waiting around for Walter to call or come home. He was so busy with his meetings and their aftermaths that he forgot time and time again to check on her.

The bartender placed her drink on the counter. Alexis forced a smile, then took a sip. Been a long time since she had a drink as good as this one. She grimaced as the cold liquid slid down her throat. She placed a ten-dollar bill on the counter and was quickly lost in her thoughts again.

She was almost finished when she felt a tap on her shoulder. She jumped. Her drink sloshed about in the glass, but she moved her hand to keep from spilling it on herself. Her mouth twisted in annoyance. What kind of idiot snuck up to people in a bar?

She sucked her teeth, double-checking to make sure that she hadn't gotten any on her conservative, lawyer-type pantsuit. It was one of her favorite outfits. She looked up.

"You drink in bars by yourself often?" JaBari smiled at her.

Alexis felt her annoyance fade. She used her drink napkin to clean up the few drops of martini that had escaped. "You sneak up behind women in bars often?"

"I didn't mean to surprise you. We seem to keep running into each other."

"We didn't run into each other this time." She paused. "I forgot you were staying here. I'm meeting Paris for dinner."

He nodded. "I see. You starting without her?" He motioned toward her almost empty glass.

"No, I was a little early. I needed to be away from my house and decided to have a drink while I waited."

There was an awkward pause between them. Alexis was acutely aware of his closeness. How could Paris not find him attractive? The man oozed sex without even thinking about it. She cleared her throat.

"I've got a while to wait yet. You can sit." He needed to move away from her. Alexis felt awkward with him standing as close as he was. She could smell his cologne, but didn't need to. She bit her lip, then looked away. Truth be told, she didn't want to. His scent was just too damned intoxicating, even through his cologne.

In one fluid motion, he pulled out the massive barstool next to her, then slid onto it.

"Aren't you back early? I would have thought you would be working way into the night, the government being in session and all."

He was slow to answer. "Normally, I would, but I had something to take care of. And this is a special session. The only thing they are really arguing over is education. I'm working on a lot of outside things right now."

"And home equity things. I know a little about that, too."

He nodded.

Alexis felt the alcohol begin to warm her, all the way down to her toes. "What outside things are you working on?" She smiled.

"I wouldn't want to bore you."

Her face darkened. "Are you implying that I am not intelligent enough to understand you?"

"I never said that. Boring stuff, really. Besides, it's top secret—"

Alexis held up her hand. "Don't give me the if you tell me, you have to kill me line, okay? You can save that for one of your girlfriends." She laughed. She could not resist looking at him from head to toe. From the looks of things, he must have plenty of girlfriends. Her eyes paused on the outline of his groin area. And with good reason, too, she decided.

"Is that what you and everyone else were talking about at my aunt's house the other day? What makes you think I wouldn't be interested? You talked to everyone else about this 'boring' stuff, except me."

"Feeling a little left out?"

She nodded. *Why am I flirting with this man?* "As a matter of fact—"

"We wouldn't want that." JaBari studied her face. "Well, I was talking to them about investment opportunities. I don't do this full-time you know. In the off-season, I invest in things."

She nodded. "I see. So you are saying that I might not want to hear about any ways I could make money—"

"No." He paused. He was beginning to get the feeling that she might be a little too easy. How had he overlooked this before? "It's just that I already talked to your husband. Or almost husband. I thought he might be talking for both of you. I didn't think—"

"That I had a mind of my own? Do he and I look like the same person to you?" All of her frustrations with Walter came rushing back at her. Why should she discuss anything with him? He was out doing his own thing all day long, without any regard whatsoever as to how it might be cutting into their time together. "Just because we are engaged does not mean that we are connected at the hip. I invest my money separately from his. We are not married yet. Besides, our objectives don't overlap one hundred percent."

Her nose flared, and her lips spread into a thin smile. She couldn't get any attention from Walter and she still felt like she was suffocating in his shadow. What she said was not exactly true, but JaBari didn't need to know that. She and Walter always talked in terms of his being the one to take care of their joint money.

JaBari ran his eyes over the petite woman next to him. He had not meant to anger her, but it was obvious that she was annoyed at being so dismissed. She was different from her cousin Paris, but she was attractive in her own right. He tilted his brow and looked at her with uncertainty. It was clear that she was craving some attention. Why else but neglect would a woman as good-looking as she be in a bar, alone, when she didn't have to be? He put his hand on her wrist to steady her hand. He touched her softly, like he knew she needed to be. It was so easy for him to read what women needed. It was a talent he had.

It couldn't hurt to pitch his idea to her. She would probably think the movie industry was as sexy as everyone else had and want to jump right in. He had not really thought about that before.

"Well, I owe you an apology then. I certainly would not want to offend a woman as charming and intelligent as you." He licked his lips. "I'll tell you what. You said you had some time before Paris arrived. Would you mind listening to my ideas now? Several people in your family have already invested." He smiled softly. "And who couldn't stand to make a little extra cash?" JaBari hadn't planned on it, but hell, if Alexis was interested, he could be that much closer to getting the money he needed to pay off his debt to Wesley, and then some. He ran his tongue over his lips and tried not to blink as they made eye contact.

Alexis looked up into Jabari's face. What was she getting herself into? "I do have a wedding to pay for." She smiled.

He nodded. "I have proposals in my room if you'd like to see them."

Alexis poked her head to the side. "Okay, you are really insulting me now. Why would I go to your room? I barely know you." Her lips said one thing, but her body was screaming that she should run, not walk to the room with him. How could she not want to? Any woman would. Alexis envisioned JaBari with his muscular arms wrapped around her.

"You have got to give me more credit than that. You know I'm harmless." He chuckled. "All I am going to do is talk." She was damn attractive, but he wasn't desperate. He gazed into Alexis's eyes and waited for her response.

For no particular reason other than he was sexy as hell, Alexis wanted to trust JaBari. She couldn't help it. As fine as he was, he probably had women throwing their panties at him anyway, and no wonder. Too bad he probably really only wanted to talk about investing.

Alexis glanced at her watch and contemplated going to his room. She might be able to trust him, but could she trust herself? He was fine, smelled good, and she was horny.

"If you are worried about Paris missing you, we can leave her a note with the maître d'. But I don't think what I have to say will take that long." He blinked slowly, then smiled, a warm, sexy smile.

Too bad for me, Alexis thought. She was being silly. He was not interested in her that way, just her money, right? Besides, she was almost a married woman. *She* was not interested in him. Or at least she shouldn't be.

He motioned for her to go ahead.

"You go first," she said. There was no way she was going to let him walk behind her so he could look at her behind all the way to the room. She suddenly wished she had worked harder at exercising.

Alexis nodded, slid off her stool, and followed him to the elevator.

They paused in front of his door. The dimly lit hallway was thick with the awkwardness that hung between them. They made eye contact briefly, then winced like they had touched a flame instead of just looked at each other. JaBari smiled awkwardly. The sound of his breathing seemed to echo down the hall along with that of the air-conditioning. He slid his card key into the door and opened it, then stepped away so that Alexis could go through first. He couldn't forget his gentlemanly manners.

She flicked on the lights and walked into the room cautiously. If this was all so innocent, why was her stomach doing flip-flops?

JaBari's phone hummed. He pulled it from his pocket and glanced at the caller ID screen. He frowned, then slid it back into his pocket. Why did Wesley have to call him now? He was doing the best he could.

Alexis leaned on the standard brown hotel desk and waited.

He grinned at her sheepishly. "I can call him back later."

She glanced at her watch. What was she thinking? If Paris knew where she was, she would be very pissed off. Paris would think that she was cavorting with the devil himself. She shook off the strong feeling of attraction that keep pushing its way into her head. Of course the man was sexy and charismatic. He was so damned good-looking, how could he be anything else? He made his living being charismatic, getting people to trust him. *Business*. She repeated the word over and over in her head until it became a mantra.

If everyone else was going to be in on the deal, why should she miss it? She cleared her throat. "I only have a few minutes." She would rather that Paris did not see her coming from a hotel room, especially one that JaBari was in.

"I have a minibar," he said. "I don't suppose you want another drink?"

She shook her head. "I tell you what, why don't you just

give me a copy of the investment information and let me go over it later. You aren't about to leave town or anything yet are you?"

"No, I'm kinda liking Austin. I'm thinking of relocating here. But it will only take a few minutes for me to go over the proposal. Why don't you sit here, at the desk, and we can look at it." He smiled at her again, then slowly licked his lips. He was getting mixed signals from this one.

JaBari pulled out the desk chair and motioned toward it. He stepped aside so that Alexis could take a seat. His proposal was lying there, and he straightened it so that it lay in front of her, open like a textbook.

He stepped behind Alexis's seat and slightly to the side and reached over her. He placed his hand on one side of the folder and cleared his throat.

Alexis shifted in her seat. The hair on the back of her neck stood at attention. A few beads of sweat popped onto her nose, and she used her index finger to remove them.

Her movement drew JaBari's eyes downward. Light blue lace peeked from the top of her square-cut blouse. He looked away, but his breathing became deeper. His thoughts wandered off before he had even gotten started on his pitch. He imagined slipping his hands inside her shirt and caressing her breasts. He took a deep breath, then blinked.

"I'm sorry. I'm a little distracted. These notes are just sketches, really. Not much of this is really written down, and I want to keep it that way. You understand what I am saying?"

Alexis nodded.

"Private sort of thing—" JaBari placed his hand on her shoulder.

Alexis tensed. This was a bad idea. When would she learn to follow her first instincts?

"Take it easy." JaBari's voice was calm. "You are just so amazing, and it has been a while for me. I'm sorry. I'm distracted. I had a long day."

Alexis frowned. A long time for what? She glanced at the door. What had she been thinking? She stood up suddenly and attempted to close the folder in front of her. "I really have to meet Paris. She'll be worried. I'll just take this with me, okay?"

JaBari did not move. He smiled, more softly now. Was she rejecting him? "But you will want to hear this. I promise you won't be disappointed." He moved in so that their bodies were touching and slipped his arm around her waist, pulling her to him.

Alexis felt his body against him. He was hard and smooth, like Texas limestone. She held her breath, her eyes opened wide. She opened her mouth to protest but he stopped her. Before she even realized what was happening, JaBari clamped his mouth over hers and pulled her closer. He forced his tongue into her mouth.

Alexis was overcome with panic. The feelings of attractions she had for him turned to disgust. What in the hell was going on? She struggled and attempted to push him away. She was too close even to knee him in the groin. "Stop it," she almost shouted at him. Her eyes burned with anger.

She pulled away from him with all the force she could muster.

He was holding on to the edge of her shirt, and just as she pulled back a tearing sound caused them both to gasp. They stood frozen, mouths open.

"What the hell were you thinking?" she shouted.

"I'm sorry," he said. "But you know you were attracted to me."

"You are unbelievable!" She attempted to put her shirt back together, unsuccessfully. "You are a bigger bastard than I thought." Alexis glared at him.

"No need for name-calling." His voice softened. "I don't know—"

He was interrupted by a knock on the door. They both jumped, startled.

"Oh, my God." Alexis whispered. "How could you when you were expecting someone?"

"I wasn't," he hissed. "Just be quiet, and it will be okay. This will all just go away, and we can go on with our lives." He rubbed his head. A headache was coming on. What the hell was he thinking? He pulled the door open.

Alexis grabbed a shirt from his closet and ducked into the bathroom to change. She had to learn to listen to her sixth sense. This was all her fault. What had she been thinking?

JaBari opened the door a crack, expecting to just peer through it out into the hallway. It was kicked open, and he stumbled backward as Paris stormed into the room.

She looked around and swallowed. She needed to be calm so she could try and remain as composed as possible. "You want to tell me what you were doing when you were asking my parents for money for your harebrained scheme?"

"Whoa, whoa, whoa," he stammered. "I don't know what you are talking about." He glanced toward the bathroom.

She stepped into his face as if she were ready for a fight. JaBari backed up as far as he could. "Let me refresh your memory. I don't know what you did, but you should be ashamed of yourself." She pointed her finger at him as she spoke. "You somehow managed to charm my mother out of twenty thousand dollars of her hard-earned money. Well, they need it back."

"Paris, it's not that simple." A sinister smile spread across JaBari's face. "That money is gone. Invested. As I promised."

"And what about a return? When will they see that?" Paris was not surprised.

JaBari shrugged. "You never can tell about these things. I told them not to expect to see anything for a year."

"A *year*? What kind of shit is that?"

JaBari chortled. "They can handle it. Besides, if he loses it, it will be turnabout anyway." His eyes darted around the hotel room nervously.

"What in the hell are you talking about? What turnabout? My mother and Brian don't play dirty like this—"

"You sure about that? Maybe you ought to ask some of their associates."

Just then, the bathroom door handle jiggled. JaBari held his hand up and tried to move toward the bathroom door. "Wait—" he shouted.

Paris looked over at the door. "Was I interrupting something? Does your friend know about how you con old people?" She was shouting.

JaBari reached out to grab the door handle. He was too late. Alexis walked out of the bathroom, talking, but stopped short when she saw Paris.

Paris's mouth dropped open in surprise. "Alexis. What—"

"Paris. It's not what you think. I can explain." She pointed a finger at JaBari. "This motherfucker—"

"What? He dragged you up here by your hair? You wanted him the minute you saw him. I knew it. All that talk about him being perfect for me was just talk." She looked from JaBari to Alexis and back again. "I told you he was sleazy from the beginning. But I am surprised at you. I thought you were my friend. And furthermore, what about Walter? He is the one I feel sorry for in all of this."

Alexis opened her mouth to speak, but Paris interrupted her. "Save it. I can't stand the sight of either one of you. But you know what? You deserve each other."

She turned and headed for the door. Alexis followed her, pleading. "Please. You don't understand. He tried to—"

"Uh-huh. You save it. I hope you are happy together. My only advice to you is to make sure you keep separate bank accounts."

SUGAR-COATED

There was a small but eclectic crowd in the waiting area of the café. The eatery was open twenty-four hours, unusual for Austin, and was popular with the local downtown business community. Tyson glanced around. The work of local artists decorated the walls, some series that involved tinfoil and paint. The bold colors, combined with the tin dinosaurs suspended from the ceiling, had an unsettling effect.

He sat on the wooden chair in the small waiting area and stared up at the ceiling. A pterodactyl-looking creation was suspended over his head, a little too close for comfort. He squirmed in his seat and checked his watch. She had better show up soon. He wasn't sure that this was his kind of place. His put his finger inside the neck of his shirt and moved it around. His neck itched from the combination of the heavy starch from the dry cleaners and the tie that he had tied just a little too tightly.

A waiter leaned over the four-foot-high podium, making

eye contact with Tyson. He was white and thinnish, and wore a standard-issue restaurant apron over his Goth uniform. Black jeans a little too tight in the hips for Tyson's taste, with a black T-shirt that did not quite reach the top of his jeans. His waist-length hair was twisted into dirty-looking dreadlocks. Tyson tried not to let his disdain show. This man's hair somehow seemed to be a mockery of his own clean and well-maintained tresses.

"You ready yet, man?"

Tyson stared at the small ring in his bottom lip and wondered how he managed to eat with it in. Probably the reason why he was so thin. Tyson cleared his throat and resisted the urge to ask him just that.

"Not yet."

He nodded and called the next person on the list. As soon as Tyson looked away, he spied Sarah approaching and stood up. Finally. He was tired of sitting shoulder to shoulder with the man next to him. It was hard not to stare at his business jacket and floor-length skirt.

Sarah looked apologetic as she swept through the door.

"I always underestimate the downtown traffic. Sorry."

"No problem," he lied, then nodded to the waiter. He had other things that he could be doing, but he didn't tell her that. The waiter led them to a corner booth.

He took their order for coffee, then shuffled away.

"Why did you choose this place? It's a little . . . different."

Sarah chuckled. "True. But they make good scones. I can't believe you have never been here."

Tyson was not in the mood for small talk. He shook his head. This was just not his scene, and he was surprised that Sarah suggested it.

"Actually, this place is quite popular with the politicians

and others working at the Capitol. Just sit here for a while, and you will know more than you ever imagined about the inside workings of state government."

Tyson sat back in his seat. "That all sounds interesting, but why would I want to do that?"

"You want to know about JaBari." She paused as the waiter returned with their coffees. "There are quite a few interesting people in here right now. Look over there. See the man with the whitish hair? He is a well-known lobbyist around here. And to your right, a state rep from the Dallas area." She used her eyes to motion toward a booth to their side. "He is well liked and well-known. Having a little fun, perhaps making some kind of deal. His family was independently wealthy before he got into politics. Owns a few barbecue restaurants up in Dallas. Big ones."

Tyson tried to be discreet as he glanced in the directions she indicated. Sarah went ahead and made full eye contact with the gentleman she was talking about. Smiled, then waved. She spoke to Tyson through her teeth. "Our families go way back."

"I'm seeing that everybody in Austin is related or knows everybody else. More than I ever realized."

She nodded. "Not so much as before, but people tend to run in small circles here. Not so many degrees of separation as one might think for a city of this size."

Anxiety crept over Tyson. "Okay, I know you have something for me, or you would not have asked me here."

Sarah paused for what seemed an eternity as she gulped her drink. She let the mug hit the table hard, like a beer stein.

Tyson jumped in surprise. He had become increasingly edgy over the past few days.

"Well, it wasn't too hard to pull up information on

JaBari. Not too many Black lobbyists around. Turns out that he has been independent for a while."

"Independent?"

"As in he doesn't work for any of the bigger lobbying firms. He really did come from the investment banking world as he claims, although the full story isn't quite clear. One day he was on Wall Street, then he was in Texas." She sipped her coffee again.

Tyson did, too, then grimaced and reached for the sugar. Sarah continued. "He takes on a lot of the speculative jobs and controversial issues. Things a lot of firms just don't or won't do. Everything from animal rights to unpopular things like representing court reporters. From what I understand, he does a lot of nontraditional wheeling and dealing, too. Anything he needs to get the job done. Makes lot of enemies in the process.

"He was in Houston last. Some of my friends tell me that he left town because of some deals he did around Houston airport concessions. He got what his client wanted, but his techniques made him very unpopular there for the moment. So his clients now are from somewhere else. No one could really tell me anything about that right now. All they knew was that he was working for some concern outside the state that did not favor the proposed new banking legislation in its current form."

"But I thought he was from New York—"

She shrugged. "From what I understand, once upon a time he was. But apparently he hasn't lived there in some time."

"So he is as shady as we thought?"

"Questionable. I couldn't prove shady. Everyone would think so except Athena. She has him pegged as a golden child."

"Why only questionable? He seems to have something up his sleeve."

"Well, he is known to be a charmer, for sure. There is no crime in that. But I can't say he has ever been caught openly doing anything wrong. He is not from money or anything like that, but he is well educated. It's just that his lifestyle is not congruent with the money that he would be making with the types of clients he seems to represent."

"Why? Lobbyists do well."

Sarah looked around the restaurant quickly, then leaned over the booth, lowering her voice. "True. When they have big contracts or work for big firms. But according to my sources, when you look at a list of the things he has worked on, it just doesn't seem to fit."

Tyson shrugged. "Maybe he saves well. Or has a sugar mama. There are a lot of rich old women in Texas who would welcome attention from someone as good-looking as JaBari. He is quite the pretty boy."

Sarah chuckled. "Do I sense a little resentment?" She paused. "Maybe so. Or maybe he has a *sugar daddy*." Sarah stirred her coffee, then took her time licking the spoon clean. She wanted the full impact of what she was saying to sink in.

Tyson's eyes grew wide with surprise. "You can't know that. And so what? Lots of people swing both ways nowadays."

"You're right. I can't. But my gay cousin who is a lobbyist in Houston might. And he might have mentioned it to me, too. But I would never repeat it. Not my business. But I will tell you this. We know that isn't too popular here in conservative Texas."

His face darkened. "Paris—"

"She would never believe it. I'm not sure I do. I got no

indication of that whatsoever, and I'm sure she didn't. Her mother certainly didn't. In her mind wedding bells should be ringing and all. Kinda thing you see on television, huh?"

"Tell me about it." Sarah nodded and stood up. She threw a few bills on the table as she did. "Well, I gotta go. Careful how you handle it."

Tyson rubbed his temples. "Damn. I just wanted to confirm if he is a criminal or not. This type of information just makes a bad situation worse. If I mention it, Paris will just think I have sour grapes or something."

"And I don't have to tell you we did not have this conversation."

He nodded, then paused.

Sarah smiled at him, then picked up her purse. "By the way, you should have a check soon. We have a lot of faith in you."

"Thanks." He stood, then shook her hand. "I'm gonna stay a while. Gotta think things through."

"I would, too. You are about to be busier than you ever have been before. Not to mention that your bank account is about to swell." She smiled. "Don't let yourself get too preoccupied with all this soap opera stuff."

"Means nothing if there is no one to share it with, know what I mean?"

"I do. Just go slow, okay?"

He nodded, then hugged Sarah. She was turning out to be more genuine than he ever imagined.

She returned his hug. "Don't get all wishy-washy on me. I don't like him either, and Paris is my friend. This is as much for me as it is for you." Sarah patted him on the back and left.

NO HONOR AMONG THIEVES

Footsteps echoed on the concrete behind JaBari as he walked back to his hotel. He tensed, and his heart rate quickened. He looked over his shoulder and did not see anyone unusual. JaBari quickened his pace anyway. Never could be too careful, but he was probably imagining things. He had been so on edge since his encounter with Alexis yesterday. What had he been thinking? All the bad luck he was having lately, he should have known that Paris would show up. Now she wouldn't talk to him at all. Neither would Alexis. He had somehow managed to screw things up royally.

It was clear that he would not get another dime from Paris or her family, so he had given up on that. But he still had to figure out how to do what Wesley wanted. Good thing he was creative. He smiled. The same technique that had gotten him lucrative information could also be useful in spreading misinformation.

The footsteps were back. The hairs on the back of his

neck stood up. What in the hell was going on? JaBari spun around and stiffened.

"Wesley," he said, "you are the last person I expected to see." He paused. "You look good." A nervous grin spread across his face. *What in the hell is he doing here?*

"Am I? Is that why you haven't been returning my calls?"

JaBari shook his head. A small nervous laugh escaped his lips. "You are implying that I have been avoiding you. You know that isn't the case. I have just been really busy, that's all."

"Busy is good, right? Getting stuff done I suppose? Or are you just spinning your wheels, wasting your time and mine?"

JaBari licked his lips. His eyes darted around. They were on a small side street, not far from the Capitol building. It was late, and deserted. The closest person he could see was almost a full block away. There were not as many people around as he would like. No potential witnesses to anything that might happen. He knew of Wesley's temper well. He was not afraid of Wesley, but he was not totally comfortable around him either. The years and shady dealings had left them less than friends.

His body suddenly felt heavy, and his palms were sweating. He rubbed his hands together. He was tired of the games. "Let's not make small talk. Why are you here?"

Wesley looked surprised. "I can come to Texas, too. Don't forget, I have ties here. My ex-wife is here."

JaBari shook his head. "That's right. Your car went off a road. We didn't think you would walk again after you went down that embankment. And look at you, you don't even use a cane anymore." He smiled. "Physical therapy must have been good to you. No one would be able to tell that you broke your leg in so many places in that crash. You were pretty banged up." He paused. "Or was it the memory of me that helped?" He licked his lips again; this time, it was more provocative.

Wesley's face darkened. He lunged forward, suddenly seeming much larger than he was. "You motherfucker. You are the lowest kind of bottom feeder there is." He pushed JaBari up against the building they were standing in front of. "I am not crippled anymore, and I will personally tear your ass apart if you ever mention that incident again. It was years ago, and I was very young. I am not one of your little twisted friends who can't decide whether they are a male or female. Nothing happened, remember. I am not some kind of homo—"

JaBari pulled free, then dusted off his clothes. He wasn't afraid anymore. He knew that if Wesley was angry, he himself had the upper hand. "If you say so. Just be calm. I told you I wouldn't tell anyone about our past. That is between us." He stepped back. "Unless I have to. They might not believe me, but it will make them wonder. Put some questions in the minds of your ultrahomophobic friends. But we shouldn't have a need for that, right. Your skeletons will stay in the closet." JaBari paused, staring at Wesley, with a steely look. "As long as I am not harmed."

JaBari wondered why he hadn't thought of using the few tender moments that had occurred between them all those years ago before. He liked having the upper hand and was enjoying the look of terror that he saw on Wesley's face. He had suddenly moved to the other side of the threats, and it felt good. Too bad that he didn't know that one experience didn't make you gay. Wesley was as homophobic as they came.

"That is what I am talking about. I knew you couldn't be trusted. That's why I came down here to take care of things myself."

"I told you I would handle it." He clenched his fists, hissing as he talked.

"Like you have been doing? First you lost my money. Then you couldn't even get a simple job done."

He held up his hands. "Wait. I have already taken care of that. That bank is going to be dropping Benton and Associates any day now. They are going to have to find someone new to lobby for them."

"How can you be so sure?" Wesley paused. "What did you do? Make up some lie and whisper it in the bowels of the Capitol, hoping someone would hear it?"

JaBari gasped. It was hard to believe that Wesley knew him so well. "Not exactly, but something like that. They aren't going to want someone they perceive as being less than ingenuous representing them."

"There goes that fancy education again." He shook his head. "But just how long do you think it will take your little girlfriend to prove that they are still the last bastion of squeaky clean in the business?"

JaBari's heart raced. The street sounds seemed louder than before.

"Oh, are we speechless now? Let me answer that for you. Not long enough. Don't worry. I may not have a fancy education, but I still seem to be the brains of this machine. As it turns out, you may have spread the rumors, but I took care of it for real. I don't like loose ends."

"I don't understand."

"You wouldn't. Turns out Benton and Associates does funny things with their money. Things that the FTC wants to know."

"That's not—"

"Doesn't matter. They are going to have to go through a whole bunch of rigmarole to prove otherwise. That gives me the time that I need. Much more time than fooling with them and their customers."

"But wait just a minute. That may implicate us. They will look for the paper trail, and I took money from that woman. Money which I, in turn, gave to you."

Wesley chuckled. "You must think I am a dumb-ass. It won't lead to me or my partner." He paused. "Can't say that about you though."

JaBari gasped. A shiver of panic shot through him. He should have known that Wesley would not waste an opportunity to hang him out to dry. He knew too much about Wesley's shady dealings. Not just this lending scam, but he knew about his crazy airport concessions in Houston, too. He ran his hands nervously across his hair. "No honor among thieves, then, huh? What happened to being friends?"

Wesley's mouth took on an unpleasant twist. "You use the term too loosely."

CHAOS MAGNET

The office was buzzing. With Brian in the hospital, everyone was working the maximum time possible to take on the challenge of their new client. Paris looked around and sighed, glad that everyone was pitching in the way they were. The only bright spot in the whole thing was that Brian had woken up from his coma this morning. Paris was glad of it, but he wasn't out of the woods yet. The doctor told her that he would be recovering for a while. That still left Paris running things.

Paris closed her eyes and rubbed her lids. *Be careful what you ask for.* Her mother's words echoed in her head. Now that she was actually doing the work, she wasn't sure she loved it as much as she thought she would. The reason she had been so gung ho about the bank was because she thought it would be good for Austin, East Austin in particular. The bottom line was that she cared more about the underlying issue than actually helping the client persuade the legislators to decide in their favor. And Brian suddenly didn't seem too interested in expanding the business at all.

Her eyes were burning, and her head was killing her. She had had an ongoing headache over the past few days, and her stomach burned. An ulcer would really put the icing on the cake. It had been one thing after another. Through it all, Paris had done what she thought she did best—thrown herself into her work to avoid thinking about all of the things that were happening around her. Unfortunately, work had now become one of those things making her head pound and keeping her up at night. Not only was she suddenly in charge, but she found herself having to juggle creditors for business accounts that she knew nothing about.

She picked up the yellow slip of paper the temp she had hired put on her desk. Brenda had left a third message about her workout schedule. She had not been to a session since she found Alexis and JaBari together, and had no intention of going. She just didn't want to talk to Alexis yet. She might wring her neck. Or worse.

The bad part was that she could not figure out why she was so angry at Alexis. Was it because of JaBari, Walter, or because she had violated the girlfriends' code of honor? Paris wasn't sure which. She could feel herself getting fatter by the minute because of her missed exercise sessions. Couldn't Alexis see how messed up what she had done was? It had been days, and ripples of her betrayal would run through their friendship for a long time. Not to mention that once the family found out about it, the incident was sure to become a legend, one of those things whispered about at gatherings. Paris crumpled the piece of notepaper between her fingers and tossed it into the trash can. But she had no time to dwell on that right now.

Her e-mail pinged, announcing the arrival of new messages. As usual, she couldn't resist looking. A red exclamation point drew her attention to one of the messages. She clicked on it, and the message enlarged to fill the screen. It was from the bank.

Ms. Montague,

I regret to inform you that we have to cancel our briefing meeting that is scheduled for tomorrow morning. We have decided not to continue our relationship with Benton and Associates. Details will follow in a formal certified letter. Thank you.

It was signed by the government liaison officer.

Paris stopped breathing and read the note again. A lump welled up in her throat, and her chest hurt. What the hell was going on? There was no way she could construe this note to be good. Especially not the certified letter part. When was the last time anyone had gotten good news from one of those? She grabbed the phone and dialed their offices immediately. The note was so cold. She thought she had done a better job cultivating their relationship than that. Apparently, she was mistaken.

She tapped her foot impatiently as she listened to the phone ring. The receptionist answered it, and she asked for the liaison officer by name.

"Who's calling, please?" Her words were drawn out and flat, with a particularly un-Austin, Texas twang to them.

"This is Paris Montague from Benton and Associates."

The woman cleared her throat. Her voice became more formal. "He isn't available. In fact, I think he will be in a meeting the rest of the day. Would you like voice mail?"

Paris felt her headache intensify. That was office speak for go to hell. She would probably never be put though if he were available. "That won't be necessary. Would you mind relaying the message that I called please."

By the tone of that woman's voice, Paris doubted that she would hear back from the man anytime today if ever. It was clear that she had done something to piss them off, but what?

A heaviness centered in her chest. This was bad. She had never gotten an answer from JaBari about her mother's money either and had just about written that off as gone. And what was that other cryptic bullshit JaBari had spewed at her? All the talk about turnabout would imply that Brian and her mother were involved in some shady dealings, and she just couldn't make heads or tails of that. And none of the research she had done could pull up any information on the so-called investment JaBari had her mother invest in, so it was not a good time for any customer, much less the best one they ever had, to cancel any contracts. She was counting on the money they would get from that contract to help put the company and her family back in the black.

What else could go wrong? Her parents were counting on her to help, and so far all she had done was alienate her mother and help to run the business further into the ground. She was obviously a chaos magnet. Everything was falling apart as quickly as possible.

Paris pulled open her lower desk drawer and grabbed her handbag and keys. If she didn't get something for her head soon, she was sure it was going to explode. The temp was on her way into the office, and Paris almost knocked her over on her way out the door. She had to get some relief and get it soon, or she might be the next one in the hospital.

"Be right back," she muttered.

The woman stopped in her tracks, but Paris kept going, leaving her standing there with a handful of papers and her mouth open.

It was rude, and Paris knew it, but the pain was almost too much for her. She was just going to have to go with the flow and understand. There would be time for apologies later. After she got some drugs for her head.

She drove her car down Eleventh Street and crossed over I-35 at a speed that was much too fast. She couldn't afford another ticket. Paris headed for a convenience store. It wasn't very far away, but certainly too far to walk.

A woman cursed at Paris through her window as she pulled into a parking space in front of the store. Paris had cut her off, but at that point she was a woman on a mission. She looked down, avoiding eye contact as she dug into her bag. As usual, her wallet held no cash. She sighed. She was going to need to find an ATM first. Experience told her that she was parked in front of the only convenience store in the United States without an automatic teller inside. Her headache would have to wait a few more minutes.

There was no line at the bank. Paris stuck her bank card into the ATM machine and keyed in her number the same way she always did. She held out her hand, in anticipation of the little door opening and crisp bills being pushed out at her. Nothing happened. The machine did not complete the transaction.

Confused, Paris glanced at her watch. It was too early for them to be doing anything to the ATM computers. They were usually unavailable for a few minutes each day for service, but that ordinarily happened closer to three. That was over two hours away. She frowned. Odd. Something had to be wrong. She didn't do overdrawn. Usually, she could virtually balance her account in her head, almost to the penny, just like her mother could.

She tried again, this time she used the card that was linked to the Benton and Associates account. Nothing. Same message on the screen. That didn't work either. What in the world? She had no choice. Headache or not, she was obviously going to have to go into the bank and find out what the hell was going on. Most certainly not her favorite thing to do in the middle of the afternoon. For Paris, going inside the bank ranked right up there with grocery shopping. Necessary evils. She hated them both.

All the money she paid in banking fees, it seemed they could at least have machines that worked for their customers. She sighed heavily and put her cards back in her wallet. Her neck was stiff with tension. She thrust her wallet into her bag and rubbed her neck.

Paris stormed into the bank, her mouth drawn into a thin, tight line. Thoughts of her headache were suddenly not so important, and she relegated her pain to the back of her mind.

The bank seemed full of people, but there were actually very few customers waiting to see anyone other than window tellers. Paris signed in, then was immediately summoned by a teller in a cheap-looking blue suit. Scorch spots had made the fabric shiny in several places, and she had hair that was streaked blond and the roundest glasses that Paris had seen since the eighties.

She smiled up at Paris from her desk. Paris started to speak before the woman could open her mouth.

"I'm trying to figure out what is wrong with my bank accounts. None of my ATM cards seem to work."

The woman waved toward the seat in front of her desk. "I need your account number or card and your driver's license." She paused and swiveled her computer screen. "Let's see what we can figure out."

She was just doing her job and trying to be cordial, but her overly nice manner annoyed Paris. She took a deep breath, then reached into her bag to get her driver's license. She slid it across the table as requested.

"I don't have to tell you how annoyed I am. I just planned on running out of the office for a minute to pick up a few things. I ended up having to come inside the bank because the bank seems to be holding my money hostage." She glanced at her watch.

The woman smiled again, more thinly this time, and began entering information into her computer. "I understand," she said. She stared at the computer screen. Paris watched as she hit a few buttons. "Hmm." She cleared her throat.

"Well?" Paris was trying to be as patient as she could.

"Well, it looks like you couldn't get any money from your account because your primary checking account is showing a negative balance."

"Not possible." Paris searched her brain to figure out what was going on. "I haven't bounced a check in years. I just don't do that."

The woman smiled at her thinly. "It happens to the best of us. If you like, I can print a statement for you so you can figure out what happened."

She nodded. "I guess that will be fine. What about this other account? My company account. I couldn't get any money from there either. I know that isn't overdrawn."

"I see a problem here, too."

"You're kidding." Paris gasped.

"In this case, we are not holding your money hostage, a federal agency is. A hold has been placed on that account." She pressed a few more buttons. "Frankly, if there had been anything in your regular account, they would have placed a hold on that, too. I'm surprised they didn't do it anyway. Usually, in cases like this, they place holds on the personal accounts of all the people who have primary access to the accounts in question. It looks like that would mean you, and your boss, too." Her eyes were full of pity.

"What?" Paris hissed at her. "What do you mean?" What in the world was going on? She wasn't in any kind of tax trouble that she knew about.

"You don't know anything about this?" She swiveled the screen around so Paris could look at it.

She stared at it in disbelief. She shook her head.

"Well, it looks like it is a hold by the IRS or FTC. And it is not on your accounts now, but as soon as you put any money in it, it will be. Count on that. Usually, they are very thorough about these things."

"So what do I do now? I have no idea why they would be interested in me."

"It's probably a mistake or something. I wouldn't worry too much. But trust me when I tell you that someone will contact you soon."

Paris stood up to leave. She put her information and her wallet back in her bag. She was stunned. Her cheeks flushed from embarrassment and humiliation.

"Look, I hope it works out." Her tone was apologetic. She slid the statement that she printed across the desk to Paris. "Here is your information. I know you said you don't make mistakes, but trust me when I tell you that it happens to the best of us. Even if they go ahead and put a hold on your account, you can check it out online, okay? You will be able to see entries, even photocopies of the checks you wrote." She paused. "I'm sorry I couldn't be of more help."

Paris nodded and stumbled her way out of the bank.

FADED FAIRY TALES

Rocky road ice cream was a long-lost friend. Alexis removed the top from her latest pint and smiled. "Where have you been girlfriend?" she muttered. The spoon bent slightly as it hit the top of the creamy confection.

"Huh." The ice cream was rock hard. "You need a hot bath." Alexis touched the pause button on the TIVO remote and sprinted off the couch and headed toward the kitchen. This one must have been hiding in the back of the freezer a long time. She kept these things around, almost hidden from herself, just in case she might need them. Usually, Alexis was very strong. The need for sugar didn't hit her often, usually just once a month, and a bar of chocolate would suffice. But since she and Paris had stopped speaking, sugar was calling her name left and right. Although the pint of ice cream had been a find, she knew she had better get it together soon, or she was going to have to start shopping for fat clothes. Just lovely. Paris would surely have something to gloat over then.

But right now, the ice cream was just what she needed. Her mouth watered as she thought about how good it was going to taste sliding across her tongue. Mental note, put some more on the grocery list. She would feel guilty later, but for this minute, she could not remember why she had been depriving herself of something she loved so much.

Fifteen seconds should do it. She tapped her foot on the floor and waited for her treat to melt a little. What had people done before microwaves?

Her musings on the nature of ice cream were interrupted by Walter entering the kitchen.

He cleared his throat.

Alexis grunted, but didn't speak. She was not in the mood to talk to anyone. Especially not Walter. If he had been there for her, none of this would have happened anyway.

"Haven't seen you in a while."

"Really? Now why do you suppose that is?" She reached into the microwave and removed the ice cream, immediately digging into it with her spoon.

He raised his eyebrows. "*You* are eating real ice cream?"

"Everybody in America eats ice cream."

"Not you. At least not since you reached the revelation that carbs are evil. Can't remember the last time I saw you do that." He leaned back on the counter. "Doesn't Athena always say that it would be easier just to smear that on your hips?"

"I didn't ask you or *her*." She pouted.

He grunted in response.

"Not everyone in this family does what Athena says. Or even cares what she thinks."

"You sure? When did this happen? You and Paris always

seemed to be real good at it before. I shouldn't complain though. If it weren't for her, I might not have been around as long as I have. I seem a little 'safe' for you sometimes."

They had gone weeks, months even, without having a conversation that meant anything, and she certainly wasn't in the mood for one now. A shadow of annoyance crossed Alexis's face.

"Don't go get all sensitive and empathetic on me now."

"What are you trying to say, Alexis? I see that you are upset, and I'm just trying to help."

"Why would you do that now? You have been so absorbed in whatever it is you are trying to prove by working yourself to death that I'm not sure you have said two words to me since you moved in here. I will work this through myself. Don't you have some work to do or some late meeting or something? For the record, I was planning on enjoying an evening alone with my ice cream and the TV remote."

"Things must be bad."

"You wouldn't know." She swallowed hard, then lifted her chin to meet his gaze. Her eyes blazed with anger. For some reason, she could not stop blaming him for everything, even what happened with JaBari.

"I see."

"What?" Alexis shoved more ice cream into her mouth.

"It's obvious that I can't win, no matter what. You are mad at Paris, and you are going to take it out on me." He paused. "So, I think I am going to go and sleep in the spare room."

Alexis jutted out her lip. That would be good. She didn't want him near her anyway. "Who told you about me and Paris?"

"Who do you think?" His eyes softened. "Sarah. She told me that the two of you were angry at each other and that neither one of you had met to work out together at your regular time. That's all."

"She is clueless, too." She held back her tears of anger and disappointment. In a defensive gesture, she crossed her arms in front of her.

"Whatever happened, we didn't really get into it. She just told me that it looked like you two weren't speaking and that Paris was really having a hard time. Now out of the three of you, Sarah seems to be the most sane. After her scare with cancer, it's clear that she is the one with the most clarity in her life."

"Psychology 101."

"See, that is what I am talking about. You and your cousin get so caught up in doing the right thing, you lose sight of the things that really matter. The things that you want the most. And you let Athena dictate your lives so much."

"I don't want to talk about it."

"Right."

"I didn't ask you."

"And therein lies the problem. You didn't. You just assumed that I was going along with your program. Never asking me about the things I want. How can you have a relationship with anyone if you are not clear on things yourself? With anyone, Paris included." He shook his head. "You are all that way."

Her eyes flashed a warning. "Where are you going with this? Paris and I will work this out."

He held up his hands. "I'm sure you will." He paused. "You are more like her mother than she is, and you don't even see it. You are so quick to tell her what she should be doing and whom she should be doing it with. I don't know what happened, and I am not sure I even want to know, but your whole family is so good at throwing up that facade and only letting people see what you think they should, you even hide from yourself."

"Just because you have known me for a while doesn't make you an expert. There are things that you will never understand."

He nodded. "You are right about that. But everybody has a deeper motivation for the things they say and do, even if they are not aware of it yet. Do you even know what yours is?" He cocked his head to one side, waiting. "For instance, I see you and Paris competing with each other constantly, vying for your family's approval. It's like the two of you are in a race, and the finish line is matrimony. You think I don't know that you are in a relationship with me because I was handpicked by Athena, too? It's not like you fell head over heels for me and couldn't be without me or anything. Ours was like an old-fashioned matchmaking. Athena told you that I was the one, and you said okay. And you wanted me to move in here so that you could be one step ahead of your cousin. More like a corporate merger than a fairy tale, huh?"

Her jaw dropped open in surprise.

He nodded. "It's okay though. I figured the real you would come out eventually. But I'm getting tired of waiting."

Alexis covered the ice cream. The taste for it suddenly left her mouth.

"I'll sleep in the back room. You obviously have some things to think through."

Alexis didn't stop him. She returned the ice cream to the freezer. Walter didn't usually speak up about her family business too much, and she wasn't used to it. And how much did he really know? If he knew what happened with JaBari, he wouldn't have kept that to himself. That meant that Paris hadn't told Sarah the whole story.

She sat back down on the sofa and flipped the channel absentmindedly. She should be more upset about his possibly finding out, but for some reason she wasn't. He was right about one thing. She did have a lot of things to mull over. More than he realized.

UNUSUAL MENUS

The office was empty. Everyone had long since gone home. The light over Paris's desk was the only light in the otherwise dark building. The click of computer keys and the rustle of paper were the only sounds.

Paris pored over her bank statement again and again. She had painstakingly gone through almost every check presented against her account, checking and rechecking to try and find out where she had made her mistake. Her method was simple. She made sure that everything was entered into the register properly, then looked at the actual check online.

So far, so good. Everything had been just as she thought it was up to that point. Part of her wanted the mistake to be the bank's fault. But there was a nagging feeling in the back of her head that JaBari was involved in this somehow, she just couldn't figure out how he would be.

A hoarse whisper broke the evening silence that enveloped her.

"Hey. I should have known this is where you would be."

Paris jumped in response. She raised her eyes to find Tyson standing in the doorway, watching her. Her stomach immediately drew up in knots.

"You shouldn't sneak up on people. How did you get in?"

"You left the door unlocked. Not exactly safe. I thought I would try to catch you. Offer you a late dinner or something." His tone was odd yet gentle, as if he were trying to find a way to get past the awkwardness between them quickly.

Paris rubbed a hand on her stiff neck. "I'm not—"

"Uh-uh. You gotta eat. Nothing fancy. And this seems to be the only way I can catch you since you have been avoiding me."

"I haven't been. I have just been busy with a lot of stuff. Brian. My mother. Money. You have no idea."

Tyson walked around behind her and began to massage her neck. "You are right. I don't. You haven't told me anything. The only way I know what is going on with you at all anymore is if Sarah tells me. We at least used to have pillow talk. I don't even get that anymore."

Paris felt some of the tension in her shoulders begin to subside. Her body received his soft touch willingly. She suddenly realized that she missed the time she spent with Tyson. A lot. A soft tingling began in the pit of her stomach, and she could no longer remember why she had been angry at him.

"Sarah? You two buddies now?"

He let out a low, throaty chuckle. He had been there a whole five minutes, and Paris had not bitten his head off yet. A good sign.

"I wouldn't say we were friends just yet. But we are well

on our way to being business partners. Along with her associates, of course."

Paris paused, then turned around so she could look into Tyson's eyes. "When did this happen? And why didn't you tell me?"

"Today. It happened today. I thought you would have heard about it by now the way your family talks about things." He paused, allowing his fingers to savor the feel of her soft skin. "We signed on the dotted line an hour or so ago. And I did try to tell you what was happening, several times. But you wouldn't let me. First you stood me up. Then you could never seem to spare a few minutes away from what's-his-name—"

"I'm sorry about that. It wasn't what you thought at all. It's just—"

"Was that your choice or his?" Tyson bit his lip and stopped himself. He had not come for a confrontation this time. "No apology necessary. I do understand that you have a lot going on. But that is why I am here. To tell you in person."

Before he knew what he was doing, Tyson had reached up to smooth her hair. It was automatic, natural.

Paris leaned into his touch just slightly. After all the stress she had been under, she welcomed a pleasant sensation for a change. Her mind burned with the memory of how intimate they had been before all the drama started. She felt a twinge in the pit of her stomach. She missed that.

"I appreciate that. But I'm not sure I can go to dinner. Our bank accounts are all screwed up. Overdrawn *and* frozen."

"That doesn't sound too good." He shook his head.

"Tell me about it. I have been sitting here for hours trying to straighten it out, or at least figure out what the hell happened before I get invaded by a bunch of guys in government-issued suits and dark glasses."

Her forehead furrowed. Tyson could see the stress and panic that stretched itself across her face.

"There are holds on all my accounts. We are about to be investigated for heaven knows what."

A shadow of concern crossed his face. "Well, nothing is going to happen tonight." He reached over and pressed the print key. "Let's just take this with us and see what we can find. I have a good head for math. Maybe I can help."

"But—"

"You work too hard. You tell me about it over dinner. A diversion will help to clear your mind so that you can focus on the problem." He spoke quickly. He didn't want to give her any time to resist. "I will tell you about all my news. We can go from there." He gathered up all of Paris's papers and statements as he spoke.

"I'm just not used to—"

"Someone helping you out? I know." He recognized now that her aloofness had more to do with her being cautious than anything else. "But you can't control everything. You are only human, Paris. Sometimes you have to let people help you. It doesn't mean you are weak if you accept help when you need it. You need a break. Let me help."

Part of Paris wanted to argue with him, but she didn't have the strength. He was right. The last few days had exhausted her, both physically and emotionally. Instead, she let him continue and just stood there with a blank stare on her face. Mixed feelings washed over her. Just a few days ago, things were as normal as they ever had been. Now she just felt overwhelmed.

Tyson sensed that he had won a small victory. He nodded. "Let's go. I think you will like the restaurant I picked."

Exhaustion hit Paris like a ton of bricks. They rode in Tyson's car. She had to fight to stay awake, and the muggy evening air did not help. Drowsiness pulled downward on her eyelids, making them feel heavy. She rolled down the window to try and get some air.

He could see she was tired, and because she was, he didn't try to make conversation. He just wanted her to relax. He had spent so much time waiting for her to do something, letting her take the lead, that he had almost lost her. Now it was his turn to be in control. But he knew she wouldn't come easy; instead, he expected her to fight and scream the entire way. That was okay though. That would make it all the more worth it.

She was asleep. He paused a minute and watched the gentle rise and fall of her chest. *Damn, she is beautiful.* She was so tired that she hadn't even noticed that the car had stopped.

She jumped. "Oh," she said. Her eyes flew open, and she looked around, confused. She blinked to try and clear her vision. Instead of a restaurant, they were sitting in front of Tyson's apartment.

He lived in South Austin, in an older area. The gray building in front of her used to be white. Its faux-limestone exteriors had faded from neglect and time. Scattered patches of dirt hinted at the ghost of grass and vegetation long gone.

The apartment complex was one of the newer additions to the area. Once considered prime rental property, the buildings were now marketed toward college students, almost as fancy dorms. The concrete lake of a parking lot that stretched around it held a smattering of mostly older and dilapidated cars and student hoopties and was pock-marked with potholes left unrepaired.

"I thought we were going to a restaurant."

"We are." Tyson was already on his way out of the car. He opened her door to help her out, and a secretive smile hinted at the corner of his mouth.

She hesitated.

"It'll be fine, I promise."

Paris sighed, too tired to argue, fight, or care. She was so hungry that it felt like the two sides of her stomach were rubbing against themselves; she felt exhausted and needed a glass of wine in a bad way.

"I know you don't like coming here. But I needed to stop for something."

"Can't I just stay in the car?" she whined, and raised her finely plucked eyebrows in weak protest. She was too exhausted to do much else.

"Not in this neighborhood. C'mon," he said. "Do you need me to carry you?"

"I am not *that* tired." She forced herself from the car and followed him. There was no way in hell she was going to let him use her to make a scene.

It was dark inside his place. Paris waited for him to flick on the lights, inhaling the comforting smells. Warm, musky, and familiar.

Pale light flooded the room. Paris stood in the doorway transfixed as she absorbed what lay before her. For the first time in a while, she was at a loss as to what to say.

The furniture was pushed back out of the way, leaving

the center of the small living room open. A blue-and-white-checked cloth was spread out in the center of the floor, and a mock table was set in the middle, complete with two place settings. Two small, white candles burned in holders. Paris could tell that they had not been burning long. Already, their vanilla scent was taking hold of the air in the small room.

Tyson cleared his throat. "Don't be fooled by the simple furnishings. I hear the food is good. Excellent actually." He reached his hand out to her.

Her heart thumped loudly in her ears as she took his hand. The stresses of the day and past week were forgotten. How could she not have seen that this was what she needed? Her body immediately felt less tired, and she relaxed some.

"You have never done anything like this before," she said.

"You would never let me." His voice was soft and tender.

He was right. In the past, their meetings had always been her call, not his. She had never really given him the opportunity to take the lead. Now she let him guide her to the blanket and help her to sit down on the pillows he provided.

"What's on the menu?"

"Sushi."

"You don't even like Japanese food."

"True. But you do. I wanted to help you relax so it seemed only natural. I can tolerate it for one meal."

Paris swallowed, her throat full with emotion. She had been so selfish, and he still found a way to be selfless. And he had obviously put a lot of thought into the evening he had planned. He was that way in bed, too. Full of thought and purpose. Part of her missed that purposefulness. "Careful," she said. "I might like this."

"That is the plan." He was glad that she was so tired. The fight seemed to have gone out of her. He wanted to help her to relax and take her mind off things. A part of him knew that Paris cared for him more than she was able to admit to herself. He wanted her to be comfortable and let herself go.

They ate in silence. Paris did not realize how hungry she actually was. She had been working so hard and running back and forth between the office and the hospital, she had barely eaten anything at all over the past few days. She knew that it was beginning to show, too. Her clothes felt a size too big already.

He watched her as she ate, his brow creased with worry. She looked gaunt. Her eyes had taken on a deep-set, tired appearance since he had seen her last. He was glad that she seemed to be enjoying the food. He was enjoying watching her.

Paris finished her meal, then wiped her mouth with her napkin. "That was the best meal I have had in a long time," she said. "My headache is already starting to go away."

"Yeah, from the looks of things, I would say it was the only meal you had in a long time. That headache was your body screaming from neglect." He paused. "You know that if you don't take care of yourself, you can't take care of the other people in your life effectively, right?"

They made eye contact, and the smart reply that Paris was ready to throw at him was lost. His eyes were full of gentleness. He was looking right to her core. *Had he looked at her like that before?* It was pointless for her to continue to deny her attraction to him for senseless reasons. She shivered. What she was feeling was bigger than just sexual attraction. For the first time, she felt apprehensive about being with him. Nervous. Somehow, she had relinquished more than just control of her evening to him.

Tyson moved to her side. He ran his hand down her hair, then let his finger trail along her cheek, stopping at her mouth. With his fingertip, he drew her to him. Then paused. He looked into her eyes again. He wanted to be sure that she understood the meaning in his gaze.

She saw an intense, smoldering flame in his eyes that both startled and warmed her.

Tyson used the tip of his finger to angle her face, then he kissed her sensuously and gently. First her mouth, then her neck, then her mouth again.

Electricity from his kisses sent shivers through her and Paris's lips parted.

Gently, he moved his tongue in and out of her mouth, tasting her.

She arched her neck, and he trailed kisses down her neck to the neckline of her simple blouse. She didn't want him to stop. In one motion, she pulled it over her head.

He moved her back until they were lying on the floor. He gazed at her, enjoying the view. He had not seen it in so long.

He ran his hand down her smooth body, down to the top of her bra, then followed with a trail of kisses.

Paris gasped. She was powerless to resist. He felt familiar to her, yet different than any other time they had been together. The level of intimacy between them felt new. Foreign, almost as if they had somehow started over. This was much more than just sex. His body was talking a new, much more intimate language than before. It scared her, and it felt good.

He kissed her again, then gently ran his fingers over the lace of her demibra. It seemed to melt away under his touch. Tyson threw it to the side, then kissed her erect nipples and circled them with his tongue.

Heat raced through her body. Before she knew it, the rest of her clothing had disappeared, along with his. She relished the feeling of his warm, hard body against hers. She sank her fingers deep into his locks, down to the scalp. His nearness was overwhelming. She was lost.

He was merciless. Tyson trailed his tongue down her midline, then planted a warm, hot kiss right below her navel. He had no plans to hurry. He wanted to savor her softness.

Her involuntary reaction surprised her. She arched her back, then drew her knees up, pressing her feet down into the soft carpet. Her breath came in short, fast bursts.

Tyson place his hands under her rear, then drew her up against his mouth.

Paris could not breathe. They had been together many times before, but this time, it was obvious that he was deriving as much pleasure as she was. She clutched his hair. Her hips began to thrust wildly. This was unbearable.

"Please stop," she pleaded.

He acted as if he didn't hear her, and instead of stopping, increased the intensity.

Paris felt herself rising and falling at the same time as waves of release flooded over her.

Tyson paused, then planted gentle, tiny kisses on her stomach.

Each one sent tiny shocks of electricity through her. She

looked into his face, wanting him in a way she never had before. Still holding on to his hair, she tugged, silently urging him to rise.

In one motion, they were face-to-face. Tyson eased himself into her gently, then paused.

Paris exhaled more heavily than she had even done in any exercise class. He filled her more tightly and completely than ever before.

They both stared, wide-eyed, into the depths of the other's soul.

Slowly, they moved together. The pleasure they felt was pure and explosive.

Gently, she wiped the sweat from his brow and welcomed him into her body, time and time again, arching her back to meet him with each of his movements. She wrapped her toned legs around him, kissing him gently on his chest and neck, her fingers examining the curves of his muscular arms.

She savored his body, he savored hers. Time melted away, and when climax was imminent, she let him be in control, clinging to him, surrendering to him in a way she never had before.

THE THIRD STRIKE

JaBari had not heard from Wesley since their last encounter on the street near the Capitol. His nerves were on end. He didn't know what was worse, Wesley calling him all the time, asking him when he was going to get his money, or silence from him. He knew him well enough to know that he wasn't satisfied yet, either about the money or about the way he had handled the Montagues. And it wasn't too smart of him to remind him of their teenage experimentation, either. He turned off the lights in his hotel room and let the door slam behind him.

It hadn't been a big deal, and in his defense, Wesley had been so drunk he didn't remember what happened until days later anyway. JaBari knew he had taken advantage of the situation.

He smiled. It really was a stroke of genius that he thought of that angle, using the situation as a way to get Wesley to leave him alone. He knew that Wesley was an old-fashioned macho kind of guy, and the idea that someone might even question his masculinity would scare the shit out of him.

Wesley had been itching for a drink, so they went to the city, to New York. Back then, if you lived in Queens, going to the city to go out was a big deal. And Wesley had insisted he pick the place. And he did. He went out more than many of the other kids his age, he always looked older than his years and rarely got asked for any identification. But Wesley was another story. He looked much younger than his nineteen years.

The bouncer ushered them in, just as he knew he would, and they passed down the long entry hallway for what seemed like an eternity. He remembered holding his breath for the entire length of the hallway. The room was dark and smoky, and the dance floor was filled with bodies gyrating to the eighties music. JaBari smiled as he remembered dancing by himself for hours, until daylight back then.

They made it all the way to the bar before Wesley realized what was going on. JaBari could not help smirking as he remembered the astonished look on his friend's face. His eyes were as wide as saucers. There were men of all shapes, sizes, and colors, dancing together, hugging each other. JaBari had never discussed this other part of his life with Wesley. JaBari was used to it, but for Wesley, it was like something from television.

Wesley grabbed JaBari's hand in a vise grip. "There are no women in this place," he had hissed.

JaBari swallowed, looked him in the eye, and said, "No, there aren't. It's not that kind of place. We just came for a few drinks, it will be cool."

And it was. Wesley had loosened up after a few drinks.

And it might have been something they would laugh about for a long time. But Wesley didn't stop drinking until he was sliding off the barstool. They'd taken a taxi all the way back to Queens and stayed at Wesley's house overnight. In the same bed.

Nothing happened really. But when Wesley woke up with a stiff dick and JaBari in the same bed, he lost his mind. And to make it worse, he couldn't remember what happened the night before. He made JaBari promise never to mention it if they were going to remain friends. And he hadn't. Until now.

Dusk had fallen quickly. The night air was filled with the cawing sounds of the grackles that swarmed the downtown mesquite trees. He cringed. He hated those birds. They were creepy, like something from a horror movie. JaBari looked across the parking lot. As usual, it had cleared out, and his was one of the only cars still parked there. The streetlights flickered to life, and he jumped. He had to get himself together. Maybe moving to Austin was not such a good idea after all. There were other cities in Texas. He could commute. Or start over in another city if necessary.

His car was parked next to one of the streetlamps that lit the parking lot. As he approached it, the light went out. The way his luck had been going, it figured that his car would be the only one shrouded in darkness. He didn't mind that so much, but he discovered that downtown Austin had bats at night. The idea of walking around in the darkness with flying rats whizzing around his head was not a pleasant one. *Strike two for this city.*

He put the key in the lock of his rental car and opened the door. If he kept being this jittery, he was going to have to stay at the hotel to eat.

JaBari slid into his car and slammed the door. His hands were sweating again. He rubbed them together, then on his pant legs. He needed to calm down. Or have a stiff drink. He was so keyed up that he was sweating like he had already run a race. He reached forward to put the key in the ignition, and when he sat up, he felt a rope whip around his neck.

It tightened and drew his head back to the headrest. He clawed at it, gasping for breath. He felt his eyes bulging from his head. "What do you want?" he gasped.

No one answered. He hit the horn, but no sound came out. His eyes darted around the parking lot in vain. Cold metal pressed into the back of his neck just as he pissed in his pants. His legs kicked about in the floor well of the car as he struggled.

He should have known that Wesley was not finished with him. His last thought was that bringing up the incident between them might not have been such a great idea, after all.

DRAMA—FULL

Cottonwood pollen floated through the morning air. Paris sneezed. She wiped at her tearing eyes.

Tyson handed her a tissue. "You okay?" he asked.

She nodded, then looked down at the floor as they made their way to Brian's hospital room. A few weeks ago, she wouldn't have even gone to his apartment, much less spent the night as she had last night. It felt so good to wake up in Tyson's arms. All her thoughts about her mother's ideas of his not being right for her seemed silly now. Her mother was just going to have to understand that she could not make her life decisions for her daughter. Sure, she had said it before, but now Paris meant it. She wanted to walk the walk and see who she liked. And Tyson was who she liked.

He was silent as he watched her from the corner of his eye. He knew this was hard for her. "I can wait in the car if you like."

"Don't be silly. It's hot. Why would you have to do that? I'm a grown woman."

"I don't want to cause any problems."

"I need you here. Besides, I wanted to get here as early as possible to check on Brian, and I left my car at the office. So, if you don't mind, you have to be my chauffeur for another few hours."

Tyson didn't mind. In fact, there was nothing he wanted more. He gently brushed his lips against her cheek. Even dressed in his T-shirt, she was beautiful.

The elevator door swished open in the hospital lobby, and they entered it. They were silent as they waited for it to ascend.

Paris swallowed. She hoped she was doing the right thing. What JaBari had said the other day was nagging at her, and she planned to confront her mother about it. And while she was confronting people, it made no sense to go through the extra struggle of acting as if she hadn't been with Tyson last night. She wouldn't. Athena would just have to get over it.

It just didn't make sense to her anymore. Her mother's so-called standards were the farthest thing from her mind. If Athena didn't like the fact that Paris was going to date whomever she wanted, without regard to her mother's approval, too bad. Paris lifted her chin in defiance as she thought about how ridiculous it was for her to let her mother push her around the way she had. She was a grown woman and was tired of kowtowing to what her mother or anyone else thought.

The struggle that Paris was going through was all over her face. Tyson wasn't going to ask her about it, but it was time she finally started to make some decisions on her own. The way he saw it, all he could do was support her if she needed it and try to help her get through the mess she and her family were tangled up in.

They passed the nurses' desk. One of them looked up and smiled at Paris, but didn't speak. The door to Brian's room was closed. Tyson grabbed Paris's hand and squeezed it. "I'll be here if you need me," he said.

"Thanks." Paris nodded, then pushed open the heavy wooden door.

She gasped. Brian was not in the bed. Her eyes darted around the room. The curtains were wide-open. Sunlight was streaming in. She opened his small locker. Personal items were still there. *What in the hell was going on*? Last she heard, he was barely out of a coma and still hooked up to an unmentionable number of monitors and machines. If something was wrong, surely someone at the nurses' station would have alerted her, right?

She turned on her heel, prepared to head down the hallway to get some answers, and almost ran headfirst into the opening door.

"What in the world is wrong with you? You never have been a very careful person. Why are you running out of here like a bat out of hell?" Athena ran her eyes down the full length of her daughter's body. She assessed her daughter's less-than-perfect appearance.

"Where's Brian? Did something happen?" Her voice shook as she spoke.

"You are so overly dramatic. Yes, something happened. I told you he woke up. He is already walking. One of the nurses is with him, exercising him. He was too ornery for me."

Her temper flared. She took a deep breath to calm herself. "Why didn't you call me?"

She stood by the side of the hospital bed. "I wasn't ready

to have you up here worrying me half to death. Besides, I knew you would be here this morning."

"Mother, your selfishness amazes me."

Athena waved her daughter's comments away. Lowering her voice, she asked, "What is what's-his-name doing here? I wasn't aware that he even knew your father other than meeting him at the house that day at dinner."

"Tyson *doesn't* know him. He came with me."

Athena opened her mouth, and for a split second, the two women stood stock-still, staring each other down. Athena nodded. "I see. So, is there something you want to tell me?"

Paris raised her eyebrows and shook her head. "No, not really." She cleared her throat, but did not flinch as she looked her mother in the eye. "I have a few questions for you, though."

"Who is this young man? Isn't he the one whose business Walter and his partners are financing? That is kind of up in the air, don't you think? You really should be dating men who are more established—"

"I don't know why, but I thought you were better than that, Mother. Or at least I'd hoped you were. You have proven yourself shallow and self-serving once again." Paris found herself taken over by a sudden anger.

"Don't raise your voice to me like that," Athena shouted. "You know better than to embarrass me that way. I just want the best for you that's all. JaBari is—"

"A crook, Mother. He is a crook." Paris hissed through tightly clenched teeth. "He stole your money and heaven knows what else. He doesn't have any job you or I could define, and he is a womanizer. Tyson is a good man, and I have been seeing him for a while, and I knew you wouldn't approve. But I don't give a damn about that." She paused as Athena stood there in shocked silence. "You don't know a thing about anything. You talk all that shit about making an investment in my future; well that is what I am doing, making an investment in my future happiness." Paris slammed the locker door shut.

"You better—"

"I'd better *what*, Mother? I didn't come here to talk about me or to stand here and let you belittle my decisions or imply that I can't make them for myself. I came here to ask you some serious questions about JaBari and your dealings. He said some things that left me wondering. He implied that there was some *reason* that you gave him that money. What was it?"

"I told you that was none of your business. Brian and I will handle that."

"I don't even think you told Brian. Matter of fact, I would bet you had no plans to discuss that with him at all. But guess what? It is my business because *I* am running the business now, at least for the time being, and this whole mess is affecting Benton and Associates in a big way."

"And what way is that?" Brian stared at the two of them, a nurse at his elbow. "What whole mess are you talking about?"

Paris glared at her mother, her arms folded. She raised one eyebrow, waiting for her to answer.

Athena was silent. She stepped back against the doorway, cowering in her corner.

Brian made his way to the bed and sat on the edge of it.

The nurse scanned their faces. "If you want to go home tomorrow afternoon as planned, you still need to take it easy, Mr. Montague." She glared at both Athena and Paris, paused a minute, then left the room.

"Well, apparently, my mother has gone and invested a large sum of money in some movie company, at the advice of JaBari—"

Brian's face looked pained. "How much is large?" he asked.

"All of your operating capital. The business has no money to operate on, and, as far as I can tell, you have no savings to speak of."

"Athena, I never said I wanted to make that investment."

Paris's eye grew wide. "You knew about it?"

"Of course I did. JaBari told just about anyone who would listen about his hot opportunity. But I never got a chance to see anything in writing before I ended up in here." Brian rubbed his hand on his chest.

"Can I say something in my own defense?" Athena was still standing. Her face was beet red. "I did what I thought was best to protect your hard work and the investment you have made in Benton and Associates. I did the right thing, finally. Did you really think I wasn't aware that I would not get that money back? How can you let her stand there and be disrespectful, pointing her fingers at me when I was trying to help you, Brian?" She swallowed hard as hot tears began to slide down her face.

Paris stood stock-still. It pained her to see her mother so upset. It was as if all of those pent-up feelings were pushing their way through. A part of her had known all along that there had to be more to the story.

"What are you talking about, Athena? I fail to see how what you did was an attempt to help anything. Let's just talk to the man and tell him you've changed your mind." His face looked pained. "And what are the terms of this so-called deal?"

Paris shook her head. "I went to talk to him, but I found him with Alexis in his hotel room."

Athena gasped. She opened her mouth to speak, but Paris stopped her.

"I was so upset that I just left." Paris looked away from her mother. And she surely didn't need to hear her say the things she knew she would about Alexis. Paris didn't want to talk about her at all. "I didn't know what to think. And now, I can't find him. There is no answer at his hotel or on his cell."

"We should just let it go. You don't even know who JaBari is, do you?" Athena paused again. Her tear-stained face was somber. She looked hard at her husband, then swallowed. "JaBari is Michael Benton's son, Brian."

Brian stood up suddenly. "What? But his last name isn't Benton."

"But it's him. His mother remarried not long after Michael died."

"Brian, please calm down. The nurse said you should take it easy," Paris said, her face clouded with worry.

"Let me guess, you felt like you could somehow make amends. Is that why you were trying to push him and Paris together?" He shook his head. "I told you that wouldn't work."

"What?" Paris's head whipped around. "I was some kind of consolation prize?" She seethed with anger. "I knew you had issues, but that is just sick." She fought back her tears. "Who in the hell is this Benton? You told me there *was* no Benton. And what happened?"

"It's ancient history," Brian put in. "Benton has been dead for years. I can believe that your mother still thinks we owe that man's family something. Way back when I was first getting started, he was the major partner in Benton and Associates. A friend of mine from college. The company is named that way because it was his first. But it was no big deal then. I joined up, helped him put the business in the black, and everything. Things were going well, but he had money problems, gambling debts. Your mother and I bought him out. I took over, and he was just going to be a smaller player in the business." He paused. "He died not too long after that, and it was a big mess. He hadn't told his wife the truth about everything, and she thought they had a bigger ownership in the business than they did. She wanted more money. But our papers were legal and rock solid."

"But I thought JaBari and his family were from New York. And if they lived here, why don't I remember them?"

Brian cleared his throat. "She was from New York originally. She was so angry afterward. And they had no money. So she moved back home to be near her family. All this happened right after your mother and I got married. You were very young then. But even I don't understand why your mother would just turn over our money like she did. It wasn't much, but I worked hard for it."

They both turned to look at Athena. She was leaning against the wall with her head in her hands. She looked up, and her makeup was streaked down her face from crying. She sniffled and wiped at her nose with a tissue.

"JaBari knew all about the whole thing. It might be in the past for you, but it certainly wasn't for him and his mother. You might think we did the right thing, but his family still does not. He threatened me, said that he would make it harder and harder for us to do business if I didn't do what he asked." Athena paused to collect her thoughts. "What was I supposed to do? We have been so looking forward to retirement and to Paris taking over the business. I didn't want that messed up. I didn't want all of your hard work to be for nothing."

"That is ludicrous, Athena. What are we going to retire on now? It's bad enough that I didn't save enough, but why didn't you ask me first?" He rubbed his chest again.

"I wanted to. But then *you* were suddenly having heart surgery." Her eyes hardened.

Paris looked at her mother in disbelief. If she didn't know better, she would think that her mother was angry at him for being sick. A sudden realization hit her. What if JaBari did have something to do with the banking and client issues they were having? She hadn't even discussed any of that with Brian yet, and it didn't look like this was going to be a great time to do so. If she brought it up, it would only serve to upset him and her mother more.

"Okay, look. My ride is waiting outside to take me to the office. I feel like a ton of family skeletons have been dumped on my head at one sitting, and we are not solving anything by sitting here and bickering with each other."

Brian leaned back on the bed.

"I'm going to leave so that you two can talk, and Brian can rest. You heard what the nurse said."

"Rest isn't going to help Benton and Associates," he said.

Paris nodded. "You are right about that. But I need to get to the office to sort things out. Maybe I can come up with a way to approach JaBari and reason with him. Whatever the case, we need to move forward." She kissed Brian on the forehead and turned to leave.

He called out to her. "Keep me updated, okay?"

She nodded, then pulled the door open, leaving her parents to sort through things.

She found Tyson by the nurses' station. The previously quiet occupants were now rolling with laughter. She could hear his voice, deep and warm above everyone else's. Paris felt a twinge of jealousy, then was annoyed with herself for it. She tapped him on the arm.

"Let's go. I leave you here for a few minutes, and you charm all the ladies."

There was a flicker of amusement in his eyes. "I thought you would be in there a while and didn't want to sit by the door so I could be accused of eavesdropping or anything." He waved good-bye and they walked away from the desk. "Don't tell me you're jealous." He grinned mischievously. He wasn't sure if he was reading Paris right, but he had to admit that he was enjoying the thought of her being even a little bit jealous. This possessiveness was another new thing between them that he could get used to. "You okay?" he asked.

"Not really. I thought that talking with my mother would make things better. But I only discovered drama and more drama." She shook her head.

"Anything I can do?" he asked.

"I don't think so. Unless you can figure out a way to get JaBari to return my parents' money, call off the holds on our bank accounts, and get our clients back."

"When you put it all together like that, it sounds bad. Real bad. But you gotta look on the bright side of things."

"I guess that means you think there is one." She rolled her eyes. The elevator doors swished open and they stepped instead.

"Of course there is. Your stepfather is going to be okay. I was reading his chart while I was at the nurses' desk. It hadn't been filed and was in plain sight. I couldn't help myself."

Paris smiled genuinely for the first time that morning. "I guess that is a good thing. But I have to get to the office and figure out what we are going to do next. Brian might be coming home, but that still doesn't solve our money problems."

They stopped in front of the car, and Paris waited for Tyson to unlock the door. He turned the key in the lock, then paused before opening her door. He stood there, blocking her way.

Paris looked up. "What?" she asked.

"Nothing. I just hope you let me help you through this." His voice was filled with warmth and concern. He had finally broken through Paris's cool exterior. Her complexities captivated him but made it hard to get to know her intimately.

"I'm not sure you can." One of Paris's eyebrows rose. Part of her was eager for his help and glad to have someone to help relieve the pressure she was feeling. But she was also still cautious and insecure.

"I plan to try," he said. Tyson held the door open and waited for Paris to get in. He closed it behind her, again, making eye contact with her through the window. He recognized the uncertainty on her face, but was determined to keep her from closing him out again.

THE BEGINNING

"So, you aren't a little bit mad we decided that you should move out? You must think I am nuts." Alexis was wide-eyed as she looked at Walter.

"You want the real answer or the right answer?"

They had come a long way, and Alexis liked the new openness they were experiencing, even if the truth seemed to take her a step further away from getting married. She wasn't even sure anymore if that was really what she wanted.

Walter shook his head. "I don't have a reason to be." He smiled. "I really feel this is a good thing. We need to sit back and take some time to reevaluate what is important to us. And I'm glad you were truthful with me about what you really want, even if you aren't sure yet."

Alexis watched him as he packed his things. Until now, she hadn't realized how little stuff he had at her place. It was almost like he had not really moved in, only come for an extended sleepover. "It was a hard decision for me, with everyone expecting a wedding and all."

"Well, they ought to like this better anyway. I think your aunt had mixed feelings about me moving in here anyway. Me moving out should make her happy."

Alexis shook her head. "I don't think so. She isn't going to understand it. She'll think this means that we have broken up. But she will get over it. We are the only ones whose feelings really matter in this."

He walked over and slid his arms around Alexis. He put his nose in her hair and inhaled her scent, then kissed her on the forehead as she looked up into his face, smiling.

"You know, I think this may be the first time you are thinking for yourself since I met you."

"I think you may be right. But I'm still going to miss you stealing my shower in the morning."

Walter palmed her behind playfully, and she jumped, laughing. "We'll be back to stealing showers soon enough. When we are ready." His smile faded, and his face became somber.

"So, do you think JaBari will show up for dinner at your aunt's house?" he asked

Alexis shrugged. "Not sure. I have no idea what is going on." She looked away. "I'm not sure Paris's idea will work. I wouldn't show up if I were him."

Walter's face darkened. "I damn sure hope he does. I have some things to say to him. I still can't believe the nerve of that bastard. If Paris hadn't knocked on the door, he might have raped you."

Paris blinked back tears. "But she did. And it's water under the bridge."

"And you can stop acting like you are reluctant to go over there. You and Paris need to patch it up. She is your best friend, for goodness sakes."

Walter pulled her close, and a shudder ran through them both.

"JaBari pissed off a whole lot of folks in the past few days. We all need to confront him. Get some closure." He paused. "And you and Paris need to get back to normal."

"She may not want to. I have to admit I went beyond friendship. I was so nosey. Pushy. But we *have* been friends all of our lives. I haven't really had the time to talk to her at all. She has been helping her mother a lot *and* running the business. Doesn't leave time for much else."

Walter smiled. "Do I detect a little jealousy there?"

She shook her head. "Not at all. I do miss her, but I have to concentrate on my own happiness, don't you think? We'd better get going. You know how Athena is about her dinners. It would upset her whole status quo if we just didn't show up."

He paused, surveying the room. She had given him the right answer for a change. He kissed her again, then snapped his bag shut.

They didn't ring the doorbell. Paris turned the knob, opening the door, letting herself and Tyson into her parents' place.

"Hello?" she called back toward the kitchen. She knew that was where everyone would be. Brian had only been home a few days and it was like everything was almost back to normal.

Athena's voice rang out, and they followed it. They found her, just as Alexis suspected, back in the kitchen stirring her pot. Brian was sitting nearby in his easy chair.

Paris went over to him and kissed him on the cheek. She

was glad to see that his normal color was returning. "Looking good," she said.

"I'm doing my best. I gotta get back to that office. By the time you are done, I won't even recognize my own business."

Paris laughed, then kissed her mother, too.

Athena smiled thinly.

Paris studied her face for a minute. The events of the past few weeks appeared to be taking their toll. She looked pale, and the strain showed clearly in her tired-looking eyes. Before Paris could comment, Alexis cleared her throat. Paris looked up, startled.

Walter and Alexis stood in the doorway of the kitchen, holding hands.

Paris's mouth dropped open, and Alexis looked away sheepishly.

"You didn't tell me she was coming," she said. She pursed her lips.

"Did you think that because you two are having some kind of disagreement that I would not invite my favorite niece?" Athena asked.

Paris turned around and looked at Brian, searching his eyes for help.

He didn't comment.

"You never let me explain anything to you, Paris. You just ran off all angry and wouldn't return any of my calls."

"You really don't want to talk about this now, do you? In front of Walter and everybody?"

"Why not?" Alexis moved closer to Paris. "I don't have anything to hide. Walter already knows what happened."

"Really? So he knows that you and JaBari—"

"Did nothing. When you knocked on the door, you

stopped him. I'll admit that he is an attractive man, but I was stupid to go to his hotel room in the first place. Up to that point, I had no reason to distrust him." Tears came to her eyes. She wiped them away with the back of her hand, and Walter stepped up and hugged her from behind.

Paris stood with her arms folded, angrily tapping the tile floor with her foot.

"He attacked me, Paris. And then you turned your back on me, and I couldn't even talk to you about it."

"I thought—"

Athena interrupted. "We all know what you thought, but you were wrong. Can't you see that? I'm not exactly sure what you were angry at anyway and don't believe you would let some hustler come between you and your best friend. You two have been buddies since the crib. All I know is that you two better just get it together. Now. Today. This family has business to handle."

Paris bit her lip. She was the one feeling sentimental now and was trying her best to keep tears away. She sniffled. They were both right—in her anger, she had overreacted. "I'm sorry, Alexis. I should have listened to you. There has just been so much else going on." Paris stepped forward and hugged her cousin. The room was silent, and the men in the room all looked away.

"So, what is the plan now?" Walter asked. "I've been waiting—"

"Just hold your horses, Walter," Brian said. "We all have things we want to say to JaBari. Paris called his hotel room and invited him to dinner. We haven't heard anything, but hopefully he will show up."

"Maybe he will. But I have a plan otherwise. Tyson and I were up burning the midnight oil last night to figure out how to get us out of this hole. Even if JaBari shows up, I doubt we are getting any money back. And it will be a few days before the holds are off our accounts. It is pretty obvious that there were some checks presented, with my signature, that I didn't write. I'm pretty sure it was JaBari who took them. He was the only one who had the opportunity. I have to admit that I was thrown off, though, by the way he so innocently returned my wallet. But that will be cleared up soon."

"And since you didn't write any of those checks, then you won't be connected to any of the shady things he was involved in," Tyson said.

"Can we back up?" Brian said. "I'm not one to cry over spilled milk, and as far as I can see, all this stuff with JaBari is over and done with. What about these new plans for the business? I'm not sure I want to change anything, Paris. And as far as I can see, we can't do anything yet."

"I wouldn't say that. I propose we start a new department."

The room was silent. Everyone looked at Brian for his reaction.

"I have it all mapped out. I have actually been playing with the idea for a while. We should add Community Development Consulting to our menu of services."

"It's a good idea, really," Tyson said. "Paris has a good head on her shoulders. Community Development fits right into what you already do, except Paris will be convincing people to spend money on community improvement projects. Things we all care about."

"But what will that cost? We are already going to be squeezed tighter than—"

"I told you, I got it figured out. I roped in some investors last night. People who owe some favors." Paris grinned and glanced at Tyson.

"It sounds good, I'll admit, but I'm going to have to see what you have." Brian rubbed his forehead while he spoke.

Paris nodded. "I knew you would. I have it all written down for you. You'll see, it will be good for us. You need to be thanking Tyson though. If it weren't for him, we would have been closing our doors. He was the one that found that check with the forged signature."

Athena wiped her hands on a dishcloth. "Maybe, maybe not. We would have figured it out if the bank didn't. That credit card check was easy to trace, but of course, JaBari didn't know that. They were able to trace all the accounts it had gone to. He could have at least spelled your name right on the signature line. All that fancy education that boy had wasn't worth much."

Both Paris and Tyson tried to ignore the less-than-friendly look that Athena had given them. She was still pouting that she had not gotten her way completely. Some things were still the same.

"I just hope JaBari gets here before we have a houseful of people." Paris looked toward the door expectantly.

"There won't be a houseful. Just us. Your mother and I wanted just family. Other than the business with JaBari, we are celebrating us getting through a tough time and Tyson's new business."

Paris and Tyson made eye contact, a knowing look in her eye. She knew that the shortened guest list was Brian's idea, not her mother's. She nodded. Some things were different, after all.

"Not much to celebrate yet. It'll be a while before we really get things off the ground and turn a profit," Tyson said, "but thank you."

"There is someone at the door," Alexis called from the living room.

Paris, Tyson, and Brian all looked at each other expectantly, none of them sure that they had really expected JaBari to show up.

Paris's face darkened. She couldn't believe it herself. He must really have thought they were fools. *It's a good thing we are all peaceful people.*

Tyson practically ran to the front door and flung it open. Paris, Walter, and Alexis all followed him.

It wasn't JaBari. The man at the door had a look of surprise on his face. He was just about to ring the doorbell again, and stood, virtually frozen in surprise.

"Can we help you?" Paris asked.

"I'm looking for Paris Montague," he said. "I'm Detective Sims."

"Is there a problem?" Tyson asked.

"May I come in?"

The group stepped away from the door to let the man enter. He stepped into the house cautiously and paused, glancing around. "Is either of you ladies Paris?"

"I am." Paris stepped forward. "Let's go into the living room. Is there a problem?"

He followed Paris into the living room and sat on the sofa without being asked. The others sat in various places around the room.

"That is what I am trying to figure out. How well did you know JaBari Nolan?"

Alexis and Paris looked at each other. "Not as well as we thought," Paris said. "Why?"

"You called his hotel room and left a message for him. You invited him to dinner here today. Was he a close personal friend?"

Walter stepped up. "I wouldn't call that bastard a friend. Why are you talking about him in the past tense? Where is he? We have some questions of our own to ask him."

"That is going to be kind of hard. He was murdered night before last in the parking lot of the Hyatt. In his car."

They all gasped. "From what we can tell, he had lots of enemies, we are just trying to sort through them all. Narrow down the list of suspects if we can. I need to ask some questions."

Paris nodded. The shock reverberated through the room. "We knew he was bad news, but damn."

"I saw this on the news." Alexis's eyes were full of tears. They turned to look at her. "They said an unidentified man died in a car fire. That was him, right?"

The detective looked grim. "It was. We think they were trying to cover up the murder. Didn't work though. The fire department was able to put the fire out before all of the evidence was destroyed. Sad." He cleared his throat. "This won't take long."

The early-evening sun was already fading, turning the sparkling water below varying shades of green and brown. Paris and Tyson sat on the love seat on her parents' patio and looked out over the water. Paris snuggled up to Tyson without one ounce of guilt. She was learning to enjoy being with him around other people. They felt good together.

"You think your mother is ever going to get over being wrong about JaBari?" He smiled. The warmth in his voice was soothing.

"Not sure." She said. "And I don't care. My mother's priorities are all screwed up, and we have got to live our own lives now. I have got to take some time and slow down a bit." She shook her head. "I can't believe that JaBari was murdered. I wanted to talk with him, but I wouldn't wish that on anyone."

"Me either. But in the end, most people get what they deserve."

It was not cold, but Paris felt warmed by Tyson's closeness. They watched the sunset. It had been a rough few days, but Paris was happy that things turned out the way they did, at least for them. Tyson had his dream, and she, well, she had him. He was a good man, and she had almost missed it.

They were going to have to take some time to get to know each other better, and she was looking forward to it.

She smiled a secret smile, enjoying the way he let his fingers play in the back of her hair. It was a good thing she had learned to recognize love before it was too late. Their sex life had always been good, and promised to get better. Now they could develop a life outside the bedroom, too. She was looking forward to that most.

Want More?

Turn the page to enter
Avon's Little Black Book —

the dish, the scoop and the
cherry on top from
NINA FOXX

Nina Foxx is always being asked how she became a writer and where her ideas come from. The answer to both questions starts with her journal. Read on to hear how Nina began her career and get a special inside peek into her personal journal . . .

I was not always a writer. It found me a few years ago, at the end of 1999. I say it found me rather than that I started writing because that is exactly what happened. I always wrote things, but didn't recognize it as something I really liked until then.

I sat at the computer and started typing, then when I thought I was done, I had the need to make it better. I wanted to learn about the craft bit by bit, with the hopes that what came out would be a little better each time. Funnier, maybe, or more suspenseful or more intriguingly worded. And every time I think I am done, I have no idea if or when the next idea is coming. Thankfully, up to now, they have kept coming, sometimes too quickly for me to write them all down properly.

I keep a journal of ideas. And when an idea visits me, I jot it down, but I don't allow it to sidetrack me from the thing I am currently developing. I visit the ideas from time to time, and occasionally, I see a bigger story in one of them. When that happens, that idea becomes the next book or short story.

Most often, they start from a line or two. A catchy phrase, something someone says or does that sticks with me. My imagination takes over, and I weave that into a story. Thing after real-life thing piques my interest, and I weave that in, too.

I am a watcher of people. I put things from real life into my stories all the time, only bigger and more exciting than real life ever is. With that being said, this book is a work of fiction. All of them to date have been. No, I'm not in it. Neither are you or anyone I know or have known in the past. That is what makes fiction what it is. Made up. I heard Victoria Christopher Murray say that if we were to say it out loud, it would be called lying. Fiction writers are professional liars.

I wanted *Marrying Up* to be fun and suspenseful, and I enjoyed writing it. I hope you enjoyed reading it. I can't even begin to thank the folks I need to. I have been scolded in the past for doing it incorrectly.

My family, immediate, past, present, and extended. My sisters, *all* of them. All of my brothers, too. There are a lot of us. My friends that encourage me and drive me to distraction so that I can experience interesting things that spark my imagination.

And then there are those who contributed something directly to the story. My sister-niece Brandie Scott, currently in the quest. Denise Davis, House Parliamentarian and Special Counsel at the Texas State Capitol. Thank you for being the expert. Texas State Representative Dawnna Dukes, D (46), thanks to you for giving me a way to get rid of him and writing the resolution that honored me, and Amanda Burrell for letting me peer into your world. Texas State Representative Charlie Geren, R (99), meeting you intrigued me so much I had to write you in.

All of these people are fine, upstanding citizens and legislators and take pride in what they do. None of them are unscrupulous like the people I wrote about in this book.

Oh, and Pilates 360 is a real place in Austin, as are just about all of the places I named in the book. Brenda is also real, and we really like her even if we have nicknamed her the Pilatzee Nazi. She is great and wonderful and does my body good. Go see her if you are ever in Austin. The women that I met during my Pilates sessions over the past year are wonderful. Peggy, Brenda, and Debi, you are all great. We are all as different as can be but I hold you among my dearest friends. You have reminded me that below the surface there are some things that are universal. And of course, many thanks to my sorors of Alpha Kappa Alpha Sorority, Inc. and my sisters in Jack and Jill of America.

Carrie Feron, Selina McLemore, and the rest of the Avon Books family, my agent Elaine Koster and the Femme Fantastik, thank you so much for the encouragement. I think I want to be more edgy (a Jenni Hummel word) next time. I feel another book coming on.

August 30, 2004

From the Journal of Nina Foxx

Never Stand in the Way of a Femme and her Manolos

The pull of the mall was too much to resist. They had shoes there, spectacular shoes. I could smell them, hear them calling my name from across the street, all the way inside the hotel where I was attending a conference. I wasn't alone.

We took the opportunity to run over there at the first break in the conference. There were five of us in all, all writers, and we were going to do some necessary female bonding. We navigated the heavy Atlanta traffic as best we could. Cars missed our backsides by inches. Oblivious to it all, we were drunk with the thoughts of the possible treasures that lay there, in the capitalist temple. Clutching our designer bags, we tipped across the street through cars like a 1980s game of Frogger.

It was Georgia hot, but sweating was not allowed. Most of us were Southern women by birth or default. We had to supress both our excitement and the ninety-plus-degree heat to appear calm, cool, and, above all, freshly showered.

We finally made it to the air-conditioned haven and began our slow meander. We charted a course down the wing of the mall that held all of the higher-end couture shops. We "oohed" at Louis Vuitton, "aahed" at St. John and Hermès, and finally stumbled into Neiman Marcus.

It didn't matter if we purchased anything, we somehow stood taller as we hobnobbed in Prada and worshipped together, paying homage to the Manolo Blahnik shoes AKA foot jewelry. We were chronic shoppers, united and on a mission.

One of us hung back, seemingly wandering off. We huddled in groups of twos and three, admiring and commenting on shoe after shoe. My cell phone rang, interrupting our scholarly debate on the merits of one particular boot design.

"Over your shoulder. There is a guy in a bad wig. He has been following us since Kate Spade." It was our wayward member, Carmen. She was calling from across the sales floor. Confusion riddled my face, then vanished. I had to appear calm, as if nothing were wrong. My eyes became slits as I looked around. *Mission Impossible* music played in my head. I signaled to the others to take notice and be on guard.

As a group, we moved on. Sure enough, he followed.

"Maybe he is Security," Victoria whispered. She wanted to believe in the good.

I shook my head. Security didn't dress the way he was dressed, and he didn't strike me as a male fashionista. He had no reason to be there.

We came to the consensus that he was following us, and probably had his eyes on the obvious jewels we carried. Our designer handbags were summoning him like the gems they were. But he had picked the wrong group. All of us could quickly forget our home training.

We soaked up the details. More information about our would-be assailant passed quickly and silently among us. Our shoppers' telepathy was strong. We circled him and adopted the fighting poses that Charlie had stolen from us for his angels.

Unable to take it anymore, the smallest of us, Lori, stepped up to him.

"We noticed," she said, "that everywhere we are, you are, too."

We all tensed. He was completely surrounded. Victoria removed her earrings. I assumed the Fighting Lotus position and held on to my Louis Vuitton handbag, ready to brandish it like the deadly weapon it was. Jaquelin reached for her Vaseline and applied it to her face lightning fast. Time slowed down to Matrix speed.

We watched his Adam's apple travel up and then down his

neck. He swallowed hard, his eyes darting among us. He was looking for an opening.

"Is that some special kind of Atlanta hospitality or what?" Lori asked.

He panicked then. Bolted and ran. He hopped onto the escalator and took the steps two and three at a time.

Smiles bloomed on our faces as we nodded at each other with satisfaction. Carmen rejoined us. The crime was foiled. I felt a little sorry for the young man. He thought he had come to the mall to jack some easy targets, and he almost got jacked himself.

We continued sashaying through Neiman Marcus shoulder to shoulder, feeling somehow stronger than before. Empowered. We didn't speak of it among us. Instead we joked with a male colleague who showed up after the fact, about how he could have come to our rescue.

"Bosley," we said, "we needed you to protect us. Where were you?"

We really didn't need him. We all knew that. A man would not have been necessary, only served as another couture accessory. It would have been his turn to be eye candy.

And the Femme Fantastik was born.

From the Journal of Nina Foxx

Japan

For hours, I watched the monitor in front of me as it indicated my plane flying across the top of the world. Our destination—Tokyo, Japan. The pilot's voice boomed through the loudspeaker, we were finally landing. I rubbed my stomach to try and calm the butterflies and licked the airplane-sleep dryness from my lips. I was taking the trip of a lifetime; this was a business trip to exotica. I might as well get something out of the deal. I was the most educated but not the highest paid in my corporate kingdom.

I waited to pass through Immigration and Customs amidst a sea of business-suited travelers. To my right, a small group of Japanese people stood obediently inside a box taped off on the floor. This was the smoking area. My fellow passengers gawked with me. Americans were by their nature defiant, and rules were made to be broken. This would never fly in the United States. I did not want to make eye contact with the passengers disembarking with me, so I studied other parts of the immaculate, alien-feeling airport. I could feel all of their eyes on me, studying me. Almost all were Americans. All, except for me, were white males.

Their curiosity whispered about my ears. I could feel it emanate from them although none dared to speak a word. We all looked curious and road-weary; the flight took over twelve hours. But I knew I was most certainly more curious than they. Female executives sent to Asia were rare. I was a Black woman, even rarer still. I checked, I was the only one of my species anywhere on the plane.

"Is your trip business or pleasure, Foxx-san?" The immigration officer studied my passport. He flipped the well-worn pages.

I answered him in textbook Japanese. "Business." My voice was low.

He raised his eyebrows and stamped my passport. He seemed less concerned about my being a female executive than did the others standing in line. I bent to pick up my things as two or three of them nudged each other. I knew they would struggle trying to follow my lead, but it would be difficult for them. I was used to things revolving around others; being able to function in more than one cultural sphere was a necessity for survival for me. I was used to adaptation. Many believed that they should be the center of the world, even when it wasn't their world anymore. Most of them would barely have any rudimentary understanding of the Japanese language and culture.

I claimed my luggage and proceeded to the meeting area. I could not make heads or tails of the signs. On an eccentric whim I had decided to learn Japanese in college, but I was not eccentric enough to learn to read the Kanji. I felt my neck stiffen and tense from the stress. Unfamiliar smells greeted my nose and I was suddenly aware that I towered over everyone around me. I was used to being average at home. I felt like an island. But I was used to that feeling. I felt it every day as soon as I stepped into my office. I felt it every day as the body language of the engineers I worked with asked what I was doing there—the lone psychologist whose job it was to examine and question their designs. I was supposed to be the voice of the "normal" person, the voice of the consumer. The "reason" in the world of high tech.

I waited on the curb to meet my escort. I had no idea what to expect. We had only communicated via e-mail, and although I was used to the name after almost two years of correspondence, I had no clue as to the gender of its owner. I wasn't even sure which part of the multiword name was the surname. My hood-sense keep me vaguely aware of anyone passing too closely as I soaked in the things around me and ran through my plan in my mind. A Japanese national holiday was this week, giving me an extra day to explore. My mind whirled; this was an ancient culture, and I was envious. The path to my own heritage had been severed so completely by American history. The meager 150 or so years that were chronicled in my family tree book were but a blip on the face of time.

A tall slender woman approached me and stopped.

"Foxx-san?"

I was speechless at first. She was as tall as I, but Japanese. Was this her? Or was this a secretary sent to meet me?

I nodded. She grabbed my hand and shook it. "Finally, I am so glad to meet you." A smile spread across her face. Her English was impeccable. She bowed, and I followed suit. People around us stared. The deepness of her bow indicated that she thought I was her senior, very respected. My face flushed red. Although I knew of this custom, I was not prepared.

I had come to test the Japanese customer experience, to find out how different it was from that of our customers in the United States. We conducted our testing at the Japanese headquarters of our business, located in Kawasaki, an industrial suburb of Tokyo. On the way there, I was assaulted by flashing lights and color, lots and lots of color. A myriad of signs that I could not understand. Smells that I could not identify. Though I had not slept, I was wide-awake, drinking it all in.

I gave my instructions to the participants in Japanese. Most were surprised by this and answered me with very deep bows, so deep that I dared not attempt to return them for fear of falling on my head. My contact and I exchanged snippets of information about ourselves through the twelve hours we were together. She was twenty-six and unmarried. She had gone to college and never was a secretary. This caused much embarrassment in her family, but she didn't care. I was not much older, married with children and a few postgraduate degrees. And tired.

At the end of every testing session, she frowned at the bows I received. Finally, I asked her, "Am I doing it wrong? I do not want to offend."

She shook her head no and looked at the floor. "I am just not accustomed to a woman being treated this way. I usually get treated more like an annoyance than like anyone values my knowledge or skill."

"Not much different in the U.S.," I said.

It was then she revealed to me her wish. She wanted to be transferred to the U.S., so she could marry for love instead of taking part in an arranged marriage as she was expected to do.

"Is it true that they have men behind locked doors there?"

I looked at her quizzically, then smiled. Did she mean the engineers that worked in the labs? They were kept locked all the time to protect equipment and company secrets. The cache of "nerds" that we joked about was a gold mine to her. A veritable cornucopia of possible husbands, who she thought would not expect her to live a life of subservience. Now this was something I had not thought of.

Her view of relationships in the U.S. had been colored by sitcoms translated into Japanese depicting sassy women with high-powered careers who did not take a backseat to that of their men. She revealed she never missed an episode of *Friends*. I could not remember the last time I saw it.

Our testing was over. We headed to the Asakusa shrine for sightseeing. I was supposed to bathe in the smoke at the temple for good fortune and to make my wishes come true. A small donation and I could have my fortune told. She wished for a husband. I wished for a promotion and an office with a view. I had to give her the Foxx-eye view of the world.

"Well, we aren't exactly subservient to our husbands in America, but somehow I think most men expect your career to take a backseat to theirs, especially if they earn more."

"What is 'backseat'?" she asked.

"Backseat. Someone has to raise the kids, and I know very few men who volunteer for that duty. And in our companies women lag behind men in salary and status because of it."

She listened with ever-widening eyes. "Oh, like our newest

prime minister got married and his wife, who was a lawyer beforehand, had to quit her job. She knew what she was getting into. It is our way."

"It is our way, too. Except we don't know it."

She laughed at that. We spoke in whispers in the holy place as I educated her in the ways of corporate America, the Glass Ceiling, the ways of American romance, and the American feminist movement.

"It is amazing that a job so important is relegated to such low status," she said at the end of our discussion. She was referring to motherhood.

"Isn't it though?" I pitched a few more coins for extra luck. "In the 1960s we were made to believe that we could have everything, job, career, family. We are still playing catchup."

"Hmm, so I guess you could say that the feminists sold you a bag of goods then. Right, Foxx-san? It is like our job, then, no? You open the box, and you never know what you are going to get?"

I laughed out loud at this. In a short time she had gained keen insight into our culture as well as our colloquialisms. We headed for the shoe store. (We had that in common).

"Yes, I guess that is true. As much as things are different, they are the same. But here, like the prime minister's wife, at least you know what to expect."

NINA FOXX

M. Shawn Image Studio

NINA FOXX is originally from Queens, New York, and now lives in Austin, Texas, with her husband and children. Her hobbies include reading, writing, downhill skiing and shoes.